THE
HUNT

a political thriller

T0344639

JACK CASHILL
and MIKE MCMULLEN

PERMUTED
PRESS

A PERMUTED PRESS BOOK

ISBN: 978-1-68261-890-5
ISBN (eBook): 978-1-68261-891-2

The Hunt
© 2019 by Jack Cashill and Mike McMullen

Cover art by Jomel Cequina

**PERMUTED
PRESS**

Permuted Press, LLC
New York • Nashville
permutedpress.com

Published in the United States of America

TONY

He lingered in that sweet borderland between dream and reality, the warm breeze from the Tyrrhenian Sea separating the curtains and washing over him, and she, ever so lovely, leaning in and whispering, "The evil ones are in the wire." She left as soundlessly as she came, the breeze cooling in her wake. It was sharp now, and bitter. *"The evil ones are in the wire"?* he thought. He looked around. "I'm in Colorado, Angel." Yes, he was, but the sudden press of cold steel on the back of his neck reminded him that the evil ones were real and very much in the wire.

Eighteen Days Earlier—

DAY
1

TONY

Driving in to the boys' school, Tony asked himself whether he'd rather be stalking the Taliban through the unholy hell of the Hindu Kush. And he wasn't sure of the answer. He really wasn't.

Today was the first time this semester he had been called in, but the third time since Luke and Matt enrolled last year. The meeting wasn't going to be fun. He pulled his 1987 FJ60 Land Cruiser into the faculty parking lot, a sore thumb among the Priuses, Volvos, and vestigial Saabs so loved by academics everywhere. His employer picked up the tuition—that was good—but he still wasn't sure the boys belonged here. Wasn't sure he did either.

Dr. Heller was polite. She always was. And professional. Always that. In different circumstances, he might have even warmed up to her. She had that sexy librarian thing going for her—tightly bunned hair, nerdy glasses, a hint of mystery—but today that thing held no charm. Someone once told him you could be no happier than your unhappiest child, and unhappiness, he knew, killed the libido surer than any emotion but fear.

He made his way through the empty corridors to Heller's office. He was sure she meant well, but she didn't have a clue. Not many educators did. He walked through the already-open door. She stood as he entered and gestured to a pair of comfortable chairs off to the side.

"Luke's not a bad kid," she told him after some pointless small talk. "And he tests well, especially in math, but he's off to a shaky start again this semester. Even with his future here at stake, he will just not…engage."

"Can you clarify?"

"It's hard to explain. He's not disruptive, not hyper, but he's listless and apathetic. He doesn't pay attention to details, can't stay focused. He's just not…really *here*."

"Sorry to hear that." He did not disbelieve her. He had seen the signs himself.

"Mr. Acero, I think it may be time to have Luke see someone."

"Someone as in like—what—a doctor?"

"Yes, or at least a psychologist."

Tony sighed, "But you know how that goes today. Kid comes in with some symptoms, and the psychologist or whatever says he's ADD or ADHD, let's send him to a doctor and get him on Ritalin or Adderall or whatever."

"Not necessarily."

"Not always, but all too often."

"I understand your concern, Mr. Acero, but several of our students are benefitting from a controlled drug regimen."

He tried not to show his disgust, but he could not help himself. "Doctor, when it comes to drugs, I have a problem with the word 'regimen.'"

"They can be a useful tool, Mr. Acero."

"Tool nothing. They define the user. They're out." He bristled at how coolly and clinically she suggested doping his kid. She had to know how he would respond. This part of the conversation they had had before.

"I wish you would at least consider medication."

"Not happening."

"I am truly sorry," she paused, giving him that concerned guidance counselor look, "but we're at our wit's end. I wish there were some alternate solution, but as much as I hate to say this, you may want to start looking at different academic options."

He stared at her dead-eyed. "You know what he's been through, right?" Tony told her the story once before. He did not want to repeat himself. Luke was just twelve when his mother was killed, t-boned by a Ram 1500, a wasted peckerwood at the wheel. At the time, Tony was deployed at the tip of America's spear in Afghanistan. It took days before the brass could extricate him and get him home. Matt helped out as much as he could, but there was only so much a brother could do. The shock of it all rattled Luke. The moves Tony made to stabilize the situation made it worse—new state, new home, new school.

Heller's downcast eyes told Tony she remembered, and remembered well.

"Yes, and you know we've tried, but he is so stubbornly reluctant to study or participate in class. It's like he's testing us."

Tony crossed his arms over his chest. "Luke has his talents."

"I am told he's an ace at video games, but we don't grade on thumb-eye coordination here. I am not sure there's much more we can do."

He was getting nowhere. He would have to share his plan. He knew in his bones she wouldn't buy it.

"I have an idea."

"I'm listening," said Heller.

"Out in Colorado, elk hunting season begins in mid-October."

Heller arched her right eyebrow. "Excuse me for being dense, but what does elk hunting have to do with anything?"

"Let's call this a family version of Outward Bound," said Tony, leaning forward as far as he could. "To survive a week beyond the grid, you have got to engage—lots of orienteering, astronomy, basic math, physics, and following directions. Luke will come back a different kid." Thor Olafson, a hard-nosed platoon sergeant he got to know during their harrowing days in the Shok Valley, slipped him this idea just a few days ago.

"Different, I'm afraid, in that he'll be even further behind. He'll have missed days of school he can ill afford."

"No, trust me. You'll see the improvement."

Heller may have wanted to oblige, thought Tony, but she saw the world so differently she could not even fake interest.

"I wish I could be more encouraging, Mr. Acero, but you're not even close to convincing me that this is a viable idea."

He paused. It was time to play his trump card. "You know if Luke has to look at a different 'academic option' for next semester, so will Matt."

Heller looked surprised. "That would be a shame. Matt's a senior. You don't want to pull him out now. He's doing so well here."

"Yes, he is," Tony said with a smile. "If you follow lacrosse, Doctor, you know Matt was the best face-off guy in the league last year."

"I've heard something about that."

"If you follow wrestling, you know Matt led you guys to the 4-A state finals last season. First time ever."

"I'm aware."

"Matt won State in his weight class. The team almost won."

"I know that too."

"Wrestling's big in Kansas, and especially big here. If Matt doesn't wrestle this year, the team's getting nowhere near Salina."

"Excuse me? Salina?" said Heller, her eyebrows arched.

'That's where they'll hold the state championship."

Then the good doctor stared at Tony for the longest second, threw her head back, and laughed. He was kind of hoping she would. He just did not expect her to.

"So what you're telling me, Mr. Acero, is that unless I agree to your plan, I will cost the school state championships in not just one, but *two* sports?"

"Did I say that?"

"Wouldn't help me with my year-end evaluation, would it?"

"I suspect not," he grinned.

"If nothing else, Mr. Acero, you've convinced me how serious you are." She rose from her seat and extended her hand. "Let me talk to his teachers. I guess we've got nothing to lose."

"It's Tony," he answered, standing now, shaking her hand, and noticing, despite himself, how unprofessionally violet her nails were. "I'd appreciate that."

He politely thanked the guidance counselor for her time, walked out to his vehicle, and began conjuring how to break it to his bitter little couch potato of a son that he was going elk hunting in a few weeks.

* * *

The Aceros lived in a newish townhouse, designed to look old, at the apex of a cul-de-sac on the western edge of Shawnee, Kansas. His sister recommended it. She and her husband lived nearby. That helped, especially when he traveled. The town may have been a bit too white bread for his taste, but it was safe and calm and close to both the company HQ in Leavenworth and KCI—just a half hour, the Kansas Highway Patrol and the Good Lord willing. He needed to be near a major airport, especially one so centrally located. His job put him on the road a lot, often to distant parts of the country, sometimes to different parts of the world.

In a month, he would head up a team providing security for the Japanese delegation at the G7 summit in Aspen. His company had this project on the books for almost a year. When he realized that the summit timed well with elk hunting season, he and Thor, now a sheriff's deputy in Pitkin County, put in for tags in the April lottery and lucked out. Ironically, Thor had to bail when his office cancelled all leave because of the summit. Thor suggested that Tony take the kids—a timely idea. With Luke acting out, he wanted to spend as much time with him as possible.

Tony got home before the boys did and wandered around the townhouse, wishing he had the time to putter and an old fixer-upper to putter in. Maybe in a few years. He watched from behind the storm door as Matt pulled up in his ancient two-tone Camaro with Luke beside him. Matt smiled. He always did when he came home—almost always anyhow. Luke hadn't smiled, not really smiled, since his mother died.

MATT

Luke looked at his phone and then at his older brother. "New slow low, bro," he said without emotion. "You may have set the negative land speed record for a Camaro in the State of Kansas."

If the shrimp only knew, Matt thought, but said nothing. The boys exited either side of the car and slammed the doors behind them. As he walked up to the front door, Matt put his game face on. Luke didn't have one.

"Hey," Matt said with a grin as his father opened the door for him, "heard you were at school today." In passing, he looked at his father close-up and thanked whatever strains of his mother's DNA spared him those scars. Tougher times. Acne must have been a bitch. But the buzz cut? Couldn't blame that on the genes.

Matt kind of liked being taller than the old man too. Had him by a good two inches now. Still, he gave away about twenty pounds, and the difference wasn't fat. As fit as Matt was, no one was more fit than his father. He never kidded himself. Push come to shove, the old man would kick his ass.

"Yeah? Who told you I was there?"

"Just about everyone who saw the ZAM in the parking lot." ZAM was Matt's shorthand for "zombie apocalypse mobile." His dad had even begun to use the acronym himself. "Kind of stands out."

"You think?"

"It's not just the pre-historic paint job, Dad, but you got the only vehicle in the lot with a winch on the front, rock sliders on the sides, and a cargo rack on top."

"Hey, don't forget the swing-out fuel and tire carrier on the back."

"No, gosh, my oversight."

Tony invited his sons to grab a drink and meet him in the family room. They had something to talk about. Matt looked at Luke and Luke at Matt, each accusingly. Luke shrugged and went off to get a soda. Fearing the worst, Matt figured he would get it out in the open before his brother got back.

"Anything wrong?" Matt asked.

"Nothing new." His father seemed content to kill time.

"That's good, I guess."

"When's practice start?" his father asked.

"Officially, mid-November, unofficially, next week."

"How you guys looking this year?"

"Good. Deeper than last year."

"That'll help."

"Yeah, it should." Matt was beginning to feel confident this meeting wasn't about him. He loosened up. "I asked coach if I could move up to 195."

"195? Man, you're fearsome at 182. That's your natural weight."

Uh oh, thought Matt. His father was giving him that look, the penetrating stare that preceded a major life lesson. He'd seen it before.

"Yeah, maybe," said Matt, "but if I went to 195, I could eat more, bulk up, live like a human being my senior year."

"What's your team's primary mission this year?" said Tony, now leaning in.

"This year? To *win* State." He knew where this was heading, and it was too late to turn it around.

"Do you guys have a better chance with you at an unbeatable 182 or you at a chubby and iffy 195?"

"Chubby?" protested Matt. Still, he could feel himself surrendering. The old man had him on the mat, shoulders down.

"The team comes first," Tony smiled, "but I didn't have to tell you that either."

"Maybe you did," Matt conceded.

Luke took his sweet time returning to the room. With his drink in hand, he collapsed sullenly into his favorite chair. Matt marveled at how well his brother was able to communicate boredom and alienation without saying a word. The kid was getting easier to dislike by the day.

"I've got good news for you, and maybe some better news," said his father once Luke had settled in.

Matt breathed easier. Now he knew it wasn't about him. He had been waiting for the other shoe to drop since "the accident." It hadn't yet; maybe it never would. Strange thing, though, sometimes, especially when he lay sleepless in the hours before dawn, he almost wanted to be found out. He wondered if he would somehow feel better the day a police car pulled into the driveway and took him away. It would shatter their world, he knew, but it just might save his soul.

Tony

"The good news?" asked Matt.

"I'm going to take you both out of school for a week."

"That's cool," said Luke, almost smiling. Tony knew he meant it. He hated school. "And the better news?"

"We're going elk hunting in Colorado."

"That's the better news?" Luke groaned.

"Yes!" said Matt.

"Yeah, right, like I'm going elk hunting," Luke protested as though he had a choice.

"Excuse me?" said Tony.

"I'm not going," said Luke.

Tony stood up and motioned to Luke. "Come with me, please." Luke shrugged but offered no resistance. Tony led him out to the kitchen and sat him down on a kitchen chair opposite his own.

"There's something you are never going to do again in your life," he said in a tone that had chilled many a battle-hardened grunt. "You're never going to talk back to me. Understand?"

Luke nodded, his eyes locked on the tabletop.

"And when you become a parent, never let your kids talk back to you. That is the worst thing you could ever allow them to do. Understood?"

"Yes."

Tony bored in with an icy stare.

"Yes, sir."

"Good. Now get your sorry little butt back to the living room."

Fully composed, Tony followed his son and spent the next hour explaining the why of the elk hunt. Matt listened intently. He was the classic older son, Tony thought, always dutiful, almost always anyhow. Humble too—usually, at least. That part surprised Tony a little bit. The kid had picked a winning lottery number in the family gene sweepstakes: smarts, height, athletic ability, looks.

Tony tried to conjure up the term from some distant biology class; "hybrid vigor"—wasn't that it? Matt had pulled just the right combination from him and Angel. With his dark, swept-back hair and rugged features, he could pass as a native in just about any country in the western world and turn heads in all of them. And yet for all that, Tony could not fail to see the sadness in the boy's eyes. Unsure of its source, he chose not to probe, at least not for now. At seventeen, he had needed space, and figured Matt did too.

Luke was problem enough. As usual, the boy zoned out. He had found solace from all that was new, strange, and disturbing in his Xbox. There, he was master. Outside of it, he was his mother's son, fair-haired and undersized. Once too sweet for his own good, he had turned cynical, just another insecure, self-loathing kid on the cusp of adolescence, one who spoke only when spoken to and then just barely. Tony was not about to let him drift. Or get drugged. Luke was going elk hunting. He had no choice in the matter, and he did not have the *cojones*, thought Tony, to resist.

DAY 3

PEL

"Whose streets?"

"Our streets!"

"Whose streets?"

"Our streets!"

"Whose streets?"

"Enough already," Pel grumbled. Marching down Boylston Street towards Copley Square, dressed in black from head to toe, the balaclava revealing only his piercing, dark eyes, Pel was gripped by an emotion that he had been feeling more and more during these marches—boredom. He was too bored to even respond "Our streets" anymore. He had done this too many times in too many places for too many causes.

"Whose streets?"

Please! These streets aren't ours. Who are they kidding? In fifteen minutes, these streets would not know that he and the rest of the Black Bloc had ever been there. Hell, the only people who had made an impression on Boylston Street since the Revolution were the Tsarnaevs. Jahar may have been a clown, but Tamerlan was kickass. The Boston Marathon? That took some balls.

Pel joined the mixed martial arts center where Tamerlan worked out a year or so after Tamerlan went down. A lot of guys there knew Tamerlan, and at least a few of them bragged about it. Pel got close to one of them, a tough little dude from Azerbaijan, who put Pel in touch with a tougher character still, a guy who had the clout and connections to make things happen.

If this guy bought Pel's plan, in a few weeks time he and Moom were going to make the Tsarnaevs look like—what did O call it?—yeah, the junior varsity. *That's it*, he laughed. *The "JV."* They'd show these reformist pussies how to protest the president. Full of unspent fury, Pel kicked a newspaper dispenser on the side of the street. It wobbled and gave him an idea.

MOOM

"You sure you want to do that, bro?"

Pel was in a deep squat, trying to yank a newspaper box off its mooring.

"Yeah," he answered without looking around.

There was no stopping Pel when he got an idea in his head. The man was a bull, bullheaded too. Moom knew what was going to happen next. Yup, Pel picked the box up over his head, marched it over to the Uno Pizzeria on the north side of the street, and threw it through the plate glass window. Moom watched in awe as the glass shattered, the customers screamed, and the Black Bloc turned and cheered. His big brother did some crazy shit from time to time. No doubt about that.

"We got a lot going on, man," said Moom as Pel rejoined the march. "Shouldn't we be careful?"

"Don't be such a...liberal," Pel snickered, wiping some glass shards off his black-gloved hands. Pel never tired of telling Moom

how much he hated those sham anarchists and fake revolution-
aries who lacked the courage and integrity to confront fascists.
"Let's blend." He grabbed Moom by the arm and led him into
the crowd. The two ducked and weaved through the anonymous
Black Bloc swarm.

Pel laughed, "No security camera is going to pick us out."

Moom knew this to be true, but he knew, too, that his big
brother could be one scary dude.

DAY 5

On the road before first light, Luke sulked throughout the drive, much as expected. Tony let him be and quietly counseled Matt to do the same. He'd put up with worse, and Luke needed the preparation that a camping trip in Missouri could offer.

It took about four hours for them to reach the campground in the Mark Twain National Forest. The Ozarks weren't the Rockies, but they could test you. In fact, any backpacking trip could make you eat your mistakes if you weren't careful. He planned to throw as much outdoor knowledge at his sons as he could—fire starting, shelter building, some uphill hiking, orienteering with topo map and compass, anything and everything to survive in the woods, navigation included, day and night. No car camping here. Humping the ratlines in Afghanistan, he learned that if you couldn't carry your gear on your back, you didn't need it.

He observed the boys closely but discreetly. He had confidence in Matt. He had been old enough to get the benefit of Tony's outdoor knowledge before his last deployment and their subsequent relocation. For Luke, who was too young to absorb much back then, it was pretty much starting from scratch. In setting up the campsite, Luke was close to useless. Tony said nothing. He wanted to let the glory of an early October Ozark day work its magic on the boy. He was confident it would. On their late afternoon hike, Luke began to loosen up, just a little. When they reached a ridge overlooking some nameless valley, the oblique rays of the sun casting a magical light on the autumn-tinted slopes and the meadow below, Luke let loose with an almost involuntary, "For Missouri, this doesn't totally suck."

LUKE

"Awesome!" agreed Matt, now draping his arm over Luke's shoulder.

Luke shivered, uneasy at the touch. Matt had not done anything that big-brotherly since their mother's funeral, and Luke wasn't sure how he felt about it. He had begun to find the rhythm to his isolation. Alone, he could be as cool as he wanted to be. In the world, he was the loser.

Luke had had enough of losing: losing his mom, losing his home, losing his school, losing—and this he had a hard time framing even to himself—losing his boyhood. In high school, especially his snobby-assed prep school, he was encouraged to be someone he wasn't—someone who cared about girls and clothes and cars and beer and ski vacations in Colorado. He did not much care about any of those things. And if he did care, who at this school would notice? At fourteen, his voice hadn't changed, and his father bought his clothes at Walmart.

To him, an elk hunt sounded like one more opportunity for someone to force him to be what he wasn't—a hunter, a sportsman, someone who gave a rat's ass about nature. His father once described his son's idea of the "great outdoors" as that unhappy space between the front door and the car door, and Luke had to admit he wasn't far off.

He preferred the surreal world of Call of Duty. There, he was not the pitiful Luke, the kid bullied at school, but the powerful and mysterious "DefCon762," the envy of all his cyber enemies and allies. Luke only wished his dad appreciated how good he was at what he did. Whether he was fighting terrorists or zombies, DefCon762 could join any game and swing the odds in his team's favor. Almost no one could beat DefCon762, and no one at all could intimidate him.

TONY

Back at the campsite that evening, the three sat around the fire and mostly just stared into it. There was not much else to do, and no place else to go. For some time, they were silent, each deep in his private thoughts. When they did talk, they talked about nothing of consequence. Tony was content with this. He appreciated the mindlessness of their conversation. Some things he chose not to think about, Angel's death chief among them. The wound was still too raw.

Luke shocked him when he introduced her into the conversation. It was not like him. Not at all.

"How did you meet mom?"

"I haven't told you?"

"You told *me*," said Matt as he pushed a stray cinder back into the fire.

Matt seemed eager to change the subject. Tony wondered why. He chose not to ask.

"You haven't told *me*," said Luke, "at least not when I was old enough to remember."

Tony hesitated. "Let me compress this for Matt's sake," he said. "I was in church with your grandmother. She'd dedicated a Mass to my father who died ten years earlier on that day."

"How old were you?"

"Eighteen."

"You were eight when your father died?"

"Yup, but that's a story for another day," said Tony. "Anyhow, I looked over and I saw your mom a few pews ahead of me. The sunlight sort of flowed through the stained glass and lit up her hair like gold. She was so prayerful and peaceful I swore she was an angel."

"That's why you called her 'Angel'?"

"From that first day on. I hadn't been to a weekday Mass in years, but I went the next day, hoping she was one of those 'daily Mass' Catholics, and there she was again. The third day I sat in front of her so she would notice me. I tried to look as pious as I could."

"That's a stretch," said Matt, grinning.

"Hey, smartass, I was in love."

"Did she notice you?" Luke asked.

"Yeah, but you've got to remember, I was this poor, pock-marked homeboy." That he was. Truth be told, though, he had felt less burdened by his poverty or by his ethnicity than he did by his complexion, living as he had in Southern California where looks mattered more than race or class.

Tony added, "About the only thing I had going for me was, well, persistence."

"Persistence?"

"Don't underestimate it. I went to Mass for six weeks straight, seven days a week. Your grandma was convinced I was going to become a priest. It was when she started making noise about sending me to the seminary I got up the nerve to talk to my Angel. And then, of course, my charm kicked in. Who could resist?"

For a minute the three teased each other like old times. Luke broke the spell.

"Why," he asked with a seam of anger running through his voice, "did she have to die?"

Luke looked at his father and then his brother. Matt looked away. Tony thought, *Why does anyone have to die? We all die someday. Every bullet has a name on it.* These were all clichés, he realized, each equally meaningless. He cached them for another, lesser occasion.

"I can't tell you why she had to die," said Tony, "but I can tell you this…that since she died, I've really come to believe that there's a heaven, and that she's in it."

DAY 6

At first light, Tony noisily stuck his head into the pup tent the boys shared. They didn't stir. He coughed. Still nothing. With his headlamp, he threw a beam first in Matt's face, then Luke's. They grumbled. He took his canteen and held it over Matt's head. Matt got the message, popping out of his sleeping bag like a jack-in-the-box in long johns and shivering visibly. All the more reason to dress quickly.

"Dang," said Matt, "what's the temperature?"

"Somewhere between a witch's tit and a polar bear's right nut. Doesn't matter. Git up!"

Despite the ruckus, Luke slept—or more likely, pretended to. Not wanting to yell, Tony leaned over and whispered, "You better get your butt out of that sack or you'll regret it." When Luke still refused to move, Tony drizzled a little water into Luke's nose, the appendage sticking most visibly out of his mummy bag. That absolutely got his son's attention. When Luke started to shout, Tony clamped his hand over Luke's mouth and in the process made him feel a little bit as if he were drowning.

22

"Hate to do this," said Tony, his headlight beam full in Luke's eyes, "but when we're hunting, hollering is not an option."

After Tony removed his hand, Luke sprung up, unzipping his bag and sputtering. "I'm calling family services when we get back."

"Yeah, what are you going to tell them?"

"I'm going to tell 'em my old man waterboarded me."

"That just might make the evening news," Tony laughed. "Not many parents spank their little snowflakes nowadays, let alone waterboard them."

"But back when you were a boy," said Matt, stifling a laugh as he parodied his father's penchant for childhood poverty tales, "I bet parents routinely waterboarded their kids."

"Oh yeah, and much worse."

LUKE

By the time Luke was dressed and out of the tent, Matt was already eating, and his father was heating water on a mini camp stove. Once hot enough, he poured the water directly into an instant oatmeal packet.

"Try this," his dad said, handing over the sticky container gingerly. "Careful, it's hot."

Luke was impressed. It made for surprisingly good grub, but better still, clean up meant licking off the spoon and putting the empty pack in a trash bag. That was it.

"Want some more?" asked Tony. "You'll need all the carbs you can get. I'm going to work your excess flab off today."

"I don't get it," said Luke. "How much work can there be to hunting? You sit in a tree all day or something and fire a couple of shots. Can't be that hard."

His father's hearty laugh caught Luke off guard. "Oh, man," he scoffed, "you're going to regret even thinking that."

"Why?" he said.

"Shooting is the easy part. The real work begins after you shoot something. A bull elk weighs about seven or eight hundred pounds. I bring a block and tackle just in case one drops into a tight spot."

"Block and tackle?"

"Yeah, you know, a device, a couple pulleys and a rope. Makes it easier to move stuff."

"And then what? We drag it back?"

"No, no, no," said his dad, the exasperation altogether obvious to his son. "We've got to field dress the thing on the spot. That means taking the hide off, cutting and quartering it. Then if the terrain's too rough for the horses…"

"Horses?"

"Oh man, you've got a lot to learn. Anyhow, we've got to carry about two hundred pounds of meat back to where the horses are."

"I don't have a choice in this, right?" said Luke with as much defiance as he could muster.

When his father turned to answer, the warmth had drained from his face. "No," he said much too quietly. "You don't."

Luke understood right then, as a thousand young soldiers must have understood before him, that he would do what he was told whether he liked it or not. And so began one very long, very hard day on the trail, a day that ended with blistered feet, sore shoulders, and a grudging respect for his father's will.

PEL

Pel strode purposefully on a northeast angle towards the Frog Pond. Moom struggled to keep up.

"C'mon," said Pel, "I don't want to keep this guy waiting."

"You trust him?" said Moom.

"Not really."

"What did you say his name was?"

"Didn't. Don't know. Just the letter R. That's all I know."

"So that's what we call him, 'R'?"

"Yup."

"Just R?"

"Yup."

"Wish you told me more about him."

"Wish I knew more."

"Local?"

"Been here a while but still has an accent from some backwater Asian country."

Pel spotted his contact sitting on the grass, facing the pond, on the Beacon Street side. Pel nodded in recognition. R nodded back.

MOOM

R surprised him. He was older than Moom would have thought and almost suburban looking.

"Please give your brother your phone," R said to Pel. Pel looked confused for just half a second and then handed Moom his iPhone.

"Now we hug," said R as he stood and embraced Pel, patting him carefully.

"Just one phone?"

"Yeah," Pel answered.

R turned his attention to Moom. "Circle the Commons, please," he said. "When you see us stand up again, come back."

Moom looked to his brother for confirmation.

"Yeah," Pel said. "Do what he asks."

"Okay," said Moom. "Whatever." He took a last look at R. His hair was neatly combed and grey-streaked, his face weathered. He guessed him to be Pel's height—a little north of six feet—and not quite as thick through the chest, but someone you wouldn't want to mess with. The accent was the giveaway, the occasional dropped "a" and "the," but Pel could hear almost as much Boston as wherever the guy was from. Not the most musical of combinations.

What impressed him, though, and it struck him as weird that he was impressed, was the kindness of the man's eyes. Moom never noticed those kind of things. This time he did. He wasn't sure what it meant. Probably nothing.

PEL

With Moom gone, R sat down on the grass and signaled Pel to do the same. They sat in silence for a minute, maybe two, both starting at the Frog Pond. Pel did not want to be the first to talk.

"Just a couple of nancy boys taking in an October afternoon," said R casually, breaking the silence.

"What?" said Pel with a startled laugh.

"That is what people say when they walk by and look at us. Just a couple of nancy boys taking in an October afternoon."

"No, not in Boston," Pel smirked. "Even if they knew what a nancy boy was, especially if they knew, they wouldn't dare even think the word."

"No," R corrected him. "They do not say it, but they do think it. When you are not allowed to say something, you think it. Privately you even joke about it. That is how our people survived Soviet days. It is our little rebellion."

"You'd know better than me."

R fell silent again. Pel felt as if he were being tested. When R spoke again, all the irony had drained from his voice. "You are sure of your information?"

"Yeah."

"Your guy in the travel office, you trust what he says?"

"Totally."

R fell silent, staring directly now into Pel's eyes, the window of his soul. "Okay, your idea is good," R said. "I like it. It is bold."

"Great," said Pel, suppressing the urge to jump up and punch the air.

"But is just an idea, not a plan," said R. "To turn idea into a plan will cost."

"Can you give me a ballpark?"

"Ballpark?"

"Estimate."

R scratched the number "200" in the dirt with his finger.

"K?" asked Pel.

"Kay?"

"Thousand."

"Yes."

"Seriously?"

"No, asshole," said R, his tone changing on a dime. "I am just pleasuring myself."

"Sorry." Pel did not know what to think. The man threw him off balance.

"Of course, I am serious. This is serious business."

"Two hundred is the cost to me?"

"Yes."

"I was kind of hoping you would underwrite it."

"We are. I am volunteering my time and equipment. What do they call that? In-kind donation? Two hundred is my out-of-pocket cost—your cost."

Pel fell silent. He did not know quite what to say.

"You are never allowed to talk details," R filled in the void. "Not even with your brother, no specifics. Uncle Sam has no balls, but he has ears."

"Understood."

"Ears everywhere."

"Got you."

R fell silent again. He picked up a stone and flung it into the pond.

Pel spoke up. "D-Day is a fixed date."

"Yes," said R. "You do not have much time."

"No," Pel sighed. "True enough."

"I know what you are thinking," said R. "Where in hell do I raise this money?"

"You're right about that."

R told him.

MOOM

Moom saw R spring to his feet from across the pond. *Pretty nimble for an old dude*, he thought. He watched the man stride away as if the world turned at his command. Pel stood now too. Even from a distance, he looked anxious.

"Yo, bro," said Pel as Moom approached. Then, lowering his voice, "We're a go."

"Man!"

"But…"

"But what?"

"We got to raise some money."

"How much?"

Pel hesitated, then whispered, "Two hundred."

"Thousand?"

"Yeah."

"Damn. Where's that coming from? Mom?"

"No."

"You know she's always been *down for the cause, man*," said Moom, imitating his mother's old-timey rhetoric.

"Yeah," Pel said. "You name your kids after cop killers, that's something of a commitment. No, we need more than that old hippie bitch has got in this world, and we got to raise it pretty damn quick."

Moom winced at the "bitch" line but said nothing.

"How quick?"

"We have to deliver it to Colorado within two weeks."

"Two weeks?"

Pel pulled his brother close and tousled his hair. He did this often. Moom wasn't sure how he felt about it. Yeah, there was something big-brotherly about the gesture, but it was also Pel's way of reminding him who was bigger, who was stronger, and who, finally, was in control.

"R gave me an idea," said Pel. He grabbed his phone and walked off a few feet to make a call in private. When he turned around, he had a big smile on his face.

"Let's pack up the truck, Moom. We're going to New York."

DAY 7

PEL

"I missed this," said Pel, lying on his side, happily spent, rubbing Chelsea's shoulders from behind.

"*You* missed it?" sighed Chelsea. "It's been too long. Way too long."

"First time I've been to the city in a year," he said as wistfully as he could fake. "They've got us going all over the place."

Pel was telling the truth, in a limited way. He had not been to New York in a year. The direct source of his subsidy, the Coalition Against Fascism, had delegated him to various hot spots around the country to organize actions.

"Boston's only a few hours away," she protested. "You could have called."

"Sounding a bit bourgeois there, aren't we, sweets?"

With that, Chelsea reached over to grab a cigarette and a lighter and sat upright, the sheets sliding indifferently off her breasts.

"I have my bourgeois moments," she said, almost in the way of apology, as she lit her cigarette.

"I noticed," he laughed, leaning on his elbow and waving his free arm at Chelsea's well-appointed Boerum Hill rental, now nicely revealed by the first hint of daylight.

"Our mutual friend set me up," she smiled ruefully.

Pel raised his eyebrows, saying nothing. He didn't need to.

"He has me infiltrating Wall Street."

"What's this," said Pel looking around the room, "your honey trap?" He was joking.

"Yes." She wasn't.

"Really?" said Pel, unable to hide his chagrin. He had yet to kill his inner moralist. It bugged the shit out of him. "Is the trap working?"

"You don't want to know the details."

"Damn, girl!"

"Who's being bourgeois now?"

She had him. He was. He hated the idea of what they had her doing.

"You've come a long way since DisruptJ20." Pel switched the subject lest he betray his unease.

"I miss those days," said Chelsea. "The inauguration was a trip. I'll never forget it. The Nazis wore blue, and you wore black."

"We'll always have Washington," Pel added, picking up on the *Casablanca* riff.

Chelsea put down her cigarette and pulled on Pel's dirty blond dreadlocks.

"You're too good-looking, Pel. It's corrupted you."

"Aw, c'mon."

"Corrupted me too. I let myself fall in love."

He knew she meant it. "I wish I could have allowed myself that privilege," he lied. At the time, he considered Chelsea so much roadkill. Yeah, she was lithe and young and pretty, but there was always someone as lithe and young and pretty in every city and on every campus he visited. He leaned his head against her shoulder. "You were one of a kind."

"Thanks, Pel."

"You *are* one of a kind."

Pel knew Chelsea wanted to believe him, just like every other woman he had used that line on. He learned over time that he could strip a would-be feminist of her ideology almost as quickly as he could remove her clothes. It was sexist to think that way, but hell, he took a certain rebel pride in the maleness of it all. Feminism was a trick on liberals, a drain on the antifascist cause.

"I need your help," he said.

"What's up?"

He told her—told her much more than R would have approved.

TONY

"Rise and shine," said Tony, shaking Luke awake. "We're going to the range."

Monday was a teacher in-service day. They had a lot of them. Too many, Tony thought, especially at that tuition rate. But this one came in handy. Luke made some minimal progress on the weekend camping trip, but he needed to make a whole lot more. The boy tried to pull the covers over his head. Tony pulled them off. "Get your sorry butt out of bed," he said with enough authority to make Luke listen.

Both of his sons had been to the range before, but not recently, and neither was keen on going in the morning, especially after an exhausting weekend. It didn't matter. When Tony was ready to roll, so was his company, or at least it better be. He had his guns and gear at the ready. He always did. Live on a firebase long enough—and "long enough" could mean one day—and you learn to stay prepared. Your life depended on it. Literally. What happened to anyone happened to everyone.

Tony kept his rifles in the "refrigerator," code for the two gun safes in the basement. As the boys dressed, he pulled out his stainless steel Ruger Redhawk .44 Magnum, a bigger, heavier gun than the Kimber he typically carried. He could use the practice. He didn't plan on bringing a rifle to the range or on the trip. There was no need. He wanted the boys to have the bragging rights.

Opening the next refrigerator, Tony smiled at his sentimental favorite: a vintage military 1903 Springfield rifle, less the upper handguard and about a foot of the forestock. Years ago, Angel's father bought it as army surplus and modified it. A history buff, Tony liked the idea that the .30-06, a cartridge designed in 1906—thus the "ought six"—was still downing more game in North America than any other.

Tony took out both of the Remington 700 .280s he had bought for the boys. The first one he got for Matt, but when a friend offered to sell him a nearly identical .280, he jumped at the chance—even if Uncle Sam wouldn't recognize their ownership until the boys turned eighteen. Tony liked the fact that the Remington would hold a tighter group than his Springfield (or any of his other rifles for that matter). For ammo, his favorite was a Barnes 140 grain TTSX, a solid copper, low-drag bullet that launched at almost three thousand feet per second and shot like a death ray. He kind of enjoyed the feel of that.

LUKE

At the Foggy Creek Gun Club there were a couple old guys on one of the pistol ranges, but as Luke hoped, he and Matt had the rifle range to themselves. If he could transfer his Xbox skills, he thought he'd do okay, but he wasn't sure.

He and Matt set up while their father walked down range and posted targets at the two-hundred-yard mark.

"Don't forget to—" said Matt.

"I know," Luke interrupted. "Open the bolt before setting it on the bench."

"Yeah, especially with Dad down range."

"You don't have to tell me that."

"Ease up, douchebag," said Matt. "I'm just trying to protect the one parent we got left."

"I get you, but I'm sick of being…patronized," Luke grumped. He regretted using that word the moment he said it. He knew how his brother would turn it against him.

"Patronized, huh?" said Matt. "Patronized? You're paying more attention at school than they give you credit for."

Matt was right. Luke was paying attention. He just saw no good reason to let anyone know he was.

TONY

With the targets up, Tony headed back towards his sons. It had been a year or so since he had taken the boys shooting. He was sure Matt would do well, but he wasn't so sure about Luke. The kid had a great eye, he knew that, but he also had a confidence issue. Shooting was kind of like sleeping or making love, thought Tony. The moment you start thinking you can't, you can't.

As Matt got ready to shoot, Tony shared some further words of wisdom. "Wind shouldn't be a factor," he said. "Fear shouldn't be either." He sometimes wondered if he piled too much advice on his kids, but he wasn't going to have them around too much longer to work on.

"This is a one-way range," he added. "Targets don't shoot back. Neither do elk."

"Some elk do," Luke deadpanned.

"Okay," said Tony. "I'll bite. Which elk?"

"Elk Qaeda."

The groans could be heard in Missouri.

MATT

Matt sat down on the folding metal chair to the left of his rifle and started adjusting the sand bags so the crosshairs of the rifle's scope would rest on the target. He relished the precision of it all.

"One last thing," said Tony. "I've been messing with the trigger."

"I got it, Dad. I'll figure it out."

"Alright then, Matt, you're good to go."

Matt put four rounds in the magazine well, pushed the bolt forward to chamber a round, and pulled the butt into his shoulder. He made a few minor adjustments, clicked off the safety with his thumb, took a good breath, exhaled and took another, let some air out, held still, and slowly applied pressure to the trigger to take up the slack, but there was no slack to take up. To his surprise, the rifle discharged and sent the round screaming downrange.

Matt looked up at his father. "What?"

"Nice touch, huh? I installed new Timney triggers. Not cheap, but they're crisp."

"I think you got your money's worth."

"Tried to tell you."

Matt reset himself and settled back in behind the rifle. This time when he squeezed the trigger he was ready. The bullet spiraled towards the target. It felt good. He jacked the bolt back, ejecting the brass case, then chambered another round and repeated the process.

"How does it look?" said Matt to his brother who was manning the spotting scope.

"The three of them are pretty tight, but that first one was, like, way off."

"Another inch or so," Tony laughed, "and that flyer would be orbiting the earth."

"C'mon, Dad, cut me some slack. What do I got to do?"

Luke yielded the spotting scope to his father, who made the calculation. "Ten clicks up and right eight clicks," he said to Matt. "Looks like you're a little over one MOA," said Tony.

"MOA?" said Luke.

"In the field, it's all jargon and acronyms. MOA means minute of angle, just over one inch at one hundred yards, 1.047 inches to be exact—so a little more than two inches at two hundred yards, three inches at three hundred yards. You get the picture."

Matt made the adjustment to his scope and didn't ask any questions. By his third round he put all four shots in the rough center of the target with none more than two and a half inches from the others. His father took another look through the spotting scope.

"Good going, Matt. I wouldn't want to be standing down range with you shooting at me."

"I wouldn't want to be down range with anybody shooting at me," said Matt.

"Got a point," said his dad. "Luke, you're up."

LUKE

When Matt finished, Luke sat down, extended his rifle, and began to twist the zoom on the scope.

"Leave it at 3X. We'll practice like we'll shoot in the mountains," said his dad with authority. No surprise. Everything he said at the range, Luke thought, he said with authority.

Luke wasn't about to argue. Once settled in, he adjusted the front bag and looked through the rifle's scope. Then he adjusted the rear bag and looked again through the scope. He pulled the chair in closer, took another look, adjusted the front bag, looked again, pushed the chair out just a bit, and took another look. He moved his chair to the right, looked again, and slid the rear bag forward just a little bit.

"C'mon, Sergeant York," Matt ribbed him. "Pull the freakin' trigger."

Luke wanted to do well. He didn't need any more pressure than he already felt. In combat, his father had told him, fear could turn a crack range shooter into a totally useless loser, and he had a deep-down fear that a loser is what he was and always would be. He had heard that word enough at school that he had begun to believe it. He got angry thinking about it, got angry at his parents for skipping him ahead a grade. No matter how smart they thought he was, they messed up his life. Being the youngest kid in his class totally sucked.

"Remember," Tony eyed Matt and said softly, "you guys are a team." Luke nodded. So did his brother.

"Come on, Luke," said Matt, now gently placing his hand on Luke's left shoulder to calm him. "Pretend it's Call of Duty. No one makes a better sniper than you do. This is your game." Luke smiled a little and settled down.

"Just straighten your back now," said Matt, "and rotate your head to relax your muscles." Luke caught the change in tone and did as asked, this time without resistance.

"Ready?"

With the crosshairs resting in the center of the target, Luke knew he was ready. He nodded slightly. Matt looked through the spotting scope.

"Okay, send it."

Luke thumbed off the safety, took a deep breath, and let it out. He then took another breath, let out some of the air, and started carefully increasing the pressure on the trigger with the tip of his finger. When the trigger "broke," and the gun drove into Luke's waiting shoulder, he relaxed, straightened up, worked the bolt, loaded a cartridge, and repeated the process. After four shots Luke looked over to Matt, who was staring through the scope.

"Well?" Luke flicked a bead of sweat from near his eye.

"I'd come down three clicks and right one," said Matt. "Inch and a half high and about a half left."

While Luke settled back in behind the rifle, Matt got up from the spotting scope and gestured for his father to take a look. Tony put his eye to the scope, looked, blinked his eyes, and looked again.

"The kid can shoot," Matt whispered to Tony just loud enough for Luke to hear.

Luke moved to the second target and repeated the feat. His anxiety was melting away. He was back in front of the Xbox, kicking ass and taking names.

"How did he do?" his father asked Matt when Luke had finished.

"See for yourself," he said, moving out of the way so his father could see through the spotting scope.

"How did I do?" Luke chimed in, sounding to himself a little more eager than he wanted to.

"Not bad," said his father. "We'll measure when we take the targets down, but I'll bet a half dollar could cover all four shots."

"This kid's a natural," whispered Matt to his father. Luke wasn't sure he was supposed to hear that, but he did. He heard his father's response as well.

"No," his dad whispered back, "he's unnatural."

MATT

"I tell you what," said Tony to his sons. "We couldn't get away with this normally, but since no one is here, let's try shooting prone."

"Prone?" said Luke. "Like right on the ground?"

"No," said Matt. "We'll go to the Rent-a-Center and get you a futon."

"No need. I got ground cloths and pads in the Land Cruiser," said Tony. "You never know what you need to lie on or sit on when you're out shooting in the wild."

Matt volunteered to grab a ground cloth. The guy who owned their house before they did left a five-foot wide roll of Tyvek in the garage. Of all the crap he left behind it was the only useful thing. It was lightweight, water repellant, and supple after a trip through the washing machine. Tony used sheets of it as ground cloths, as tarps, even as an emergency blankets when push came to shove.

"Here it be," said Matt on returning. He handed his father a sheet.

"Love this stuff," said Tony, petting it like a dog before placing it on the ground.

"You know, said Matt with a straight face. "Tyvek being all white and wonderful in every which way, I was wondering if when I got married my bride could make her wedding gown out of this stuff, assuming we still have some left over?"

"Sure," Tony snapped back, "assuming you marry a woman?"

"Aw, man, that's cold."

"You deserve it," said Tony with a smile. "Now get your sorry butt over here and let's get started."

TONY

While shooting prone, Matt's grouping widened. That was to be expected. Luke's grouping stayed tight. That was unexpected. Satisfied that they had absorbed about all they could in a morning, Tony led them over to the pistol range. Here, today at least, they were going to watch and learn. He laid out the massive revolver with its eye-popping six-inch barrel and invited his sons to pick it up.

Matt didn't hesitate. "You must like this cannon a lot," he said. "Pretty heavy to haul up a mountain."

"Not too heavy."

"Expect to use it?"

"Never know. With a few hundred pounds of elk meat on your saddle, we might have some uninvited dinner guests."

"I hear bears don't have particularly good table manners," said Matt.

"It's our job to teach them some."

"Will bear spray help?" asked Luke. Matt laughed, but Tony hushed him.

"Stuff works," he said. "Let her rip for about five or so seconds, and you can stop a bear at about twenty-five feet. Won't hurt to bring some."

"And if the bear spray doesn't work?" asked Luke.

"Then it comes down to guns and prayers," said Tony. As he loaded the .44, he explained that to be fast you had to shoot on the way up and stay focused on the front sight.

"Just as the sight reaches the target," he said, "you pull the trigger straight through in one smooth stroke." He then fell silent and demonstrated to the boys what he had just told them. They didn't always listen to their father when in teaching mode, but from the wide-eyed looks on their faces, Tony could tell that this monster had caught their attention.

MOOM

Moom saw the sign for Dean Street up ahead and breathed easier. He had been hanging around Brooklyn all day and into the evening, killing time. He drank lots of coffee and played a thousand games of Candy Crush on his iPhone, but mostly he just moved from one ten-minute or twenty-minute or thirty-minute parking place to another. The way he figured, there were only about twelve parking spots in the whole damn borough and at any given moment a million people in a million cars were circling around hunting for them.

He turned left on Dean and eased his way down the quiet, tree-lined street. He found the number to Chelsea's building but didn't see Pel. He was supposed to be out front. Moom stopped and waited. Although one-way, the street was still too narrow. Cars had to finesse their way around him. He quickly learned that New Yorkers—even nice liberal millennial New Yorkers—

had little patience, and they were not afraid to communicate that impatience by some combination of horn, mouth, and middle finger. If Pel were there, Moom suspected he would have dragged at least one of these clowns out of the car and reminded him—or her—why not to call someone you don't know an "asshole."

Better to just move on. Moom drove around, stopping here and there, waiting for a call or a text. He wished Pel would have told him what they were doing in Brooklyn, but maybe he was better off not knowing. After a few minutes of aimless circling, he was relieved to see Pel's name surface on his cell.

"I'm out front, pick me up," Pel barked into the phone.

"That's what you said twenty minutes ago."

"Sorry, this time I really am out front."

Moom did as told. He always did. Pel was there as promised. He hopped in the car, typed an address into his phone, and waited for instructions. A British lady told them to turn right at the end of the block.

"Where we going?" asked Moom.

"Brighton Beach."

"What's there?"

"A poker game."

"You playing?"

"Nope," said Pel, pausing for effect, then slipping into a little gangsta talk, "We be robbin'."

"Hmmm," Moom grunted at a loss for words. "We've never exactly done that before."

"There's a lot we're going to do that we haven't done before."

"I suppose."

"Suppose nothing. You better come to terms with that."

Moom stared ahead and drove, waiting for Pel to say something next. This whole project scared him. If he had a home to go to he'd go, but his mother was a head case and his father was a memory. Pel was all the family he had, and had been since his parents split so many moons ago. Pel had always been there for him, always stood up for him. He could not imagine letting Pel down.

"What's the plan?"

"That remains to be seen. We'll know more when we get to Brighton Beach."

"Chelsea in on this?"

"Yeah."

"How much did you tell her?"

"Too much."

"R won't be pleased."

"R doesn't have to know."

Moom fell silent for a moment. "I always liked Chelsea."

"Good. Because we're staying at her place this week."

"Beats sleeping in the truck."

"Where did you end up?"

"Under the highway, down by the waterfront. Spooky place."

"You survived."

Interesting choice of words, thought Moom, "survive." Surviving one night in a truck was no big deal, even in Brooklyn. Surviving this whole damn adventure was another thing altogether.

PEL

Pel had a hard time believing how big Brooklyn was. They had been driving forty minutes in pretty light traffic and had not yet gotten to Brighton Beach. Along the way, he had the chance to fill Moom in on the details of the job ahead. No need to burden the boy with too much information in advance, though.

Yes, R was the one who told him about this game. He knew these Russians played for high stakes—very high on Friday nights—at a place called "The Caspian," a boutique hotel in the Russian enclave that was Brighton Beach. "Little Odessa," they called it. From what Pel had gleaned, R loved to see Russians get screwed. He hated them even more than he did the Great Satan. Moom listened, but said little.

"You think this is like a test?" asked Moom out of nowhere. He turned to Pel when he asked this. Pel could read the anxiety in his eyes. The kid was so young, so fair. Sometimes Pel regretted pulling Moom out of school. With his sweet Anglo features and floppy blond hair, Moom could have been prom king this year at just about any dipshit suburban high school in America. Still, he wished the boy would muscle up a little, put on some weight, add some spine.

"Yeah, probably," said Pel. "If we pass, the show's on. If we fail, R figures we weren't cut out for this shit in the first place."

"Turn left on Brighton Beach Avenue," said the British woman in Pel's phone.

"Doesn't look much like a beach town," said Moom.

"Doesn't," said Pel. "Brooklyn *de la mer*."

"Turn right on Brighton Beach 4th Street," said the woman.

It was mostly just apartment buildings, not new cool ones with terraces and the like, but old brick ones that could have passed for housing projects in a different neighborhood. A lot of the signs were in Russian.

"Turn left on Brightwater Court."

Pel pulled a blanket out from behind his seat and a crude cardboard sign that read, "Vet, homeless, please help."

"Look for Coney Island Avenue," said Pel. "Just drop me on the corner and keep going."

"Then what?"

"Stay with the truck, keep close, and listen for a call. I may need you."

Moom stopped as told. Without a word, Pel jumped out of the cab and walked south into the wind whistling off the water. The Caspian Hotel stood at the end of the street, which dead-ended at a boardwalk. It looked like one of those fancy shore homes that someone could no longer afford and sold out to someone who could. Immediately across the street from the Caspian was the YMHA. Jews were soft touches, thought Pel. They wouldn't dare ask a homeless war vet to up and move, especially one who sat so quietly and humbly in the shadows.

He took off the Red Sox cap he was wearing, placed it in front of him, and put a few singles of seed money in it. With no better plan, he watched and waited. He was not sure what he hoped to see, but he knew he needed to see something.

The occasional passerby threw him some change. One young woman asked him if he had a place to stay. He was tempted to say, "Is that a proposition?" but thought better of it. The last thing he needed was attention. Besides, the bitch had spiked orange hair and about fifty pounds more than she needed to get through life. Pel laughed to himself, *Yes, beggars can be choosers.*

After about an hour of nothing, a large, bald fellow in a tight-fitting black suit walked out in front of the hotel and stood there unmoving. Pel looked at his phone. It was exactly eight p.m. No more than five minutes later a car pulled into the hotel's circular drive—a Lexus—and a man got out the driver's side. This man was older, stouter, shorter, grayer, and better dressed than the man who was waiting for him. He gave the keys to the big man who, in turn, gave them to a young guy in a valet jacket. The valet drove the car away.

Without being asked, the older man held his arms out at his sides parallel to the ground. The big man patted him down and nodded when he was finished. He made no attempt to hide what he was doing. The older man nodded back and entered the hotel. In the next half hour, six other men pulled up in front of the hotel and repeated the ritual. None of the men were young or appeared particularly fit. All dressed halfway well, either sport coats or sharp leather jackets. All drove nice cars—one, unmistakably, a Maserati. These guys, thought Pel, had to be the players.

For about a half hour after the last man entered, nothing happened. No one left the hotel or entered. The big man, however, still stood vigil. Soon enough, Pel saw why. A skinny, young guy on a red motor scooter pulled up in front of the hotel, grabbed a large red warmer bag from the red box on the back of the scooter, and approached the big man. As if on cue, the kid opened the bag, and the big man casually looked inside. He patted the kid down and sent him into the hotel.

At the sight, Pel pulled out his phone and called Moom.

"You nearby?"

"Not far, why?"

"In a couple minutes, a kid on a red motor scooter will leave from in front of the Caspian. I need you to follow him."

"I'm on my way."

"Be discreet."

"Understood."

"Don't talk to him. He's delivering pizzas. I want to know where he comes from. So stay with him even if he makes other stops.

"Got you."

"Sure?"

"Yeah."

"Okay, just don't fuck up."

MOOM

Damn, why did Pel have to say that? Why did he have to take that last parting shot? Here he was, on a kamikaze mission to rob a Russian poker game, and his brother had to make him feel like dog shit. *Pel didn't mean it,* he thought, he hoped, *but damn!*

Moom pulled up to the corner where Brightwater Court dead-ended at Coney Island Avenue. Since Brightwater was one-way heading east, he figured the kid had no real choice but to continue north on Coney Island. He would simply turn left behind him. His heart skipped when he saw the kid pull out from the Caspian, and skipped again when the kid turned left past Moom, heading west, the wrong way on one-way Brightwater.

"Damn," shouted Moom.

Pel would kill him if he lost this kid. He thought for a second of executing a K-turn in the middle of the intersection and speeding down Brightwater after the kid, but that would blow whatever cover he had. Instead, he did the only thing he could do: track the kid through his side view mirror until he turned right two blocks down.

His phone rang. He looked at the name. It was Pel. Moom ignored the call. He had no time for his brother's bullshit. He turned north on to Coney Island Avenue, sped up the street to Brighton Beach Avenue, blew through the red light, and turned left into traffic. Racing down the street he saw a pizza place on his left at 5th, and—*hot damn!*—the kid was pulling into it.

Moom U-turned into a ten-minute pick-up spot in front and called his brother.

"He works for Pizza Hutch. It looks like some kind of Pizza Hut knock-off."

"Good job," said Pel. "Come get me."

"On the way, bro."

Moom had to laugh at his own pathetic self. Just one little stroke from Pel was all it took to get him back in the game.

DAY
8

Moom pulled up hard in front of a weary brick warehouse by the Lafarge concrete plant off the Gowanus Canal in Brooklyn in the shadow of the Gowanus Expressway.

"This is it?" asked Pel skeptically.

"This is it," said Chelsea, sitting between the brothers on the truck's bench seat.

"What's the guy's name?" Pel asked.

"Not sure. We call him 'Rainman.'"

"Rainman?" gasped Pel. "Like in the movie?"

"Afraid so."

"That's not very encouraging."

"He's pretty high functioning though," said Chelsea, "and I wouldn't call him Rainman to his face."

"Thanks for the tip."

"Honk three times," she said. Moom did as told, and the door groaned open in front of them. Moom pulled in slowly. The opening was barely wider than his truck. In the abrupt shift from noonday sun to semi-darkness, Pel could see almost nothing, including the hand that pulled open the passenger-side door. He jumped.

"Didn't mean to alarm you, alarm you," the man said. He was tall—Pel could now see—balding, and a little stooped. He had curly mutton chop sideburns and wore a pair of safety glasses on a string around his neck. *Strange looking dude*, Pel thought. *Could be any age between 30 and 70.*

"No problem," said Pel, sliding out of the truck and shaking the man's leathery hand. Chelsea slid out behind him.

The man made no effort to introduce himself. "Chelsea tells me you need some assistance," he said without inflection, "assistance."

"Yeah," said Pel.

"I can help, can help," said the man.

Pel liked to think he could size people up quickly, but this man defied easy assessment. Chelsea referred to him as the movement's "technician," a guy who knew everything about everything technical. Pel expected someone younger, hipper, more comradely. This guy was definitely none of the above. Standing in the midst of a cluttered workshop, thinking out loud in his greasy mustard-colored jumpsuit, the man would have seemed more at home at a small town chop shop or at an institution for people half a bubble off plumb.

"Tell him what you need," said Chelsea. "You can trust him."

Pel looked over at his brother, now standing on the far side of the truck and leaning on the hood. Moom just shrugged. That was no help. Pel decided to plow ahead. If the Feds were going to run a sting, they would have used someone a notch or two lower on the autism scale.

"Okay, here's the deal," said Pel. "I need two guns, one scary but small enough to fit inside one of those pizza warming bags."

"And the other, the other?"

"You know, just a regular handgun."

"Why do you need them? Why?"

Pel looked to Chelsea. She nodded.

"We're going to rob a poker game," said Pel.

"Where?"

"Brighton Beach."

"Russians?"

"Yeah."

"You're right," the man sputtered. "One of those weapons better be scary, be scary."

"Can you help us?" asked Chelsea.

"When do you need them by?"

"Friday," said Pel.

The man rubbed his chin as though he were playing the old geezer role in some '30s screwball comedy.

"For friends of Chelsea, yes, yes I can," he said after due reflection.

"Great," said Pel. "And the cost?"

"Don't worry about it," said the man, still smiling. "We have the same paymaster, paymaster, the same."

"Whatever," said Pel.

The man looked over at Moom.

"You guys hungry?"

"Kind of," said Moom shyly.

"Good," the man laughed slyly. "Let's order some pizza."

"Pizza," said Pel. "Pizza."

MOOM

Driving more or less randomly around Brighton Beach, Moom found himself laughing every time he thought about the meeting with Rainman earlier in the day. *What a trip!* Mostly, though, he was waiting for a call from Pel, who was camped out again in front of the YMHA. He passed by the Pizza Hutch on Brighton Beach Avenue a few times, but not so many times as to call attention to his truck. In this borough of precious little cars, a pickup kind of stood out, especially an old, ratty one with an oversized camper shell on the back.

His one task was to find a spot off the street where they could hold the pizza kid in the camper while they robbed the game. That spot wasn't going to be on Brightwater. Like most streets in the neighborhood, Brightwater was dark and narrow and faced on both sides with apartment buildings. There was no commerce on the street, no place to idle, not even for a minute.

Coney Island Avenue was a different story. Moom had pulled into a BP station just a couple blocks north of the Caspian and looked around. The space was tight, but there were half-a-dozen cars squeezed in away from the pumps. After gassing up, Moom went into the seedy little shop on the premises to get a coffee. They didn't have any made. *Weird*, thought Moom. He bought some Peanut M&Ms, his personal weakness, and approached the little foreign dude skulking in a glass-encased booth that looked like it could withstand an RPG attack. Moom paid through a tray that slid in and out.

Above the man on the right were a few closed circuit screens. They did not show much beyond the pumps and the store entrance. This place had possibilities. If the man was too chickenshit to come out and make coffee, he wasn't about to roust Moom for parking on his property for ten minutes.

Pel called about ten. When Moom picked him up, he could see his brother was pissed.

"Nothing," said Pel. "No bouncer, no poker game, no pizza delivery."

"Maybe it's every other night," Moom ventured. "Monday, Wednesday, and the big game on Friday."

"Maybe," said Pel.

Moom drove by the BP station on the way back to Chelsea's and had Pel check it out. His brother approved. The evening wasn't a total loss.

DAY
9

MOOM

At a minute or so after eight o'clock, the phone buzzed. Moom picked it up while navigating traffic on Coney Island Avenue. It was Pel.

"Doorman's back," he whispered.

"Good," said Moom, reflexively. He was not sure it was good.

"Get to the Pizza place and look for the kid from Monday."

"Okay."

"Can you pick him out from the others?"

"Think so. Skinny, greasy little dude."

"Follow him."

"I'll do my best."

Moom wasn't sure he could ID the kid. He wasn't even sure the same kid would get the call. He drove back up Brighton Beach Avenue to the Pizza Hutch and pulled in to a ten-minute spot and waited. Sure enough, just about twenty minutes after he got there, the kid emerged from the store with a big floppy warmer bag, hopped on his scooter, and headed south down Brighton 4th Street. Moom followed. This time the kid was going the right way on the one-way street. At Brightwater Court, the kid turned left, east. Moom watched from a distance. He could see well enough if the kid turned right on to Coney Island Avenue. That he did. It was the same kid, the same destination.

Moom turned left when he got to Coney Island Avenue and headed for the BP station. Cool. There were a couple spaces still available. Pel would be pleased. Pleasing Pel, Moom realized, mattered too much.

DAY 10

TONY

Two days removed from range practice, Tony flew to North Carolina. He had not been back since they moved. When threat assessment training at Fort Bragg broke early, he steeled himself to do something he had not done since the day he buried Angel—visit her grave.

The morning had been dreary, the sky close and ominous. As he found his way to the small rural cemetery, the clouds parted just a little, and the sun struggled through. There was something mystical about the light—something mystical about the whole experience, for that matter.

The marker was not hard to find. It was a carved angel about three feet high. On the base was her name and the years of her birth and her death, and below them the inscription, "Our Angel." That was it. Tony knelt beside the statue. He felt as if he were supposed to cry, but that's not who he was. Instead, he prayed.

"Angel, love," he whispered, "just…just…help me look out for the boys."

PEL

Pel woke to the touch of Chelsea's fingers on the back of his neck. It annoyed him. She annoyed him. In her clingy way, she reminded him of his mother. He chose not to say anything. He needed her.

"You awake?" she whispered.

"Am now," he grumbled and looked over at her alarm. It was nearly noon. They had an appointment with the Rainman in little more than an hour.

"I need to know what my role is," she said with a touch of irritation. She had asked yesterday and the day before. Pel put her off—told her he was still trying to figure it out. She muttered some bullshit about patriarchy. He blew her off, said her liberal brand of feminism only interfered with the protracted people's war he was fighting. Besides, he knew she was too into him to play the gender card.

"You're coming in with me," said Pel with his back to her.

"I am?" Chelsea sat up, surprised and pleased.

Pel rolled over and looked up at her.

"You're the bag girl, bag woman, bag person, whatever. You gather up the money. I keep you covered. We split with a couple-hundred grand, and we're on our way to Colorado."

His goal was to spare Moom the danger he was about to expose Chelsea to. He didn't tell her that. He didn't tell her either that there was no way in hell she was going to Colorado. He hadn't quite figured out how he was going to break that news to her. Maybe he wouldn't have to.

Moom

Moom maneuvered the pickup through the narrow opening in the Gowanus warehouse and came to a stop. Rainman was there to meet them, still a little weirder than made sense.

"Welcome back," he said flatly as Moom and his brother exited the vehicle. "Where's Chelsea, Chelsea?"

Moom looked over at Pel.

"We just left her," said Pel. "She had to work today, kind of wrap things up."

Moom still had no idea exactly what Chelsea did for a living and wasn't sure he wanted to know. He didn't even know where she was. She wouldn't tell him or Pel.

"I got what you're looking for," said Rainman, beckoning the brothers over to his workbench. There he picked up an odd-looking gun and held it out in front of him, as proud as if it were his new granddaughter.

"What am I looking at?" said Pel.

"A tactical Benelli 12-gauge less the stock, less the stock, with a shortened barrel."

"We talking a sawed off shotgun?" asked Pel.

"Loaded with number one buck. That's twenty-four .30 caliber balls of pure mayhem in a three-inch magnum shell. Three inch. You start pulling the trigger with this baby, this baby, and you'll put more lead in the air than you could with two full autos."

"Pretty cool," said Moom, not exactly sure what the guy meant, but it sure as hell sounded impressive.

"Any shorter, shorter, I'd have to reduce your magazine capacity. That wouldn't be good."

"No?" said Pel.

"No, no, no. If you have to pull the trigger once, you'll probably want to pull it a few times more. And the Benelli will shoot every bit as fast, fast, fast, as you can pull the trigger."

"How many, like, shells does it hold?" asked Moom tentatively, not sure he was using the right language.

"Five. Four in the magazine, one in the chamber."

"That's it?" asked Pel.

"You won't need any more. Even if you don't hit anything, anything, you'll scare everyone to death."

"We'll hit something," said Pel.

"I thought about getting you a suppressed full auto, suppressed, but you'll like the Benelli. It's scarier and idiot proof. Close to idiot proof."

"Idiot proof?" said Moom, just a bit offended although he knew the man had him dead to rights. Pel too, truth be told.

"Yes," said the man. "You and your brother look like idiots. Most movement people, movement people, are idiots when it comes to guns. The fascists aren't. They know guns. You don't, don't."

Pel and Moom exchanged quizzical looks.

"You don't have much in the way of an internal editing mechanism," said Pel, half-laughing.

"I'm not sure I understand, understand."

"Didn't think you would," said Pel.

PEL

Pel watched carefully as the Rainman demonstrated how to operate the safety. He wished he knew more about guns than he did. The Rainman was right. The fascists had much more experience with guns than his side. Come the revolution, if his people didn't improve their game, they could get their asses kicked.

"I will leave it fully loaded, loaded," said Rainman. "You won't need to do anything other than thumb off the safety and pull the trigger. Idiot proof."

"Thanks," said Pel, with a touch more irony than Rainman would understand.

"Now let me show you something," said Rainman, wandering across the room.

Pel sidled over to Moom and whispered in his ear, "How is it that the resistance's smartest guy is a fucking retard?"

Moom smirked, "Knows his shit."

"Shit," said Pel, "knows his shit." They both laughed until the technician returned with a large Pizza Hutch warmer bag. He placed it on the workbench and opened it.

"Where did you get the bag?" Pel asked.

"Jersey, Jersey."

"Jersey?" said Pel, thinking, but not saying, *What the hell is that supposed to mean?*

"Jersey. Let me show you this."

The Rainman removed two pizza boxes. In each was a cold pizza. Underneath them was what appeared to be a third box. When he lifted the third box, Pel could see that it was simply a box top with three sides attached to a foam rubber cutout. The Rainman took the Benelli and placed it carefully into the foam rubber. It fit easily. He placed the modified pizza box in the bottom of the warmer bag with the gun inside and placed the other two boxes on top of it.

"If the man at the door wants to see whether you're a real pizza person," said the technician, opening the warmer bag as he spoke, "you open the warmer, the warmer, and show him the two pizzas boxes on top."

"If he wants to see the third pizza?" asked Pel.

"Here," said the technician, "I left a slit in the back of the warmer so you can just reach in, grab the weapon's wrist, pull the trigger, and blow the man's ass to kingdom come, kingdom come."

"Does the gun need, like, an exit hole?" asked Moom.

"Idiot, that pizza warmer isn't going to stop two-point-two ounces of lead," said the Rainman. "It'll make its own hole, hole. But hold it, hold it, like a man. If you limp-wrist it the recoil will break your wrist, your wrist."

Moom and Pel started at each other, both smiling. *This guy,* thought Pel, *is a certified madman.*

"There's more," added the Rainman, obviously proud of himself but not quite knowing how to show it. "I cut a hole in the bottom of the warmer bag and aligned it under the weapon's ejection port, port, for the spent shell to exit."

"Damn," said Pel, only half-ironically. "You think of everything."

"Everything," the man said with a hint of satisfaction. He pulled a black, .40 caliber, Glock 23 out of his waistband and handed it to Pel. "Everything."

"Cool!" said Pel.

"Know how to use it?"

"We'll figure it out."

"Just rack the slide, pull the trigger, and it goes bang."

"Bang," Pel smiled.

"One more thing," said Rainman, extracting what looked like a small glass container from the right pocket on his overalls.

"What's in the...bottle?" Pel asked.

"It's butyric acid, kind of like tear gas. And it's not a bottle really, bottle, but a 200-milliliter ampoule, professionally sealed by yours truly, truly. It fits in the bottom of the pizza warmer. Throw it against a wall, run away quick, and no one will follow you. No one."

"Thanks," said Pel.

"I made up a batch for the inauguration, inauguration, but our idiot friends got busted before they could use it."

"Too bad," said Pel.

"Oh yeah," said the man, pulling a map out of one of his many pockets and pointing to a spot circled with what looked like blue crayon. "When you're finished, dump everything, guns, everything, here."

"Where is that exactly?" said Pel, trying to read the map.

"Jersey," said the man, eyebrows raised, as if he had never heard a stupider question. "Jersey."

"Yes, of course," Pel smiled. "Jersey. Where else?"

"One more thing," said Rainman, "check the weather forecast for Friday, tomorrow, Friday. A nor'easter's coming."

DAY 11

MOOM

"He's leaving," said Pel into his cell.

Chelsea said something back to Pel, but Moom could not make it out.

"She's ready," said Pel. "Stay on top of the dude, and let's hope he takes the same route he did last time."

The pizza kid hopped on his scooter and headed south down Brighton 4th Street towards the beach and the Caspian. Moom followed close behind in the pickup, the wind buffeting the truck as he drove. Two thirds of the way down the street, Moom saw Chelsea emerge from the shadows, her hair blowing wildly over her head and shoulders. She walked into the middle of the otherwise vacant street and waved her arms. The kid came to a stop, and Moom stopped right behind him. Before the kid could get a good look at Chelsea, Pel jumped out from the cab, ripped the kid's helmet off, and threw a large drawstring bag over his head. Chelsea, meanwhile, grabbed the helmet, hopped on the scooter, and drove away.

Moom hustled around the back of the camper and pulled the door open. Pel was right behind him, dragging the pizza kid, his right arm locked around the kid's head.

"Say a word and you're a dead man," said Pel as he threw the kid into the camper and climbed in behind him, the Glock now at the kid's head.

"Let's go," said Pel.

Moom slammed the door shut and headed back to the cab.

"Damn," said Moom, prouder now than he was scared. "Did it. Gone in sixty seconds!"

PEL

The kid offered no resistance, didn't cry, didn't whimper. In the quick look he got of the kid, Pel figured he could not have been much older than Moom or weighed much more either. He had that Brooklyn look—Italian-Jewish, Jewish-Italian, dark hair, greasy, sort of a pocket-sized John Travolta.

"I'm guessing," said the kid after a moment, his voice muffled by the bag, "you haven't gone to this trouble to rob my sorry little dago ass."

"You figured that out, Einstein," said Pel. "Good for you."

After a couple of turns the truck slowed and pulled to a stop. Pel assumed that they had arrived at the spot Moom had identified at the BP station.

A second later, Chelsea opened the door and crawled in. She used the flashlight on her phone to illuminate the camper.

"Okay, kid," she said, "we need your jacket."

"Sure, whatever."

JACK CASHILL AND MIKE MCMULLEN

As the kid struggled to take the jacket off, the Glock still at his head, Pel handed Chelsea a crowbar. "Take this up to our friend in the cab and come back."

She exited without saying anything and quickly returned.

"Give the lady your jacket," said Pel. The kid didn't hesitate.

"Damn, you are one skinny little wop," Pel laughed at the sight of the jacketless pizza kid.

"That's what they said about Frank Sinatra," the kid said, "but he did all right."

"You got some brass ones, kid," said Chelsea.

"Thanks."

Chelsea put on the jacket and then pulled a pair of handcuffs out of the pouch on the sweatshirt she wore underneath.

"Okay, kid, hold out your hands," she said and proceeded to put the cuffs on the kid's wrists.

"Got these today," said Chelsea, "at a sex shop in downtown Brooklyn."

Pel shot Chelsea a menacing glare. She gave out way too much information. They might have to kill him after all.

"Sex shop? Downtown Brooklyn?" said the kid. "What's this borough coming to?"

But the kid was cool. That Pel had to admit. He pulled the wallet out of the kid's pocket and opened it.

"Tyler Carbone, huh?"

"Yeah."

"Okay, we know where you live, and if you want to save your life I need some straight answers."

"Shoot," said the kid. "Figuratively."

Pel laughed in spite of himself.

"How many pizza boxes?"

"Three."

"What do you say when you pull up at the Caspian?"

"Pizza for Medvedev."

"What's the doorman or bouncer or whatever say?"

"Not much. He grunts. Checks my warmer, sends me up."

"Where do you go?"

"Elevator straight ahead. Third floor. Turn right. End of the hall, no number on the door, big door."

"Then what?"

"I knock three times and say, 'Pizza for Medvedev.'"

"And then?"

"Another thug puts his eye up to the peep hole, looks me over, and lets me in just a step."

"What do you see?"

"Card game. Texas Hold'em. Maybe seven or eight other thugs around a table. You know the game?"

"A little."

"You gotta put your stake up for a place at the table. All the cash sits in stacks on the dresser to the left."

"Damn, kid, you're good. If we don't kill you, we might have to make you a partner."

At that moment, Moom opened the camper door, crowbar in one hand, pizza warmer in the other, and handed them both to Chelsea.

"Box is off the scooter," said Moom. "Back's flat enough to sit on."

"Okay," said Pel, as he quickly removed the top two pizza cartons from the kid's warmer bag and put them in the warmer that Rainman had given them—the one with the Benelli positioned in the carton at the bottom.

"Pizza smells good," Pel said to no one in particular. Zipping up the warmer, he added with a smile that cloaked his inner doubts, "Okay, let the revolution begin."

MOOM

Moom watched as Chelsea and his brother climbed out of the camper and hopped on the scooter. It had just started to rain, and although light, it was coming in sideways. Pel, in front, was wearing a bright red sweatshirt he bought for the occasion and the kid's Pizza Hutch hat, his dreads stuffed underneath as far as possible and into the folds of the sweatshirt's hood. The plan was for Pel to cut the dreadlocks immediately afterwards to make him harder for the Russians to track—the police too. He started growing the dreads on a memorable Election Day in the not so distant past. The outcome gave him the excuse he needed to get radical.

Chelsea, holding the warmer bag with one hand and the back of Pel's sweatshirt with the other, looked semi-authentic in the kid's jacket and helmet. As much as he hated to admit it, Moom was glad it was Chelsea on that scooter and not him. He offered just one lame protest when Pel told him that Chelsea was going in. He was sure Pel saw right through it.

Once the two were safely away, Moom climbed into the camper and closed the door behind him, the only light inside filtering through the camper's small, dirty window slits. Pel left him the Glock, but he hoped to hell he wouldn't have to use it.

The kid spoke up first, his voice quaking now, his bravado almost gone.

"You guys aren't going to hurt me, are you?"

"Not if I have any say about it," said Moom impulsively, not at all sure that anything he might say could save the kid's life if Pel wanted him dead.

PEL

Chelsea hopped off once they entered the Caspian's circular drive. Pel parked the scooter.

"Pizza for Medvedev," shouted Chelsea over the wind at the bouncer who had retreated under the hotel's canopy. She took off her helmet and shook out her hair as seductively as she could, given the wind and rain.

"You new?" grunted the bouncer in thickly accented English.

"Yeah," said Chelsea.

"The regular guy's grandmother died," Pel volunteered as he approached. "He'll be back next week."

"Who you?"

"The supervisor," yelled Pel over the howling wind. "I'm breaking the new girl in."

The doorman expressed no interest. He turned back to Chelsea and pointed to the bag.

"Open!" he shouted.

Her hands shaking, Chelsea unzipped the bag. The doorman looked at her, then at Pel.

"She's just a little nervous," shouted Pel. "First day on the job."

The doorman shook his head. Pel wasn't sure whether it was in sympathy or disgust. After patting Chelsea down, making no attempt to disguise the pleasure he took in doing so, he took a quick look inside the bag and waved his hand. He was letting them in. Chelsea zipped the bag back up and headed towards the entrance. Pel followed. When they had gone a few steps, the doorman shouted at their backs.

"You!"

"Me," said Pel, turning towards the man and pointing to himself.

"You going in too?"

"It's her first damned day," Pel snapped. "What kind of supervisor do you think I am?"

"Come here!"

Pel had no choice. He approached the man, trying not to show any fear. "Yeah?"

"Arms out." Pel knew the drill. The man patted him down.

"Does this mean we're engaged?" said Pel.

"Wise guy," said the doorman, waving them away. "Deliver fucking pizzas."

Pel would never let Moom know, let alone Chelsea, but his teeth were chattering. The elevator doors would open in a second, and he would walk into who knew what kind of hell. The face-offs with the police in the streets of Seattle and Oakland and Boston were fun and games. Worse case there, you sucked in a little tear gas or caught a police baton in the ribs. In the streets, the cops were wary of the protestors. They had pensions to protect and weren't about to risk them beating on some pampered jerkoff. Pel had never even been arrested.

The Russians were different. As Rainman told him, they did it all: racketeering, extortion, loansharking, drug trafficking, gun running, illegal gambling, and, when need be, killing. Pel saw the Caspian heist as the scary part of the larger operation. If he could survive this, the rest would come easy.

"You ready, girl?" said Pel as the elevator door opened. Chelsea nodded. When the elevator reached the third floor, he looked around for security cameras. Seeing none, he opened the warmer bag and took the Benelli out from under the pizza cartons. He also grabbed the butyric acid ampoule and stuck it in his pocket. He handed the warmer back to Chelsea and let her take the lead. Once at the door, he leaned back against the wall. She knocked three times.

"Pizza for Medvedev."

A man eased the door open just a crack.

"Let's see da pizza," he said in heavily accented English. Chelsea unzipped the warmer. As she did, Pel jumped out from behind her and kicked the door open, driving the man back into the room.

"You, down on the floor!" he barked at the guy who opened the door. "The rest of you, hands on the table!" Pel was finding his rhythm. The room appeared just as the pizza kid said it would. Eight stacked and wrapped piles of cash sat on top of a dresser to Pel's left. He counted eight men around the table, seven of them overstuffed thugs straight out of central casting, and one slim, balding, clean-shaven, impeccably dressed guy on the table's far side. Pel wondered if this Russian Fred Astaire might be Medvedev, but, like the others, the man followed Pel's orders.

Chelsea dumped the pizza boxes on the floor and began shoveling the stacks of cash into the pizza warmer.

"Hand me the warmer," Pel said to Chelsea when she finished. It was heavy. He looped the handle around his left arm and returned both hands to the Benelli. His confidence growing, he got an idea.

"Gentlemen," he said, "the lady is going to circle the table and collect your cell phones. No sudden movements or I will start blasting." Pel believed in improvisation.

Chelsea scrunched her face in confusion. This was not part of the plan. Pel nodded as if to say, "Get started." Circling the table, she put the phones into the pizza jacket's pockets one by one. In the second before everything went to hell, the thought again crossed Pel's mind that maybe the well-dressed man on the far side of the table was Medvedev, and that, if this was the case, maybe he was allowed to keep his gun.

It was, and he was.

Before Pel could tell Chelsea to watch out, the man leaped up and grabbed her around the throat with his left arm. With his right, he held a very large revolver to her temple. It was that quick.

"Amateurs," Medvedev said with a kind of crisp elegance and only the slightest of accents. "You don't hijack my room." He then started pushing Chelsea around the table to where Pel was standing. She resisted, but the man's end game was obvious to Pel. When he and Chelsea got halfway around the table, Pel raised the Benelli to chest height.

"Put the gun down," said Medvedev.

An amateur he might have been, but Pel wasn't quite the pussy that the Russian took him for. Without saying a word, he blasted the pair of them. This wasn't a plan. This was just pure tension. He didn't stop pulling the trigger until he realized the gun wasn't firing anymore. When the shooting stopped, he saw that he had killed Chelsea as well as the man holding her hostage. They both lay in a bloody heap before him, her lovely face oddly unscathed amidst the carnage. The others, some likely hit, hid as best as they could under the table.

Gathering his wits, Pel wheeled and ran through the door, turning the corner into the hall. With a sudden stop, he faced the now-closed door, removed the ampoule, threw it hard against the door, and ran like mother-loving Usain Bolt. He did not turn back to see his handiwork. He did not have to. The God-awful vomit-like smell of the acid raced him to the stairs, which he took in twos and threes. He had to get out before a card player could call the doorman, bouncer, whatever.

At the base of the stairs, he decided to leave the Benelli behind. It would do him no good now, and he knew these guys weren't about to hand it over to the cops. Opening the stairwell door, he saw the bouncer still outside, under the canopy. Pel walked by him as casually as he could fake it.

"Hey, stop!" the man barked over the sound of the canvas flapping wildly above him.

"What?"

"Did you hear shots or something?"

"I can't hear shit in this wind," Pel yelled.

The bouncer seemed to buy the answer. He had one more question left.

"Where is the girl?"

"Upstairs," said Pel, shouting back as he strode towards the scooter. "Medvedev wanted her to stay."

"And that is okay with you?" said the man, surprised by Pel's answer.

"She delivers more than pizza," Pel yelled over his shoulder.

The second he reached the scooter, the man's phone rang. Pel didn't hesitate. He blew right by him, laughing in relief as he passed by. Too bad about Chelsea, Pel thought. She had her virtues, but now at least he wouldn't have to tell her that she wasn't going to Colorado.

MOOM

Every few minutes Moom glanced at his phone to check the time, sure that the allotted thirty minutes was up. If Pel and Chelsea weren't back by then, he was to leave. What he was to do with the kid sitting mutely in the dark with him, he had no idea. Where he was to go, he had no idea either.

Exactly sixteen minutes had passed when he thought he heard a scooter over the howl of the wind surging up Coney Island Avenue. He listened intently now, and anxiously. Yes, it was the scooter. Thank God or whoever! He could hear it now right outside the pickup on the side away from the street. When Pel opened the door, he was smiling.

"All good, bro," he said as he threw the warmer bag into the back of the truck, climbed in after it, and shut the door behind him.

Moom turned his phone's flashlight on and looked at the bag.

"Is this what I think it is?"

"Yup," said Pel.

"Damn," said Moom. "You are one bad dude."

"Maybe so, but we got to get our asses out of here."

"Yeah, but where's Chel—where's our friend?" said Moom. In his relief, he had almost forgotten Chelsea had gone to the Caspian with Pel. He felt bad about forgetting.

"She wanted out."

"Out?"

"Yeah," said Pel. "She bailed before we got to the Caspian. Couldn't force her to come with me."

"Wow, didn't see that coming," said Moom, now shining the light towards Pel.

"Me neither."

Looking closely now at his brother, Moom snapped back in surprise.

"Is that blood on your face?"

"Yeah."

"Whose?" said Moom.

"Medvedev's," said Pel drily. Turning to their captive, he added, "Hate to break it to you, kid, but you just lost a customer." The kid said nothing.

"Man," sighed Moom, aware the two of them had just entered virgin territory and not at all sure what to say about it.

Pel solved that problem. "Get your ass in that cab and get us out of here."

Moom did as told. He always did. He climbed out of the camper, walked around the side away from the street, and climbed into the cab from the passenger's side.

"What the fuck?" he said out loud and slammed the dashboard. He exited the cab to get a better look at the huge square of paper plastered on the driver's side of the windshield. The rain blurred the small print but not the larger message. It read, "Tow this vehicle." He tried to peel it off by hand and made no progress at all. He climbed back into the cab and grabbed an ice scraper from the glove compartment and tried again. He did a little better, but using the scraper he figured it would take him at least an hour to get it off well enough to see. They didn't have an hour. He thought about driving down the street with his head out the window, but that would be suicide. He had to tell Pel what was wrong. He dreaded the moment.

PEL

"Mother fucker," said Pel, ripping the scraper from Moom's hand and climbing past him out of the truck. He knew he shouldn't be out here with the Russians surely combing the neighborhood, but if his incompetent little brother couldn't scrape a sticker off the window, he knew he could.

He couldn't.

"God damn it," he said, throwing the scraper across the parking lot, storming back to the camper, and climbing in wet and angry.

"Now what?" said Moom.

Pel had no answer. All options sucked. After a long moment of nothing, it was the kid who broke the silence.

"Check the pocket on my left leg."

"What?" said Pel.

"Just check," said the kid. "Left leg."

"Hope you're not fucking with me," said Pel as he felt his way down the kid's cargo pants to the pocket just above his knee. He reached in and pulled out what felt like a knife with the blade retracted.

"Give me some light," Pel said to Moom. He flicked the handle open. He was expecting a blade. What he got was a straight razor.

"Welcome to Brooklyn," said the kid.

"Damn," said Pel. "You're one surprising little shit."

"Try it," said the kid. "I've done it before. It's part of the average Brooklyn kid's skill set."

Pel handed the razor to Moom. "Get that sticker off and let's get out of here." Turning to the kid, Pel said, "If it works, you may have just saved your life."

MOOM

Moom was amazed at just how well the razor worked. He sliced the sticker off in less than two minutes and watched it blow away. They were on their way, thank God! He knew exactly where he was going. Jersey. Jersey. He had studied the route well enough to avoid looking at the map or using the GPS on his phone.

He had no trouble finding the Belt Parkway and headed west. He liked the sound of the word "west." When he saw the Verrazzano-Narrows Bridge up ahead, he shouted out, "Yes!" Once on the bridge, gripping the wheel tightly lest he be blown out of his lane, he watched Brooklyn fade away through his rear view mirror and smiled. He had never been so happy to leave a place in his life.

PEL

Pel counted off ten one hundred dollar bills from his stash, stuffed them in the kid's wallet, and stuck the wallet back in the kid's pocket.

"You got a thousand dollars in your pocket, kid," said Pel.

"Thanks, man," said the kid. Pel could hear the sound of relief in his voice, even strained through the cloth of the bag.

"Don't thank me yet. You got a lot of shit to face."

"Tell me."

"Unless I miss my guess, the Russians are going to come looking for you."

"What do I say?"

"You tell them exactly what you're going to tell the police."

"You mean about the two black guys who hijacked my scooter?"

Pel laughed.

"Not to mention my pizza."

"You are one cool little mother. No, you got to tell the police exactly what happened."

"Why?"

"The Russians will probably get a hold of the police report, and they *know* two black guys didn't rob their poker game."

"I tell the cops everything?"

"I wouldn't mention the razor blade. That would make you an accomplice, and I wouldn't admit the bit about where the handcuffs came from."

"Where *did* they come from?"

Pel laughed again. "I like you, kid. If you didn't have family, I'd advise you to get your ass out of Dodge. These guys play hardball, and they have to be very, very angry."

"You think?"

"And there is one thing above all you don't tell the police. You don't tell them anything about Medvedev being killed."

"No? Why?"

"There is a good chance the Russians won't report the robbery or the deaths."

"Deaths?"

"No," said Pel, correcting himself much too obviously, "not deaths, death. It would not surprise me if the Russians don't tell them about the *death*. All you got to report is that two white guys and a girl hijacked your scooter and your pizza, held you captive in their truck, and dropped you off in some God-forsaken swamp in Jersey.

"Jersey?"

"Jersey," Pel laughed, and he knew the kid had no idea why he found it funny.

MOOM

The phone rang. Moom picked it up out of the cupholder. It was Pel. He put it on speaker.

"Yo, bro, what's up?" asked Moom, a little afraid of the answer.

"No big thing," said Pel through the speaker. "When you get off the Turnpike, stop at a convenience store if you see one and get some water for the kid and us too."

"Need food?"

"We be good, we still got some pizza back here," Pel laughed. Moom joined him, relieved they were still alive.

PEL

"Okay, kid," said Pel, "here's the drill. We're going to make two stops. The first one is to get water for you. The second one is to drop you off."

"In Jersey?"

Pel thought he heard a hint of distrust in the kid's voice that he had not heard before. Or maybe he just imagined it.

"Right, Jersey," said Pel, almost as a way to reassure him. "I got a blanket here for you too—my panhandling blanket. It's getting cold and very wet. You'll need it."

"Thanks," said the kid, but once again Pel heard a bite in the kid's voice. To reassure him, he unlocked his handcuffs.

"Is that better?"

"Yeah, thanks."

"Keep the bag on for at least ten minutes after we drop you off, and then you're free to go."

"Okay."

Pel could think of nothing else to say. After a few minutes he picked up a slice of pizza.

"A little cold but still good," said Pel. "Want a slice?"

"No," said the kid. Now there was no mistaking the defiance in his voice. "The girl's dead, isn't she?"

"Whoa!" said Pel. "That's none of your fucking business, kid. I respect your ballsiness, but you're way out of line."

"You lied to your friend, how do I know you're not lying to me?"

"Enough!"

"Did you kill her?"

Without thinking, Pel threw a short jab at the kid's face. Stunned for only a second, the kid ripped the bag off his head and lunged at Pel. He didn't have a ghost of a chance. Pel quickly put a hammerlock on him and pushed his face into the truck's floor.

"What the fuck's wrong with you, kid?"

"Carbones don't die on their knees."

"We weren't going to kill you."

"Liar!"

Pel shocked himself. He started crying. He wasn't sure why, maybe it was because the kid's courage moved him. No other reason came to mind.

"You're a tough little dude," said Pel. "Sorry, man." So saying, he snapped the kid's neck. Only then did he notice the phone ringing. He pulled himself together to answer it.

"Nothing to worry about," he told Moom. "Just moving shit around back here. And by the way, don't bother stopping for water. We're good."

MOOM

Moom exited the Turnpike at 9 South, followed it to 616, and headed back east to Perth Amboy, a sleepy little city whose shabbiness even the sideways rain could not disguise. At Elm, he turned south again and followed the street until he ran out of blacktop. Off to his right on what was now a lumpy gravel road, he saw a large, rotting sign that read, "Soon to be Park #4." Moom laughed to himself, *That'll be the day.* Beyond the sign was pure industrial wasteland, crumbling steel frames from buildings that ceased to be or never got built, set among a homely mix of marshes and scrub trees and moraine-like piles of illegally-dumped junk.

Moom took the road until he could go no farther, braking in front of a shredded chain link fence that separated the road from the mile-wide Raritan River beyond. Eager to put this part of the job behind him, he jumped out and almost ran into Pel, who had already exited the cab and closed the door behind him.

"What now?" shouted Moom over the wind and rain.

An unusually grim Pel told his brother what happened, excluding only the exchange about Chelsea that triggered it.

"I hope you believe me," said Pel.

Moom was appalled, but what was he to say, what was he to do?

"I believe you," said Moom. He meant it. He had never seen his brother so close to tears.

"He was a ballsy little dude. I had no intention of killing him."

"I said I believe you."

"Good," said Pel, "because we've got some work to do."

"I guess so."

"Let's go find something heavy enough to pull the body down," said Pel so matter-of-factly that for a moment Moom found himself doubting Pel's story. But just for a moment. He was too anxious to meditate on Pel's character. Every sound spooked him and every siren, no matter how distant, unnerved him. He set himself to the task and got a sliver of satisfaction in finding a chunk of rusted I-beam that would do the job.

He called Pel over, and they dragged the beam to the water's edge. Pel took the lead from there, and Moom was only too happy to let him. Pel ripped a hole in the fence with his bare hands. It wasn't hard. He then pulled the beam onto a rotting little dock at water's edge.

"Okay, here comes the tough part," said Pel. He opened the back of the camper, reached in and pulled the kid's body out to the doorway. The kid looked oddly peaceful, Moom thought. Having no family to speak of, Moom had never been to a wake, never seen a dead body before. He was surprised how little he felt. Pel then reached into the kid's wallet and pulled out the ten hundreds he had put there earlier.

"Damn, I wished he had believed me," Pel groaned.

Instead of letting the body fall and dragging it, he cradled the boy in his arms and carried him almost tenderly to the I-beam. He then placed the body on top of it.

"Do we have any rope?" Pel asked.

"Don't think so."

"Then get me a few of the bungee cords, okay?" Pel asked with much less bark than Moom was used to. Moom found the cords without much trouble and backed away after handing them to his brother. Pel did not ask for help. He attached the body to the beam as best he could and then pushed beam and body into the river, which at this juncture was as wide and deep as a bay.

The body and beam sank like a cannonball. Pel stood in the rain longer than he needed to and watched.

"God love him," said Pel in the way of an elegy. Without speaking further, he climbed into the truck and returned with his own bloody sweatshirt, the pizza boxes, and the extra pizza warmer—the one the kid brought. The one without the money. He walked up river in silence and dumped them in one by one. He walked back as silently as he walked away.

"Did I forget anything?" Pel asked.

"The Glock?"

"We're keeping that. Anything else?"

"Not that I can think of."

"Good, then let's get the hell out of here."

DAY
13

MOOM

Moom looked as discreetly as he could at the speedometer. The gauge was hovering around eighty-five. This was not good.

"Slow down, bro," he said cautiously. "We don't want to call attention to ourselves."

Pel had been jumpy all day. All day the day before, too, for that matter. It didn't help his mood any that they had to waste a whole damn day in Breezewood, Pennsylvania. The truck had started to overheat on the Pennsylvania Turnpike. Moom would shut the engine off, coast as far as he could, wait for it to cool, start it up again, and drive as far as he dared. When the temp gauge was back in the red, he would start the process all over again. Fortunately, not too many cycles were necessary before they coasted into a rip-off repair shop in Breezewood, a bizarre little tourist trap where the Turnpike fused with I-70. With time to kill, Pel had Moom cut off his dreads in a truck stop restroom. Pel wanted it shaved down all the way. He thought it would make him look tougher. It did, but the new look didn't do much to improve his mood.

If that weren't trigger enough, Moom suspected his brother had popped a few bennies to keep him alert. He seemed to be crashing. Hard. Benzedrine had that effect; it was the only drug Pel allowed himself. He was always saying bennies were functional and cool, a throwback to Kerouac and Miles Davis, but they always left him ragged.

"You're right, sorry," Pel grunted, easing up on the gas.

"Any chance you could turn the music down a little?" ventured Moom.

"Now you're pushing your luck. No."

"With the dreads gone, how about something other than Reggae for a change?"

"Fuck off."

About the only kind of music Pel played was Reggae. Pel reminded him that Reggae was the only truly revolutionary music. For whatever reason, he had been laying the revolutionary mumbo jumbo on thick the last few days.

Moom wasn't sure whether that was the speed talking or guilt over killing the pizza kid, but after fourteen hours in the car he had listened to all he could stand about the need to smash fascism in its infancy with utmost brutality, blah, blah, blah. Still, as Pel had proved in spades the last few days, he wasn't all talk.

"I'm going to get some gas," said Pel.

"Good," said Moom. "We could use a break."

TONY

"Okay, guys, wake up," said Tony as he pulled his vehicle into a gas station off I-70.

"Why are we stopping?" asked Matt, rubbing the sleep from his eyes.

"Tony's rule #36," said Tony. "Vehicles run much better when there's gas in the tank."

Stretched out across the back seat, Luke was even slower to rouse than his brother. "Where are we?" he asked, sitting up and looking around.

"Bates City."

"Bates City?"

"Yup, Bates City, Missouri."

"You think there's a Bates Motel here?"

"Why, you need a shower?" said Tony.

"Not at the Bates Motel," answered Luke with an involuntary shiver.

"A shower might help. You girls need something to bring you back to life. Can't even stay awake to keep the old man company for a few hours' drive."

"Long day," said Matt. "We're hiked out."

This was the second weekend Tony had taken the boys camping. He was beginning to wonder whether they would ever be ready for the Rockies.

"I noticed," said Tony, "but if you could rouse yourself to go in the store here and get me a Diet Coke, I'd appreciate it."

"You know aspartame isn't good for you," Luke said reflexively.

"Well, neither were my four combat tours, but if I could survive those, I'm not going to worry about a little artificial sweetener."

"Our father lives dangerously," laughed Matt, exiting the vehicle, his brother right behind him.

Tony stepped out of the vehicle, stretched, and headed to the pump. Never once in his life had he filled up with anything other than "regular." He thought "premium" a trick on Yuppies, and he wasn't about to start now. As he filled the tank, he heard a loud throbbing sound from about half a klick away and watched a hard-driven black Chevy pickup follow its angry noise into the station. It came to a jarring halt about two feet behind his vehicle. The music shut off. The driver slipped out.

He was a young guy, twenty-something, about Matt's height and obviously buff even in his Army fatigue jacket. He walked around the front of the cab and looked hard at Tony. Being in the risk assessment business, Tony stared back. A young guy with a shaved head always caught his attention.

"What you lookin' at, fascist?"

"Fascist?" Tony had to laugh. "I guess, my skinhead friend, you must think I'm a Nazi too."

MOOM

"Shit," thought Moom. "Skinhead! Nazi!" He watched his brother rub his head in near shock as if he had forgotten that he had shaved it down to the nub. And now he was hassling some jerkoff on the highway who had no idea how stupidly sensitive his brother was about his new look. He knew he better do something before this thing got out of hand.

TONY

Behind the skinhead, a passenger as skinny and white as toothpaste hopped out of the cab. Younger than the other guy, he looked to Tony as if he would rather be any place than where he was.

"Chill," said the skinny kid, grabbing the arm of the skinhead.

"Get me the crowbar."

"C'mon man."

"You heard me."

"We don't need this."

"Get the damn crowbar."

The kid dutifully walked around to the back of the truck, grabbed a crowbar, and brought it around to his partner.

"Just scare him, okay?" the kid pleaded.

"We're beyond that," said the skinhead.

Damn, thought Tony. *I should not have ratcheted this up, not with the boys around.* This guy was nuts.

"Hey, I don't want any trouble," Tony said, holding his hands up, backpedaling down the side of the vehicle, trying to shield what could possibly happen next from the prying eyes of a security camera. "We cool, okay?"

The skinhead followed. "No, we ain't cool," he said. "You disrespected me."

"How about if I just apologize?" said Tony strategically.

The skinhead stepped over the fuel hose. The kid, close behind, was trying to hold him back, but the skinhead shrugged him off. He was a man on a mission.

"How about if I shove that apology up your ass."

Tony sighed, reached into his jacket pocket as casually as if he were looking for change and pulled out a 9mm Sig pocket pistol. He held it tightly against his hip to better avoid the camera and kept the slide canted away from the torso so it wouldn't jam when firing.

"How about if I blow your shiny-ass head clear off."

The skinhead's eyes bugged.

"Be cool," said the thug, holding the crowbar out as a peace offering.

"I am being cool," said Tony, "proof of which is you're still breathing. Now grab Boy Wonder," he said, pointing to his sidekick, "and get your Nazi ass out of here."

"We're going," said the skinhead, stepping backward over the hose.

"Of course you are. And next time you come to a gunfight?"

"Yeah?"

"Don't bring a crowbar."

The pair walked away slowly. Cursing, the skinhead jumped into the vehicle. The kid did the same, and the truck backed up violently, tires screeching. Tony put his pistol back in his pocket and pulled out his phone, but then thought better of it. This was not provocation enough to call 911. The last thing he wanted was to spend a night fingering perps or filling out police reports—in Bates City, Missouri, no less.

On pocketing the phone, he looked up to see his sons exiting the store, snacks in hand. The boys had no idea what just happened. Tony thought about telling them, if for no other reason than to remind them this was a darker world than they imagined it to be. You had to be ready to deal with that darkness, he had learned over time. What was that saying? "The best defense against evil men are good men skilled at violence"? There was truth to that.

But he chose not to say anything, not even about the wisdom of keeping a handgun in your jacket pocket on a long trip when an inside-the-belt holster grows uncomfortable. There were a lot of things he didn't say. Maybe he was wrong, but he hoped to preserve their innocence as long as possible, not suspecting for a moment how short that long would be.

PEL

Once inside the cab, Pel pounded the door with the side of his hand. He was as furious as he could remember being. There were no two ways about it. That man had humiliated him, and he did it in front of Moom.

He slammed down on the left blinker, preparing to turn back on to I-70, thought better of it, and pulled off to the right side of the access road. Without saying a word, he reached across Moom and pulled the Glock out of the glove compartment.

"What are you doing?"

"What does it look like?" He chambered a round.

"Are you out of your mind?" Moom groaned. "The guy's kids are with him."

"What kids?"

"Two of them—boys. I saw them coming out of the store. One about my age, one younger."

Pel made a fist as though to hit Moom.

"Fuck the kids," said Pel.

"And fuck our project too?"

Pel caught himself, dropped his hand to his side, and shook his head almost in the way of apology.

"I'm sorry, Moom. That pizza kid really jacked with my head."

"You know," said Moom. "We can always call this whole thing off."

"No," Pel insisted. "Mao says you got to face your fear and conquer it."

DAY 14

"I guess we're not in Kansas anymore," said Pel, rubbing his eyes and looking around at the mountains that flanked the two-lane road on either side. "How long was I out?"

"I think I lost you around the Colorado border."

"And you drove the whole way straight through?"

"Nah, I pulled over for a few hours at a rest stop and slept."

"Damn," said Pel. "I don't remember any of that."

"You were crashing hard, brother. How you feeling?"

"Much better," said Pel, "like a real human being. Where are we?"

"About twenty miles north of Aspen."

The pair rode in silence for a few minutes while Pel straightened out his thoughts. Odd how much better he felt about himself, and the world, when he had slept well.

"So what are you thinking?" Moom asked.

"I'm thinking we're being tested."

"We passing?"

"So far," said Pel. "The fact that R asked for two hundred thousand dollars, and we just happened to find eight stacks of twenty-five thousand dollars each tells me he knew how much was there."

"So are we being played or what?"

Pel couldn't be sure. The one thing that reassured him was that R gave him a real address to deliver the money to in Aspen. If it had been a dead drop somewhere, he would have smelled a con.

"Guess we'll find out soon enough."

Moom

Moom wished he were more alert when they pulled into Aspen. He might have appreciated the town a little more. It seemed like a pretty enough place, a little too cute maybe, but on a late October morning in the mountains, he would love to have gotten out, walked around, smelled the air.

"Stay awake there, bro," said Pel.

"I'm good." Moom shook his head to clear it and fixed his eyes on the road ahead.

"Smuggler Street should be three streets ahead on the right."

In a minute Moom saw the street sign and turned right off Seventh. "Smuggler Street," he laughed. "What a trip." He pulled into the circular drive of the first house on the left.

"Damn," said Pel, "it looks like the Kentucky Colonel died here."

Pel was right. The place had the whiff of old south about it—big porch, lots of white columns, drooping trees of some sort or another.

Moom pulled to a stop. Pel opened the glove compartment, took out the Glock, and stuck it in his jacket pocket.

"I'll do the talking," said Pel.

"What else is new?" said Moom under his breath. They both exited, and Moom trailed his brother to the front door. It opened before they could ring. Entering, all they could see was the man who pulled it open. He was huge. Moom was not sure he had seen an all-around bigger guy. He looked Samoan or Maori or something—had to be at least 6'6", 350 pounds, dressed like he was going to the beach in baggy shorts and a Hawaiian shirt, full sleeve tats on either side, wild, bushy black hair pulled back in a ponytail, and a nose flattened halfway across his massive head.

"R sent us," said Pel.

"We were expecting you," said the giant, his voice rumbling like offshore thunder. Without asking, he patted Pel down and lifted the Glock out of Pel's pocket as though he expected it to be there. The giant then removed the magazine and racked the slide, catching the 9mm cartridge in his massive hand. After placing the weapon, magazine, and cartridge on the table, he proceeded to pat Moom down and found nothing.

"Follow me."

Pel flashed a wry smile at his brother as if to say, "weird trip." *Weird it is*, thought Moom. He and Pel followed the man around the central staircase, through an elaborate dining room, and into a greenhouse filled with exotic plants and colorful birds, extracted, Moom thought, from the kind of country where, well, birds make a lot of noise.

Sitting behind a formal desk in the middle of the greenhouse was a shriveled little white man with wisps of gray fringe around his head and ears as big as Dumbo's. He wore a white tropical suit with a vest and a red tie as though he were at work and this were his office. Moom judged him to be at least seventy, though he was admittedly not a good judge of these things. The man did not stand or offer his hand. As to seats, there were none.

"The retainer fee?" said the man brusquely.

"Retainer fee?" asked Pel.

The man stared at him as though he were some idiot child.

"Oh yeah, retainer fee," said Pel, handing the Samoan his key to the truck. "It's stuffed in a pizza bag in the rear of the truck."

Moom admired how nonchalantly Pel handed over the key. He was glad he did not have to make that judgment call. The old man nodded to the giant Samoan who nodded back and walked away. Nothing was said for an awkward minute until the Samoan returned, bag in hand. He placed it on the old man's desk, nodded in affirmation, and walked away again. The old man pointed to a manila envelope on the edge of his desk.

"These are your instructions," he said in a deep rasp. Pel picked it up and started to open the envelope.

"No," said the man firmly, "not here."

Pel stopped. "If I have any questions?"

The man just shrugged and let out a throaty laugh. "That's not my department," he said.

The guy spooked Pel, Moom could tell. He reached into his desk drawer and pulled out two identical sheets of paper. "My department is law. I am your attorney. You paid me ten thousand dollars each as a retainer."

"And the rest of the money?" asked Pel.

"That's not your worry. All of our communications, now or in the future, are privileged and protected. Speak to no authority before speaking to me. Please read these agreements and sign."

Moom and Pel each leaned over the desk and read—or pretended to. It was all legalese. They were prepared to sign whatever it said. They had come too far not to. When finished, Moom sensed the giant Samoan standing behind them. He cast a shadow.

"Thank you, gentlemen," said the old man, nodding at the Samoan.

"Come with me," the Samoan rumbled. The brothers turned and followed the man out the way they came in. At the entryway, the Samoan picked up the handgun, magazine, and cartridge with one hand and stuffed them back into Pel's jacket pocket.

"We do not expect to see you again," he said in words that sounded somehow like a warning.

The brothers walked in silence to the car. Moom could feel the Samoan's eyes burrowing into his head. Once safely in the car, doors shut, Pel turned to his brother and said, "Was that real or was that just the Bennies kicking back in?"

Moom kind of wished it was the Bennies.

PEL

"First the Rainman and now a giant Samoan and some frea-koid senior citizen," said Pel as Moom looped the house's circular drive. "Let's boogie. These guys are tripping me out."

"Where to?"

"Get back on Main and look for some off-brand coffee shop or another. They've got to have a hundred of them in a place this precious."

Pel resisted the urge to rip open the envelope. He needed a jolt of java to get his head back from wherever the Bennies had taken it. Just off Main he saw a sign for Peaches Corner Café. He liked the sound of it and told Moom to pull over.

The place was brighter and neater than Pel liked, but he found a spot in the front corner with no one sitting nearby and took a seat with his back to the wall. Moom fetched the coffees.

Pel did not have to tell him what to order—black, no frills. He knew the drill.

While Moom waited at the counter for the order, Pel opened the envelope. He pulled out a map and looked inside to see if he missed anything. He hadn't. Pel shook the envelope and looked within the folds of the map. There was nothing. Moom returned with the coffees and sat across from him.

"This is it." Pel spread the map out in front of him.

"Nothing else?"

"No, just the map."

"There's a red X over here," said Moom, pointing to a small felt pen mark that Pel overlooked.

"That answers all my questions," smirked Pel, not bothering to mask his frustration. "The test continues."

R may not have needed their money, but it helped. R didn't need their presence at the site, but that would probably help, too. If they got the money and found their way there, from R's perspective, they were probably worth having there. If not, too bad.

"What's with all these lines and stuff?" asked Moom.

"I think they show, like, altitude. You know the tighter they are together, the steeper the hill, or something like that."

"I think you're right."

While Pel continued to fuss with the map, Moom pulled out his smart phone and began to explore.

PEL

Pel watched his brother search away on his iPhone. He had resolved never to tell him about Chelsea unless he had to, and the only way he would ever have to is if the Russians talked.

"Any word about the Caspian?" Pel asked.

"Let me check," said Moom, dialing up Google News and keying in the words "Caspian," "Brooklyn," and "murder."

"Nothing," said Moom.

"Didn't happen," said Pel. "Those guys know how to keep shit out of the news." He didn't dare ask about the pizza kid. He figured Moom would have told him if his death had been reported.

"I suppose the red X is where we're supposed to go. I think I can figure out how to get there," said Pel, pausing and then looking up at a presence he sensed before he saw—another friggin' giant, this one in a down vest and a cowboy hat. He was standing near the front door facing him and his brother.

"I was on my way out," said the giant, "and I saw you fellows wrestling with that topo map. I thought I could help."

In the five seconds he had to make the call, Pel read not a trace of intrigue into the guy. His offer seemed genuine. He was just some big innocent galumph trying to be helpful. West of the Hudson, he had been noticing, people were like that.

"Yeah, thanks, we could use some help. Don't know the area very well." Hell, he didn't even know what a "topo" was, but he was not about to ask.

"Happy to oblige," said the man, pulling up a chair backwards and leaning over the map. "I'm guessing you're here for the elk."

Pel was glad the question led him to the answer.

"Yeah, you guessed right," Pel smiled.

"Got your tags, I suppose."

"Got 'em," said Pel, not exactly sure what a tag was. "We're meeting up with some friends at the spot marked on the map."

"That's pretty deep in there," said the man. "How you getting in?"

"Hiking," said Pel, hoping it was the right answer.

"Your friends got the horses, I surmise."

"Yup," said Pel, not exactly sure what horses had to do with anything. The man then pulled a pencil out of his vest pocket—who carries a pencil?—and started tracing a line on the map.

"Your pals picked a good spot. This is pretty much virgin territory. They just opened a trail up to this area during the summer. Not many people are aware of it."

"Yeah," said Pel. "My friends know their way around."

"Just drive up to the Chief Blanton Trailhead here," said the man, marking the spot on the map, "and follow the line I'm drawing all the way in. The trail's not too hard to follow, but you got to pay attention." Here the man paused for dramatic effect. "When you come to this overlook," he said, pointing to a spot on the map, "and you see this gorgeous valley spread in front of you, you'll wish this valley was yours, but yours is the next one. Just climb one more ridge to the west, and your spot is on the far side of it."

"Sounds promising," said Pel with a sly grin the man did not notice.

"Keep a steady pace, stay on the trail, and the hike should take you no more than about eight hours."

"Thanks for the help," said Moom.

"No problem," said the man as he stood to leave. "Be careful out there. If you screw up, your phones aren't going to do you any good."

"By the way," asked Pel, "know where we can get some additional camping gear?" He congratulated himself for thinking to say "additional." In truth, they had almost none.

"There are a few places here in town," said the man, "but if it was me I'd go up to the Walmart in Glenwood Springs. They got everything you need at about half the price."

"Oh, Walmart," said Pel, trying his best not to snarl. Maoist that he was, he'd rather shop in the Seventh Circle of Dante's Inferno than in a Walmart. "Thanks for the tip."

MOOM

"Any idea what we should do with the vehicle?" Moom asked after the cowboy had left.

"Not really," said Pel with a shrug, "hadn't given it much thought."

The answer hardly surprised Moom. Pel had a habit—not a good one, all things considered—of not giving plans much thought, at least until the last minute.

"I have an idea," Moom volunteered.

"Yeah," said Pel indifferently.

"I'm thinking I should take you and the gear to the trailhead and then drive to Denver and park at the airport."

"What?" said Pel, now looking up. Moom anticipated the response. He was familiar with the tone. In a single word, Pel managed to express doubt mixed with more than a hint of disdain.

"Let me explain," said Moom, as calmly as he could. "We got to park the truck someplace, right?

"Yeah, but why not at the trailhead?"

"The cowboy says it's like an eight-hour hike in, right?"

"Yeah."

"Okay, if we succeed, imagine that site eight hours later?"

From his look, Moom could not tell whether his brother was more confused or annoyed.

"So why the airport? Why Denver?"

"The airport is the one place I can think of where you can leave a car for a long time without anyone even getting suspicious."

"Okay."

"Aspen airport will be hot afterwards."

"No denying."

"Denver should be big enough and far enough away."

"Okay, but why you and not me?"

"People notice you. They don't notice me. I park, walk into the terminal, come out a little later, and hop on the Colorado Mountain Express. One hundred and twenty bucks and three and a half hours later I'm in Glenwood Springs or downtown Aspen. People do this all the time, at least the Colorado Mountain Express part."

"You just looked that up?"

"Yeah."

"That's a long day for me out at the trailhead."

"Take a hike, bring a book."

"How do you get back out there?"

"Hitchhike."

"Hitchhike? You sure that's a good idea?"

"Can't exactly Uber. I'm just a clean-cut kid with a back-pack. Lots of old hippies around here. I know I can catch a ride, and they wouldn't rat me out even if they were suspicious."

"Let me think about it."

"This is something you should have thought of a long time ago," said Moom under his breath.

"Did you say something?"

"No, just talking to myself," Moom muttered. Even when he spoke out loud, he reflected, he might as well have been talking to himself.

DAY 15

MOOM

He couldn't stand his brother when he was like this. Everything sucked, and it was all Moom's fault. Why did they have to go to that God-forsaken Walmart after all? Why did they have to stay in dipshit Basalt? Why did they have to get up so early? Why was the breakfast so crappy? When Pel got into these moods, every problem was a crisis, and every crisis had a culprit, and that culprit was the person closest—usually Moom.

"How long until we get to the site?" Pel grouched.

"I think about ten minutes," said Moom, staring ahead and hoping not to run into a deer, or a moose, or whatever might jump out of the woods in the dawn half-light.

The thing about Pel was that he was a natural leader. He was born to be in charge, and he was good at it. Moom could not imagine anyone else pulling off the poker game bust the way Pel had. The problem came when Pel was not in charge. He could not *not* be a leader. Once he agreed to Moom's Denver airport plan, for instance, everything about it sucked. Moom was used to this. He could deal with it. He doubted very much, though, whether R could. He was hoping R and Pel would get along. He wasn't optimistic.

"There, up ahead on the left," said Moom, relieved he found the Chief Blanton trailhead. He pulled in and parked. There was room for about a dozen cars, but theirs was the only one there on this day.

"Looks like R didn't park here either," said Moom.

"I bet he didn't park at the Denver fucking airport," said Pel, sliding out of the vehicle and stretching. He tried his phone. Nothing.

"Give me your phone," said Pel. Again, nothing. He motioned to his brother, "Put these in the glove compartment and leave them in Denver. The phones stashed, they unpacked in silence interrupted only by the occasional "over here" and "not there, you idiot."

"I guess I better get going," said Moom.

"I guess you better." Pel walked over and gave his brother an uncharacteristic hug. "Sorry to give you so much shit. Denver makes sense."

PEL

Pel welcomed the sunrise. He wasn't scared of the woods in the dark—not really—but he was awfully damn uneasy. There were too many sounds he couldn't account for, and he couldn't be sure they weren't human.

Thinking Moom would not get back much before dark, he decided to pick a spot up the trail to set up camp. He wanted to go deep enough so that if a ranger pulled into the parking area on a routine check of the trailhead, there would be nothing to see. But he wanted to stay close enough so that he could hear if someone did pull in.

On the hike down the trail, with the rising sun at his back, Pel had what he thought of as a "smell the roses" moment. He noticed how the sun pierced through the leaves and caused something of a strobe effect, especially where the trail angled north. He thought about this for a moment and then dropped the thought. Truth be told, he didn't really give a rat's ass about nature. If pressed, he could tell pine trees from the other trees, but that was about it, and he knew less about birds than about trees. In the past he had protested on behalf of some environmental cause or another, but the cause was always secondary to the protest. His goal was to stir shit up and break stuff. Revolution followed disorder. He wanted to be remembered as the guy who brought the whole show down.

Once Pel found a good spot, he decided to set up the tent. He and Moom could sleep there that night and get a fresh start in the morning. As he opened the pack the tent came in, it dawned on him that he had never set up a tent before. He had slept in tents at various protest sites, but they were always someone else's.

How hard can this be? he thought. He was tempted to pick up the instructions, but instructions were for retards. He did, however, take a look at the picture on the package. This was apparently a dome tent with three poles. Looking at the tent on the ground, Pel could make no sense of it until he realized it was upside down. When he saw these little sleeve things, he figured the poles must go through them. Understanding that fact helped, but the whole exercise was still a sorry pain in the ass. He was glad no one was there to see him flail away.

When Pel finally got the tent set up, he took it down and tried again. With a little practice it wasn't difficult at all to put one end in the pocket and push the other through the sleeve to get the bow to form the tent and stab the other end in the pocket on the ground. By his fourth try he felt like quite the outdoorsman. This was less about discipline than about pride. He did not want Moom to see him struggle, and he sure as hell did not want R to see him do anything that would cause the man to question his competence.

Moom

Moom chose not to think about much of anything besides avoiding deer in the half-light until he got on I-70 in Glenwood Springs. From there it was another three hours or so to the airport on the far side of Denver. Once on the Interstate, he threw the vehicle into cruise control and put his mind in gear.

He thought a lot about Pel and what made him who he was—so fixed on his goals, so righteous in his anger. An anger that Moom never really felt himself. Pel said more than once that Moom's revolutionary consciousness wasn't fully formed, and Moom could not disagree. Hell, he was only eighteen. He still couldn't grow a beard.

Before he threw his life away he needed to convince himself that Pel's rage was justified. He wasn't sure he could. So much of that rage seemed to flow from the father Pel had known but Moom never did. Pel had no love lost for their mother. That was clear. But just about the only word he used to explain his feelings for the old man was "hate." Truth be told, Pel more or less hated just about every male in authority.

As he drove through the mountains on this glorious morning, one deeply subversive thought crossed his mind: all he had to do to beg off from this crazily scary plot was to head east on I-70 and keep on heading east until he got some place he wanted to go. He imagined a leafy university town in the Midwest where he could get a job, blend in, take some classes, meet a girl, and forget about fighting fascists and saving the world.

But he could not forget about Pel. When his mother went off the rails a few years ago, Pel took him under his wing. Pel loved him as much as he could love anyone, he supposed. Still, he had to admit that hate came much easier to his brother than love. Moom lost himself in his driving and in his dreams until an unwanted thought struck him like a fist to the chest: if he blew the plot off and kept on going, what would happen to his brother?

Moom knew Pel too well to think that he would give up on this plan. No, before he went looking for Moom, Pel would go find R to complete the job. And what would R do when he learned that one of the only two people who knew the plan had fled? Moom did not have to be paranoid to think the worst. Why even dream? He knew he could never abandon his big brother.

PEL

After hiking around a bit and getting bored, Pel found a spot in the sun, against a tree, protected well enough not to be seen from the road but clear enough that he could see anyone coming and going. Although he was not big on reading, all his revolutionary heroes were. If they could read, he could. Besides, he had little else to do after he got the camp set up.

The book he brought along was *1984* by George Orwell. He bought it at a used bookstore back in Boston, one of the few cities that still trafficked in used books. He bought it because his comrades were buying it. They tweeted about it and talked about it all the time. They said it helped them explain the current lay of the land. Pel joined in the conversation, hoping no one would smoke him out, but he had never read the book. He barely knew the plot.

As he waited for Moom, he plodded through the book. At one point he fell asleep and woke up anxious, fearing he missed his brother's return. He got up and looked around but saw no sign of Moom. The longer the afternoon dragged on, the more worried he grew. He told himself it was getting too dark to read. It was, but that wasn't the reason he stopped. He was too nervous. If something happened to Moom, he would have no way of knowing.

When he heard a vehicle pull into the parking area, he slipped behind a tree and watched. Moom stepped out of a beat up VW van with a peace symbol on the side. The driver, a crusty old dude with a long grey ponytail, rolled down his window, called Moom over, and gave him a righteous handshake.

"Thank God for clichés," said Pel quietly.

DAY 16

TONY

"Salina!" said Tony, pointing to a road sign up ahead.

"Good to know where it is," said Matt. "Hope to be back in a few months for State."

"I'm going to exit here, and we'll gas up. Sure you don't want to drive?"

"No, thanks. I'm okay."

Sometimes Tony wasn't sure his son was okay. Before the accident, he always wanted to drive. They had been on the road a couple hours and had about ten more to go. As the vehicle pulled into a QuikTrip, the change of speed stirred Luke awake.

"This is boring," Luke yawned, stretching out as he exited the vehicle. "We should have flown."

Luke had a way of sucking the joy out of everything. If Tony hadn't felt so damn guilty about not being there when Angel died, he would have gone full drill sergeant on his sorry ass. Instead, he throttled back.

"Boring?" said Tony. "About six hours from now, you'll think back on the first part of this trip like it was the Mamba ride at Worlds of Fun."

"Huh?"

"What Dad means," Matt clarified, "is the really boring part is just about to begin."

Before Luke could voice a protest, Matt preempted him, "I know. 'Don't *patronize* me.'"

Tony had, in fact, considered flying, but he actually enjoyed the unpretentious calm of the Kansas countryside. I-70 was largely straight, the grade soft, and the distractions few. It was boring, he imagined, only to people who had no life of the mind. On trips like this in the past, alone with his thoughts for hours on end, he had been able to work out the design of his future. Plus, the gradual climb from about a thousand feet above sea level in eastern Kansas to about eight thousand in Aspen made acclimation at least a little bit easier.

More to the point, the thought of schlepping their gear and their guns through the airport made it easy to nix flying. He would send the boys back by plane, but he would rather drive just about anywhere he could. Even when traveling by himself on business, he had little use for a screening process designed less to stop terrorists than to give fliers the illusion that terrorists were being stopped. The authorities had made "profiling" a dirty word even though the whole security business, his own end of it included, depended on profiling. Strange world.

LUKE

They were right. From the looks of things, Western Kansas was a seriously boring place. He wished he were back at Fort Bragg. There, at least, the leaves turned colors in October. Here, the only color the leaves turned was brown. Then they just fell off the trees. On the plus side, there were not a whole lot of trees to fall off of. There were mostly just silos and rusting oil rigs scattered among the endlessly drab fields of whatever. It was so dull, in fact, that the big, ugly windmill farm beyond Salina made the drive's highlight reel. Hell, he even looked forward to the billboards. "Each Kansas farmer feeds 156 people and you," read one. "Eat beef," read another, "the West wasn't won on salad."

"Dad, why exactly can't I play my games?" he asked from the back seat, making no effort to hide his frustration.

"I want you to enjoy the scenery."

"It's totally boring. I'd rather play Pong than look at this stuff."

"Okay," said his father after some reflection, "granted it's not exactly Yosemite, but it's real. And if we were traveling not at seventy-five miles an hour but, say, at five, and our biggest concern wasn't boredom but getting basted over an open fire by some chronically pissed-off Comanches, you might have a better appreciation for getting from here to there."

Uh oh, thought Luke. He felt a lecture coming, and he kicked himself for triggering it. His father did not disappoint. He told at length how the settlers from New England gave up everything they had, traveled west on steamboats and Conestoga wagons to start a new life, plow new ground, keep Kansas free from slavery, blah, blah, blah, blah, blah.

"And thanks to them," he said, "even ordinary people like us live lives that are free and rich beyond the dreams of kings. And what do we do?"

"We bitch," said Matt, finishing his father's thought.

"Exactly."

"I bitch," said Luke, mimicking a phrase he picked up somewhere or another, "therefore I am."

"That," said his dad, "is the nub of it—modern youth explained in one short sentence. And one more thing, guys."

"Yeah?" said Matt.

"Don't use the word 'bitch.'"

TONY

There was still plenty of daylight when they crossed the border into Colorado. Some endless time later they ascended a swell, and at the top of it they saw the mountains beyond. They looked almost blue from a distance as they subtly pushed their way into the sky.

"I'm not sure I understand why the settlers stopped in Kansas," said Luke, half-serious.

"Try growing wheat in the Rockies," said Tony.

"About the only thing they grow up there," said Matt, "is Coors."

PEL

"This must be that valley that guy told us about," said Moom. "It's pretty spectacular."

"Yeah, whatever," said Pel. He was pissed. They got here hours later than they might have if they had gotten an earlier start, and if they hadn't lost the trail a few times. But Moom was right. The view was pretty spectacular. The sun was just about to set behind the ridge to the west, and its fading rays covered the whole of the valley in a soft golden light.

"Their camp should be over that next ridge, you think?" said Moom.

"Yeah, I think so."

"Think we can make it before dark?"

It dawned on Pel that Moom posed almost every thought in the form of a question—a question that he was supposed to answer. Twice earlier, when they wandered off the trail, there was Moom each time, "Are you sure we're on the right track?" Pel just wished his brother would speak his mind.

"Maybe," said Pel, "but I don't want to take a chance on running into those guys in the dark. If it comes to friendly fire, all we got is a Glock, and God only knows what they have."

"Do you think we should set up camp here?"

Another question.

"Sure, why not?" It was a good chance to show off his tent pitching skills.

TONY

It was not long past dark when their vehicle rolled up to the Mountain Inn in Basalt—about thirty minutes north of Aspen and a hundred bucks cheaper. As they stepped out into the brisk night, Tony looked skyward. "Remember, the moon reads right to left," he said to his sons, "A bright right side means it's waxing. That's good. Camp will be brighter each night."

"Can we eat soon?" asked Luke, in full indifference to his father's astronomy lesson.

"Sure," Tony sighed. "Let me check in first."

The room secured and the bags stowed, they headed into Aspen. Although he had no formal responsibility for overall site assessment, he wanted to take a look around. State Highway 82 was the only land route into town. From a security perspective, he knew this to be an advantage. After the Seattle WTO protests in 1999, summit organizers chose sites that were hard to get to and expensive to stay at. No sense making things easy for the army of sea turtles, Ninjas, and other sundry whack jobs that descended on Seattle. But then again, 82 was the only way out, and that thought troubled him. If things went deeply south, a town like this could be a bear to get out of.

On this October night, though, everything was perfect. It almost always was in Aspen. The town fathers—and mothers—saw to that. In the twenty years since he had last visited, this once quaint little burg had become America's priciest chunk of real estate. He had no grudge against the rich, but something about this place bugged him. The moment Highway 82 morphed into Main Street, Colorado turned into Hollywood or some rustic facsimile thereof—a perfect playground for overfed, overpaid public servants on their G7 junkets.

Tony imagined what Aspen must have been like during what locals called the "quiet years." They meant the period after 1893 when the panic killed the silver market and took the boom out of the boomtown, and before the 1950s when the growing moneyed classes discovered skiing. To live an ordinary life in this spectacular a setting must have been, well, extraordinary.

Tony had no trouble finding Zane's Tavern, a couple blocks off Main Street. Thor Olafson was waiting for them at a table towards the back of the joint, less crowded than it would be in either summer or winter. He was hard to miss. Olafson had the face of an altar boy, but the body of a nose tackle. He stood nearly half a foot taller than Tony—not including his cowboy hat—and weighed a hundred pounds more. His red, checkered flannel shirt barely covered his gut. He sprung out of his chair and they walked towards each other.

"Thor, my man!"

"Howdy, cap'n!"

"Enough with the captain stuff," said Tony.

He never did quite identify with the officer class. In the summer of 2001, he was a JUCO grad with a pregnant wife and a decent enough future in the HVAC business. A few years down the road, if all went well, he hoped to get his own shop—a classic mom and pop, with pop running the service calls and mom running the office. To him, this was the American dream, and it was all within reach.

Then September 11th happened and war followed in its deadly wake. He figured unless someone was willing to step up and preserve that dream, that dream would collapse as surely as the buildings at the World Trade Center. So while his neighbors were hoisting their flags, he was heading down to the recruitment office with Angel's blessing. Her father was career Army. She understood.

From day one, Tony sensed he had a gift. His superiors sensed the same. There was no element of soldiering he did not master quickly. He was smart, tough, relentless, level-headed, and a natural leader—virtues that counted for a lot more in the military than they did in the HVAC business. The Army put him through college and OCS. In the upstairs-downstairs world of the military, he was headed upstairs. He just never felt comfortable with the pomp and the politics.

"Tony'll do. Besides," he added with a smile, "I exited as a major."

"Whatever," said Thor as the two embraced. "Great to see you."

"Great to see you, too," said Tony, now holding his friend at arm's length and sizing him up. "Truth is there's a whole lot of you to see. I don't remember you being this big."

"And I don't remember you being so ugly, but I can lose weight."

Tony had to smile. "These are my sons," he said, "Matt and Luke." They shook hands around.

"Nice to meet you," said Matt.

"I can see why they call you Thor," said Luke. "That's not your real name, is it?"

"No," laughed Thor.

"Should I tell them what it is?" Tony asked.

"Not if you value your health."

"Secret's safe."

"Hope you're hungry," Thor said, quickly changing the topic. "They got great bar food here."

"Any left?" asked Tony.

"Our union says we can get as big as we want."

"You didn't have to take them up on it." Tony looked Thor over once more. "Damn, man, they're going to have to cut your next uniform out of the infield tarp at Coors Field."

"All muscle."

"Bull."

"Well, mostly muscle."

"I can still kick your butt," said Tony, "no matter how big it gets."

"I suspect you can." Thor looked over to Matt and Luke. "Guys, I don't know if your old man told you, but he is a *legendary* badass."

"Huh," said Luke in surprise.

"Did he ever tell you about Shok Valley?"

"Don't think so," said Matt.

"Saved my life," said Thor.

"Shut up," said Tony.

"He did, boys. Picked my sorry shrapnel-peppered butt up and…" Thor could say no more. For an endless moment, he tried to finish his sentence but could not. Tony saw the problem he was having and resolved it.

"No way I could pick your fat ass up today. I'd need a forklift."

Thor laughed heartily, turned his head, and wiped away a tear. "Thanks, man. You saved me once again. I haven't cried since the dog ate my binkie. Let's grab a seat and get some chow."

"Guys, you good with chicken wings?" Tony asked his sons. They both nodded. "Cool. Why don't you go play some eight-ball until the food comes? Thor and I have to talk a little shop."

The two settled into a booth. After some routine flirting with a predictably cute waitress—"In Aspen, it's just a question of how cute," said Thor—they ordered a couple of beers and Zane's world famous chicken wings.

With his sons now well out of earshot, Tony got serious. "So, tell me what it is that's got you worried."

"There's been a lot of chatter. People are nervous."

"There's always chatter. People are always nervous before these things. Anything specific?"

Thor leaned in as though to answer but didn't. Instead he stopped and looked quickly around the bar. "This is going to sound nuts, but I'd like you to look very discreetly over my shoulder to about ten o'clock."

"What am I looking for?"

"You see the guy sitting at the bar under the Coors sign?"

"Yeah."

"I think he's a Haji of some sort."

"You think? Like a regular goat-humping, poppy-growing Haji or a terrorist, up-to-no good Haji?"

"I think B, up-to-no good Haji."

"What makes you think so?"

"About a week ago, I got a call from an old C Company buddy. He tells me he's at this gentlemen's club south of town."

"Gentlemen's club?" asked Tony, his eyebrows raised.

"You know, pole dancing, that sort of thing."

"Yeah, okay, gentleman stuff."

"He says there's several foreign-looking guys there throwing money around."

"That made him suspicious?"

"Not just that. He heard two of them jabbering away in some central Asian shithole language he couldn't quite make out."

"And you figured since the 9/11 guys were known to frequent such establishments, you'd go there to check out these potential terrorists?"

"Something like that."

Tony laughed. Thor joined him.

"Anyhow, I said to my buddy, 'Next time you see these guys, let me know.' The next time was two nights ago."

"You went?"

"Yeah. I swear. I'd never go there otherwise."

"Okay, I believe you," Tony smirked.

"Anyhow, there were four of them there. This guy was one of them, but it was too loud and I couldn't get close enough to hear what language they were talking."

"But you were suspicious?"

"Yes, I was."

"You weren't profiling them, were you?" said Tony with a wink.

"Heaven forbid," said Thor, "but it was more than just the language thing."

"I'm listening."

"See the way the guy is dressed?"

Tony looked discreetly at the fellow. His black hair was short and neatly parted. He wore a dark red polo shirt, khakis, and Docksiders.

"He dresses like Jake from State Farm," said Tony.

"Jake from State Farm?" said Thor.

"You remember the guy in the commercial from a few years back. They ran it a million times. The husband calls late at night.

The wife's suspicious. She asks what 'Jake from State Farm' is wearing? Jake says 'khakis.'"

"Right, that guy," said Thor. "That's what they dressed like—Jake from State Farm."

"So what's suspicious about Jake from State Farm?" Tony repeated.

"That's more or less the way the Hajis dressed on 9/11. I'm thinking they're up to something. I'm thinking their imam or whoever told them to dress like ordinary Americans, not understanding that ordinary Americans don't live in Aspen."

"Have you told anyone?" Tony asked.

"I'd like to kick this upstairs, man," said Thor, "but this town is so PC it squeaks."

"Even the sheriff's office?"

"Especially the sheriff's office. You might think I'm joking, but in this town, the more a person looks and acts like a terrorist, the less interest we're allowed to take in him."

"I don't think you're joking," said Tony. "That's everywhere. Done anything on your own?"

"The night at the club, I waited until two of them came out."

"And?"

"They got in an SUV, Jake in the passenger seat. I ran a check on the tags. The vehicle is a rental, but I don't think they're here for pleasure."

"Why do you say that?"

"I followed them, and they stopped at a very swell place on Smuggler Street."

"Is that the real name of it?" smiled Tony. "Smuggler Street?"

"Yup. Couldn't make that up. I got a make on the address. It's the home of this guy named Howard Mossman. Ring a bell?"

"Sounds familiar."

"He's a big-shot civil rights attorney."

"Civil rights, huh?"

"Yeah, at least if your idea of civil rights is pedophilia, pornography, Puerto Rican terrorism, cop-killing, or just all-purpose Jihadism."

"And you suspect Jihadism?"

"Suspect is a little strong. Curious is about right. Anyhow, they go in and each comes out carrying a bag stuffed with something."

"Something?"

"Drugs, money, guns, I don't know."

Tony stared for a moment over Thor's shoulder at the man under the Coors sign. He was nursing a beer.

"Don't look, but Jake's drinking a Dos Equis."

"Yeah, and…?"

"I think he's Latino."

"Just because he's drinking a Dos Equis?"

"No. He looks Mexican. Most Mexicans range on a spectrum from Indian to European. I'm somewhere in the middle. So, I think, is this guy. We could pass for natives in half the world's countries."

"I think he's American," said Matt, throwing himself into the booth next to Tony. "He looks like Jake from State Farm."

"What'd I tell you?" said Tony with a chuckle while turning to check on Luke. He seemed content shooting pool.

"Great minds think alike," said Thor.

"I guess so," said Tony, hesitating to pull Matt into the conversation. "How much did you hear of what we were saying?"

"Just the last part about the guy at the bar," Matt answered. "Is something going on?"

"Maybe, maybe not," said Tony somberly. "But whatever you hear from now on, keep to yourself." As Tony spoke, the man at the bar got up and appeared to head for the restroom.

"Don't turn around," he gestured to Thor. "Time for me to do a little research."

"You da man."

Tony slid out of the booth, walked casually towards the bar, and followed the same narrow path down the dark hallway that Jake had. The men's room was the first door on the left. Tony turned the handle. It was locked. Must be a one-holer, he thought. At the sound of the toilet flushing, he leaned against the wall with his back to the restroom door. When the door opened, he turned abruptly around and walked square into Jake.

"*Pendejo!*" growled the man.

He was as tall as Tony and almost as solid.

"Sorry," said Tony, holding his hands up in the way of an apology and sidling around him.

"Son of a whore," the man muttered as he pushed his way past Tony.

"Sorry," Tony repeated. "My bad." He then opened the bathroom door and locked it behind him. Once in the restroom he figured he might as well use it. Then he came back the same way he had come, careful not to make eye contact with the man at the bar.

"Well?" asked Thor after Tony had sat down.

"Well," said Tony, "our friend took the UPO test and passed."

"The UPO test?"

"Unexpectedly pissed off."

"Is that a real test?"

"No, I just kind of made it up, but I did read somewhere that if something suddenly upsets you—like me bumping into this guy—you respond instinctively in your native language, which is what this guy did."

"And?"

"Spanish, Mexican accent."

"What'd he call you?"

"An idiot. A little worse actually."

"How did you respond?"

"Apologized. In English. Then to make sure I got the message, he questioned my lineage in English. Obvious accent. You sure those guys were speaking an Asian language?"

"At least two of them, that's what my buddy said."

"Sure it wasn't the lap dancers speaking Pashto?"

"Do a lap dance in a burka," Thor laughed, "and you ain't getting much in the way of tips."

"You've heard of confirmation bias, right?" asked Tony. "We believe something to be true and, without meaning to, we finesse the evidence to fit our beliefs. We all do it."

"He told me it was Central Asian, Pashto or something like it," said Thor, turning to the bar and yelling, "Honey, two more Imperial Reds."

"I'm good," said Tony. "Those guys didn't ID you, did they?"

"No, I was in my civvies. I do all my uniformed work in the north part of the county. Sure you don't want another?"

"Yup."

"How about you, Matt?"

"Coke's good," said Matt, anxiously enough his father noticed. Thor turned again, "Make that one, honey, and a coke."

After the waitress brought the drinks, Tony raised his glass and said, "To Captain Matt Freeman."

"To Captain Matt," said Thor. "There was a warrior."

After a moment of awkward silence, Tony asked, "How do service workers afford to live here?"

"Many of them don't. I can barely afford to live here."

"Maybe our friend over there is supplying the local business community with undocumented help," said Tony.

"Wouldn't shock me."

"Or running black tar or crystal or trafficking in underage human cargo like all us Latinos do," Tony smiled.

"Don't bust my chops."

"I'm just teasing. You might be right."

"You never know," said Thor.

"You never do," affirmed Tony. "I'll keep my eyes open."

"Me too," Matt volunteered. While Tony playfully rubbed his son's head, the waitress brought over a massive pile of chicken wings and some shriveled celery stalks.

"Hey," Tony said turning to Luke and changing the mood, "move it. If I let Thor loose on these wings, we'll be down to the celery by the time you get here."

LUKE

Luke sauntered over to the table, more than a little cocky after beating the invincible Matt in three straight games of eight-ball.

"I'm hungry," he said, sliding in next to Thor.

"Matt says he let you win," said Thor.

"What!" shrieked Luke.

"He's just teasing," said Matt. "My bro's a champ, got that hand-eye thing going."

That was cool, thought Luke. He shrugged off the compliment and dug in. As Thor leaned over to eat, the letters tattooed on his chest peeked out over his shirt. Not one for tact, Luke asked what they spelled.

"Shhh!" cautioned Thor as he unbuttoned the top two buttons. "My bosses won't like this if word gets around." He pulled back the shirt to reveal the word "Infidel" written in cursive across his massive chest.

"I know what infidel means," said Matt, "but why would you want it as a tattoo?"

"Better ask your father that when he's got some time. It takes explaining."

"How come you don't have any tattoos, Dad?" Luke asked.

"He was about the only one in Afghanistan who didn't," said Thor. "Even the goats had tattoos."

Tony turned to his boys and smiled gently, "Your mom hated them. She was totally into the 'your body's a temple' stuff. Now Thor here, his body is less a temple than uh…"

"…a men's room wall at a truck stop," said Thor, finishing the thought.

When they caught their breath and stopped laughing, Luke asked, "Can't Thor come with us, Dad?" He liked the guy.

"Sure, why not?" said Tony, redirecting his question to Thor. "Don't you have like a naked picture of your boss's dog or something you could leverage into a couple of days off? You already bought the tag."

"Wish I could. But I wasn't just saying they canceled all vacation requests. They did."

"What do they have you doing that's so important, other than stalking State Farm salesmen?"

"Babysitting Japanese bureaucrats," said Thor, then added with a smile, "Oh no, that's your job."

Tony laughed. "We call it 'high level, tactical security.'"

"Well then I'll call my assignment 'strategic vehicular management,' better known to mere mortals as 'directing traffic.'"

"Traffic won't be that bad," said Tony. "They can spare you for a little while."

"We'll see," said Thor. "If it takes you about five or six hours to the site I'm sending you to, I could probably get there in three or four.

"And where exactly are you sending us?"

"This is the good part." Thor smiled, wiped the Buffalo sauce off his fingers, and took out a topographical map of the area. He then walked the three of them step by step through the process—from the trading post where they would secure their horses to the trailhead and on up the trail.

"We'll swap vehicles when we leave here," said Thor.

"Sure, thanks."

"Why we swapping?" asked Luke.

"You're going to be pulling a horse trailer tomorrow, Luke, and I got a seasoned F-450 Super Duty parked outside that could haul a herd of wild mustangs."

"Seasoned?" asked Luke.

"That's Thor-talk for 'dilapidated,'" said Tony.

"Way I figure, you should be on the trail by nine or so tomorrow," Thor continued. "That'll give you time to do some scouting and be ready to terminate some elk come Saturday morning when the season opens."

"Sounds good."

"The trick," said Thor, pointing to the map, "is that when you get to Crow Creek here, you ignore the main trail that turns north along the creek. Instead, I want you to cross the creek and look for this secondary trail which leads more or less northwest."

"Will the turnoff be obvious?"

"Probably not. Last time I came through there it wasn't marked, which tends to discourage amateurs. Cross the creek at that juncture and keep your eyes open. Once you find it, you follow the trail up to this ridge," Thor continued, now tracing the route with his finger, "and when you cross the ridge, you're looking at something like virgin territory."

"Like?" said Tony.

"Yeah, like," said Thor. "I showed this trail to a couple of young guys the other day, but they're heading into the valley beyond you."

"You know your way around here pretty good," said Matt.

"That I do. Born and raised. You'll like the hunting area I picked out. The trail is new, and almost no one knows about it. Less chance some novice hunter will mistake you guys for a gang of elk."

"Gang?" said Luke.

"Gang's the actual word for a herd of them," said Thor. "You know how it works. Some wear red bandannas. Some wear blue. Try not to get caught in a drive-by."

"We'll do our best," Matt laughed.

"Sure you can't come?" Tony asked.

"I'll tell you what. If they don't stick me with OT, I might be able to catch up Saturday and come back for a Sunday evening shift. Love to get out and do a little riding. If not, you can regale me with the play-by-play when you bring the truck back."

"Wish you could come," said Luke, surprising himself with this burst of anxiety. He hoped it wasn't obvious, but there was something very calming about Thor's presence. It was not every day he met a cowboy or a Viking, let alone both.

"I'll give it a shot, guys, but don't count on me."

"Funny you'd say that," said Luke. "Dad says you're the one guy he can always count on."

DAY 17

MATT

"Up and at'em, girls," said Tony. He grabbed each of his sons by their feet and shook them awake.

"It's the middle of the night," said Matt groggily. He wasn't as eager to hit the road as he thought he'd be. It looked way too cold outside.

"No, it's almost six. They start serving breakfast in about five minutes."

"What's on the menu, Pops?"

"Shoe leather with my foot still in it if you call me 'Pops' again. See you down there."

His father was the only other patron in the room when Matt slumped in. He looked at the breakfast bar. He hadn't spent that many nights in motels, but it amazed him that they all served the same food: coffee, juice, cylinders filled with cereal, donuts from the Jurassic age, croissants made of wallboard.

"Where can I get an omelet?" he groused.

"Denver. Don't complain. In Afghanistan, they'd be taking reservations six months in advance for a joint this swell."

Matt drained the last of the Cheerios from one of the cylinders and joined his father.

"Dang. One more Cheerio, and you'd be in the Guinness World Book of Records."

"I gave it my best, Dad." Matt laughed.

"That you did."

Stale or not, Matt dived mouth-first into the cereal. He figured there must be something about high altitudes that made people hungry. Minutes later, Luke shuffled in, fiddling with his cell phone as he entered.

"The signal sucks."

"It's the best signal you're going to have for the next few days," said his dad, "so enjoy it. And don't say 'suck.'"

"Alright."

"Or anything that rhymes with suck for that matter."

When the boys finished, now half-alert, they grabbed their stuff and headed for Thor's F-450. Their father had already checked out. "Man, it's still dark," said Luke.

"Not for long. Look off to the east, and you can see the sky starting to brighten. Get in, gents. The elk won't wait forever."

"They might die of old age by the time we get this junker there," said Matt, backing away from the passenger door. He wanted his brother to sit in the middle, but Luke, he knew, wasn't about to volunteer.

"After you, bro," Luke said.

"I'm older," said Matt humorlessly.

"C'mon you two," said their father.

"Whatever," Luke mumbled, climbed in, and slid in to the middle.

"Good call, son. That wasn't hill enough to die on."

Matt hopped in after Luke. The bench seat squeaked and stuffing popped out of it. He shut the door. Didn't catch. He re-opened the door and gave it the necessary slam to make it latch. His dad started the truck up, but not without an unhealthy belch of blue smoke. Matt had to grin. There was no emission test in the civilized world this beast could pass. He guessed being a sheriff's deputy had its perks.

The trio headed east out of Basalt on Frying Pan Road. The road ran along Center Creek, which Matt could hear better than he could see. He listened carefully. He loved the endless, unchanging hum of it. As a boy, every now and then, his mother used to take him and Luke to picnic alongside a stream that sounded very much like this one. He fought to keep that image front and center, but hard as he struggled, he knew that the final terrifying sight of his mom screaming "Matt" would soon shove it out. All thoughts of his mother ended that way. He spoke up just to think of something else.

"Almost there?"

"Five minutes."

His father turned north on Toner Creek Road for a few more miles and pulled into a gravel parking lot in front of Zeke's Trading Post and General Store. Matt had never seen any place quite like it. In the early light, it looked like something out of a John Wayne movie. He took that as a good sign.

They had hoped to get to Zeke's first, but someone beat them to it. As Matt climbed out of the vehicle, he could see the outfitter across the parking lot helping two other guys lead their horses onto a trailer.

"Dad," he said quietly, grabbing his father's arm to get his attention. "Who wears a hat like that to go hunting?"

His father looked. "It's called a Fedora."

"A little gangster, don't you think?"

"Different folks, different strokes. Don't sweat it."

"The other guy has a braid down his back. Looks like an Indian."

"Yeah…and?"

"Just sayin'."

"Don't worry. I'll keep my eye on your scalp," his father said, tousling his son's hair.

"Aw, c'mon, I didn't mean anything by that. It's just they don't look like hunters."

"They're dressed like hunters. What do they look like to you?"

"I don't know," said Matt, "cartel bosses?"

His dad laughed involuntarily. "You're as bad as Thor," he said. "I knew I should never have let you watch *Breaking Bad*."

TONY

Tony smiled to himself. Matt was right. They didn't look like hunters. They didn't look like cartel bosses either, but they did look like Mexicans. He was relieved that Jake from State Farm wasn't with them. Then he might have worried at least a little.

Working quickly, the outfitter got the two guys on the road and walked back over to Tony.

"You Zeke?" asked Tony.

"That be me," said Zeke. "What can I do you for?"

Tony once promised himself to shoot the next guy who said "do you for" but thought better of it. As they shook hands, Zeke's more thickly callused than his own, Tony mused at how much the outfitter seemed the part. A sturdy, well-weathered gent, probably in his sixties, Zeke wore his sweat-stained cowboy hat as naturally as if he had come out of the womb with it on. Tony imagined that he was one of those guys who mastered the look—boots, jeans, wide leather belt, flannel shirt, down vest, and a big, drooping mustache Sam Elliott would envy—without ever trying. Tony respected his wholeness. He looked like he actually did win his belt buckle at the rodeo.

"Tony Acero. You should have us on your books. My buddy Thor Olafson set us up. Horses and trailer."

"Great guy, Thor. Come on inside, and we'll take care of you."

Tony and the boys followed him in. While Tony went through the paperwork, Matt shopped as instructed—lots of pre-wrapped sandwiches, no mayo, and a six pack of Gatorade to supplement their powdered Gatorade, as much to provide plastic bottles as anything.

"I didn't have to sign this many forms when I bought my house," said Tony with a smile.

"We get a lot of people from back East," said Zeke. "They seemed disposed to *litigate*." He slid still another document Tony's way. "Just one more."

"What's this one say?" asked Tony, signing without reading.

"Basically," said Zeke, "it says if a horse kicks you senseless, it's your fault, not his, and certainly not mine."

Tony laughed. Zeke smiled.

"Last I checked the weather looked good," said Tony. "Any changes?"

"Little cooler than average. Maybe some flurries in a day or two. Nothing to worry about."

Tony chuckled to himself, thinking that if there were a blizzard coming, this guy wouldn't tell him for fear it would kill the sale.

"One more thing?" said Tony. "Those guys here before us. They look familiar. I think I might have known 'em back in San Antone."

Tony felt a little foolish asking. He had never even been to San Antonio, let alone said "San Antone." He hailed from Orange County, California, but "San Antone" sounded somehow more authentic than "Anaheim." Those guys were likely not up to anything, but he promised Thor he'd keep his eyes open.

"They pay cash in advance," said Zeke, "deposit included, so I don't ask a lot of questions."

"Not their first time here then?" asked Tony casually.

"They were here last week," said Zeke. "I'm guessing they wanted to scout the territory before the season starts."

"We only got about an afternoon for scouting," said Tony.

"That's about the norm," said Zeke, "for out-of-towners, anyhow. But these guys are serious. They bring a lot of equipment, and they know their horses. Hate to break it to you, but today they got four of the best ones, and they paid a pretty penny to get them."

"No big deal," said Tony. He did not much care about the horses, but the intel spooked him just a little. Something wasn't quite right but wasn't wrong enough to worry him.

"So what kind of ponies you got for us?"

"Well," Zeke said with a wry smile, "I got some veteran trail horses for you."

"How veteran is veteran, like Spanish—American War veteran or what?"

"Next stop, GlueMax," deadpanned Zeke, "but that's at least a week or two away. Give me your keys if you don't mind."

Tony handed them over. Zeke climbed into the F-450, pulled the truck out, and backed it under the open-air gooseneck trailer's hitch without once looking over his shoulder. Getting out, he cranked the trailer down and lowered it directly on the truck's hitching ball. After securing the hitch he connected the electric brakes and lights and pulled the rig over to the corral. The trailer looked only marginally newer than the truck, but as long as the brakes worked, Tony figured, it was new enough.

Zeke motioned the fellows to follow and they walked over. "Man the gate son," he said to Luke. He then entered the corral, walked up to the nearest horse, grabbed the bridle, and led him out.

"Not exactly Seabiscuit," Matt whispered to his father.

"In the real world, you get what you pay for." By no means an expert on horseflesh, Tony knew enough to be disappointed. He hoped to see a little more muscle. "I think you ate more oats at breakfast than this pony has in the last week," he said to Matt, "but he'll do. He knows the drill."

"One final thing, Dirty Harry," said Zeke, his eye firmly fixed on the .44 Magnum riding high in a cross-draw holster above Tony's left hip.

"Yeah?" He wasn't sure whether he had just been flattered or insulted.

"Should you feel the need to shoot that hog leg while you're on the back of one of these fine animals, you just might find yourself as the main event in a very small but no less exciting rodeo."

"Roger that," Tony responded. "It's our fault, not the horses."

"Alright then, go shoot something worthy of a Cabela's wall and good luck."

LUKE

The drive to the little-used Chief Blanton trailhead took about twenty-five minutes. No one said much on the way. Luke let himself doze off once or twice, and no one bugged him—

reward, he figured, for not being too big of a jerk about the middle seat.

Uncomfortable as it was, he felt oddly safe sitting between his father and his brother. In his dreamy state, he could have ridden forever. He didn't want to get there. Truth be told, he didn't want to get anywhere.

MATT

"Dad, look," said Matt as they pulled into the small parking area at the trailhead and looked at the same rig they had seen back at Zeke's. Parked next to it, he noticed, was a black, late model Ford Bronco.

"Guess we're not the only ones here after all," said Luke.

"Don't sweat it," said their dad. "They're probably taking the main trail."

"You think?"

"Yeah, c'mon. We're burning trail time. Let's stop worrying and start moving."

Matt sensed his father's impatience and got going. His first task was to help unload the horses while Luke stood by trying at least to look useful.

"Grab your day-packs, cowgirls," said his father once the horses had been unloaded and secured. Matt remembered how relentless his dad had been in making sure he and Luke had everything they needed in those packs in case one of them got separated. When fully loaded, each day-pack was pretty well stuffed. Matt double-checked his just in case. Luke couldn't be bothered.

He still didn't know what to make of his little brother. It wasn't easy being on the south side of puberty when just about all your classmates were on the north, but he could not be sure the boy would ever get over whatever it was that bugged him. But who was he to talk? In time, Luke just might outgrow his problem. Matt had no such hope. He knew his own problem was too deep to outgrow, ever.

TONY

While the boys pulled their bags out, Tony made a quick, discreet call to Thor. He tried to, anyhow. No signal. He then texted a quick message, "Bronco, Arizona plates, X3Z-9J9?" The message box turned gray and read, "Failed." Ah, no big deal, he thought. Time to tend to the horses.

LUKE

"You know you don't want to get too close behind a horse. Just talk to him when you approach and put your hand on him when you're close. You startle him, and he may kick you halfway into next week."

"I know that, Dad," said Luke. He had ridden a few times but not enough to inspire confidence. He expected a lecture and got one.

"Figured you did, but when you're a father, trust me, you won't hesitate to repeat the safety stuff until it comes out in your kid's stool."

"Look at these monster saddle bags!" said Luke, fishing for something to talk about.

"Those are panniers. The French would call them pann-yays, but as Americans we have a sacred right to mispronounce all French words."

"What do we need them for?" asked Luke, holding one up, wondering about its jumbo size.

"To carry all the elk meat you're going to harvest. They'll hang over the saddle with the weight distributed on either side, easier on the horse that way."

"If the meat bags are on the saddle, Dad, where we gonna ride?"

"Ride? Elk meat ride. Paleface boy walk."

"Aww, man!" Luke would just as soon walk—he knew he could manage that—but he'd confuse his father if he did not put up at least a little resistance. So resist he did.

TONY

Observing the world through his son's eyes, Tony began to see how trying a trip like this could be. If he took all these little preparatory steps for granted, Luke did not—could not. He did not know enough to. All the decisions that came with each step were new to him.

On a firebase, a bad decision could be a fatal one, and not just for the fool who made it. Now, he had to keep telling himself Colorado wasn't Afghanistan. He did not bear fools lightly, but Luke wasn't a fool. He was a kid. If he failed to perform well, the fault was on him, not Luke.

With the boys' help, he unloaded the rest of the gear from the vehicle and stowed it in saddlebags or lashed it to the horses. Each of the three carried his own equipment. Nothing was mixed. Tony had spent enough time in the bush to know you never wanted to trust someone else to carry gear you might need—too much chance that person wouldn't be around when you needed it.

Time to run the guys through the drill. "From here on in," said Tony, "bad stuff can happen. Shout out if you don't have each of these with you on your person. That means in your pockets. These are items you can't get separated from." Tony went down the checklist: lighter, fire starter tabs, compass, map, whistle, knife, squeeze light, Ziploc bag, orange flagging tape, survival blanket, and an orange bandana. Each checked out. He was glad to see they had been listening.

"Now for the icing on your cake, the caffeine in your coffee," said Tony, reaching into the lower pockets of his cargo pants and pulling out two small ammo wallets. Matt took his without comment. Luke looked at his quizzically.

"I only count five bullets."

"That's all you need," said Tony. Although he kept more in reserve, he did not want the boys to know that, especially Luke. "And let me remind you for the nth time, they are called 'cartridges.' The 'bullets' are what you send down range."

"Whatever, but I only got five of them." Luke strained instinctively to see if his brother had gotten an extra cartridge or two. "What if I need more?"

"If you need more, you'll already have scared the elk into the next county," said Matt.

"Sure," said Luke. "We'll see."

"Take your time and don't miss," said his father. "If you do miss, you'll be real lucky to get a second shot. And if you get a second shot, you won't get a third."

"So why not just two...*cartridges* then?"

"The last three are so you can signal for help if you need it. You shoot. Then count ten elephants. Shoot. Count ten more elephants. Shoot again. That'll make it plain you're signaling and not just blasting away."

"Why would I need help?"

"You never know," Matt smiled. "Rattlers, grizzlies, Elk Qaeda!"

LUKE

This was getting to be a drag. Luke got the preparation part, but his father was overdoing it, and his brother was sucking up to him at every step. He wished he had finagled some way out of this, but it was too late now—way too late.

"Luke, I'm going to stick the GPS in your saddlebag," said Tony. "You know how to use it?"

More grief. "If it's electronic and has buttons, I'll figure it out."

"I thought we were going old school here, Dad," said Matt.

"Yeah, son, but when you get to be a parent, you'll learn that there's no greater terror than misplacing a kid."

"Dad, if Luke gets lost, the GPS won't help us find him."

"But it could help him find his way out."

"I won't get lost," Luke protested.

"I didn't say you would, Luke, but once I got separated from Matt in a Toys "R" Us for a half hour, and I'm still having flashbacks. Besides, someone has to carry it, and your horse has the lightest load. Do this for me."

"Whatever." No word better captured his take on all this, on life in general.

"Enough with the 'whatevers.' Let's head out."

Luke couldn't leave without pulling out his cell phone. Before he could even find a signal, his father grabbed the phone out of his hands, confiscated Matt's, took his own out of his pocket, walked over to the F-450, and stuffed the three phones into the glove compartment. He then turned and looked quizzically at Luke.

"Yeah, give me the GPS back. Let's do go old school. If you get lost, you can always whistle."

Luke had no problem yielding the GPS, but dang he was going to miss that phone.

"How we gonna communicate?" he said pleadingly.

"The old-fashioned way. We open our mouths and talk. We're not splitting up. So there's no issue here."

"Dad!" Luke implored.

"Not up for debate. I'm sick of watching you guys squander your young lives on those stupid things."

"But…"

"No buts. Let's take a look at the real world."

MATT

"You guys ready to mount up?" asked Tony.

"Let me hit the head first," said Matt. He walked towards the plastic outhouse—hated them—and continued into the woods to find a likely tree, the last great male advantage as he saw it. The relief came quick.

On the way back he checked out the rig the two amigos had parked at the trailhead. He faked doing it casually, but he was all eyes. New truck, new trailer. Must be nice, he thought. He tried to convince himself they were just some rich guys from South America or somewhere, but something kept telling him they weren't what they appeared to be. He thought about sharing his concerns but then thought better of it. He didn't want his father to think him paranoid—did not want to be accused of profiling, either, especially since these guys could be distant cousins of the old man.

TONY

Matt mounted his horse as if he owned it. *There's little that doesn't come naturally to the boy*, thought Tony. Luke was another story. For him every step in the natural world was an adventure. Tony watched him take hold of the saddle horn, put his foot in the stirrup, pause for a reaction from the horse, and, getting none, climb up.

"Hi ho, Silver," said Tony. Matt got the reference. He laughed. Luke stared blankly.

"Okay guys, I know we haven't ridden much." Tony could see the 'duh' look on their faces. "But your horse doesn't know that, at least not yet. Don't let him know. All he needs to know is you're in charge."

"How do I do that?" asked Luke.

"Real simple: the reins are in your hands, not his."

"Horses don't have hands."

"Thanks for the intel, son."

"Sorry."

"Pull left on the reins if you want to go left, right if you want to go right. Don't worry too much. Your horse will be content to follow the trail on his own. Now if he gets spooked and takes off running, pull back hard and steady on the reins until he decides running's not all that much fun."

"What if I want to make him go fast?"

"Tell him the glue people are on the way," laughed Matt.

"No, seriously."

"Keep the reins loose," said Tony, "pressure his sides with your legs, mainly your heels, and say 'giddy-up.'"

"That's it?"

"Pretty much, though I don't know when you'd want to make him go fast, not on this trip."

Tony saddled up and with a quick check behind him, swiveled around, gave his horse a nudge with his heels and headed out and up, Luke behind him and Matt in the rear. The trail was well tended here, almost as smooth as a bridle path. This gave him a chance to look around and absorb the vibes in this aspen-rich woodland. Two weeks ago, it would have been pure gold. Now, some leaves still clung desperately to the trees, but they spoke only of a lost glory. Each passing cloud foretold winter.

PEL

After crossing the valley at first light, Pel stood on what he thought to be the final ridge and saw nothing; nothing, that is, but trees below, lots of them, and more ridges beyond. He pulled the map from his backpack and stared at the red X. By his imperfect reckoning, the X should have been right below him at the base of this hill or whatever you called it. The morning sun was at his back. He was facing west. He could figure that much out. If that X marked anything real, he was not seeing it.

"Moom," he yelled down at his brother, who was still ascending the slope.

"Yeah?"

"Take a look at this," he said, waving the map. "Tell me what I'm missing."

Pel could not shake the sensation he had suppressed from day one that he was being played, that the whole thing was an elaborate con. He needed Moom to reassure him.

"Am I crazy or what?" he said, handing the map to his brother when he reached the ridgeline.

"Give me a second," said Moom, now bent over and struggling to pull some oxygen from the thin air.

Pel had no patience. "The X should be right below us, shouldn't it?" He was not sure why he was asking Moom. His brother knew no more than he did, but sometimes he asked good questions.

"Yeah," said Moom slowly. "Should be right below us. What's the problem?"

"The problem," said Pel, making no attempt to hide his frustration, "is that I don't see anything."

"What did you expect to see?"

That's what he liked about Moom. He asked good questions. What *did* he expect to see? Directional signs? Balloons? An inflatable Uncle Sam waving in the wind?

"If they're here," Moom added, "I suspect they'll find us."

"I suspect you're right," affirmed Pel.

MOOM

As he followed his brother down the slope, over a stretch of bare ground, and into the trees, it dawned on Moom just how piss-poor a revolutionary he made. Pel was desperately hoping R would be there. Moom was kind of hoping he would not be. Although he had resigned himself to his fate, he wished that fate would take a twist his way.

"Don't lose me," he yelled out to Pel, already twenty or so yards in front of him. There was nothing like a trail to follow. Pel was just dodging randomly between trees.

"Hustle then," shouted Pel.

The way Moom figured, if R were not here, and things did not pan out, Pel could content himself with the thought that he at least tried something totally hard-core. If so, they could walk out of the woods as anonymous and as unhurried as they walked in. Hell, if he could talk Pel out of demanding his money back from that old lawyer—or trying to, what with the giant Samoan and all—they could put this whole misadventure behind them and get on with their lives.

"Stop!"

The shove of a hard object into the base of Moom's skull killed those thoughts in a heartbeat. From that one whispered word, Moom sensed the guy knew few other words, at least not in English. He raised his hands over his head. There was no backing out of this now.

PEL

Pel did not know quite how, but he sensed Moom was no longer following him, and the second he did, he turned.

"Okay!" he said on seeing Moom, hands in the air, confusion all over his face. Pel raised his own hands and started walking towards his brother and the man behind him. Although he tried not to show it, he hadn't felt relief like this since they crossed the Verrazzano. This wasn't a scam after all. The game was on. He was about ready to star in the single greatest anti-fascist drama since Castro kicked reactionary butt at the Bay of Pigs.

"Relax," he said to Moom, who clearly needed encouragement. "We're good."

The man holding Moom motioned for Pel to turn around and walk forward. Pel got the message and heeded it. He could hear Moom and the man follow behind. R was waiting for them in a small clearing at the foot of the slope. He was smiling. To

Pel, the smile seemed genuine. As Pel approached, R opened his arms in welcome.

"You guys are not bullshitters, are you?" said R.

"Nope," said Pel. "We did it. Wasn't easy."

"So I heard," laughed R.

"So you heard?"

R just smiled. "Follow me," he said.

Pel did as requested, just a little bit uneasy about R's comment. *'So I heard?' What the hell did that mean?* He did not have much time to think about it. R led him and Moom through the trees and into a camp he could not have spotted from above. No one could have. It was too small, too simple, too well integrated into the environment. It consisted of little more than a pop-up canopy, maybe twelve feet by twelve feet, camouflage-colored with a cammy sidewall. Beside the wall, underneath the canopy, were two piles of boxes with what looked like Russian lettering on every box. One pile Pel guessed to be ammunition. On top of that pile were several sleeping bags. The other pile he guessed to be food. On top of that were a bunch of plastic water bottles. Underneath the center of the canopy was a single, collapsible director's chair, on the back of which was written a word that Pel figured was probably the Russian word for "director."

"Nice touch," said Pel.

"Thank you," said R.

"But the *technology?* I'm not seeing that."

"It is on the way."

Pel just shrugged. He did not want to look too concerned. R then turned to the guy who escorted the brothers in and spoke to him in a language Pel had not heard before. The conversation seemed serious. The man, of indeterminate age with fresh beard growth nearly up to his eyeballs, nodded his assent and then headed back in the direction from which he came. Pel chose not to ask R who he was or which language they spoke. On some subjects, the less he knew, the better.

"Are you guys hungry?" R asked.

"Yeah, sure," said Pel. Moom echoed him.

"Have a seat," said R, pointing to the ground. Pel and Moom got the message and sat down. R handed each of them several packs of food and a water bottle, then settled himself in his chair.

"What are we eating?" asked Moom.

"Just read the label," said R. "These are Russian version of what your Army calls MRE's, meals ready to eat, no cooking." He added playfully, "You guys speak Russian, correct?"

R was jacking with them, thought Pel. He knew about the Caspian. He had to. He must have heard the Russian toms-toms or whatever. If R was from Chechnya or some other breakaway republic, his people and the Russians had been killing each other for generations. How deeply each side had infiltrated the other he did not know at all. He decided to play dumb. It wasn't hard.

TONY

The air was brittle, the trail hard and dry. It obviously had not rained in a while. About one mile in, he passed an encouraging sign. It read, "Wilderness area, no motorized vehicles." That was good, one less class of humans to share the world with. Tony dismounted and pulled the topo map from his saddlebag and the compass from his pocket. The boys grabbed theirs—he insisted they each be able to operate independently—and joined him on a thick log just off the trail.

Tony unfolded his map so they could see the entire area. He then quickly oriented it so north on the map roughly aligned with reality.

"For now, let me just lay out the basic route in rough terms. We're heading almost due west now and we'll veer northwest once we cross Crow Creek. You see these two ridges here? They run largely north-south, perpendicular to the trail we're on. I'm not telling you something you don't know, but the closer the lines get to each other, the steeper the climb."

"Understood," said Matt.

"In the field we always give these things names. So let's call the first of these two ridges, the one we cross first, 'Alpha.' The second ridge, the one on the west side of the valley, we'll call 'Bravo.' Let's be optimists and call the space in between them 'Elk Valley.' By mid-afternoon, just before we reach Alpha, we'll find a spot to set up camp and leave the horses to graze."

"Why leave 'em?" Luke asked.

"The next morning we'll need to negotiate our way over that ridge in the dark. We need to be in place to shoot before dark. So better to check the route out on foot first in the daytime and find a spot on Alpha's east slope that gives us a good angle on the elk below."

"Any chance we'll actually see an elk?" asked Luke. The kid's skepticism bled through even when he tried to conceal it.

"No guarantees," said Tony. "In any case, once we find that spot, we'll climb back east over Alpha to where we left the horses, bed down early, and head out before dawn back to our spot so we're in position to shoot at first light."

"Sounds like a plan," said Luke, with that seemed to Tony just a hint of enthusiasm. They were making progress.

"I hope it still sounds like a plan when I drag your butt out of your sleeping bag tomorrow morning," said Tony, smiling. For now, at least, he liked the way the plan was working out. He had his sons' attention. They were learning things they needed to learn. With the maps stashed, they remounted and headed out.

About five klicks ahead, on the near side of Crow Creek, the main trail bent north, and the secondary trail forked northwest on the far side of the creek just as Thor had said it would. Tony noticed they were not the first ones to have come this way, but he could not tell how fresh the horse tracks were. He kept the observation to himself.

"Remember what Yogi Berra said about this situation?"

"Who's Yogi Berra?" asked Luke.

"Dope," said Matt to his brother, then turned to his father. "No, what did Yogi say?"

"When you come to a fork in the road, take it." Tony laughed. The boys rolled their eyes. The trio now headed northwest on a trail much rougher than the one they had left. After a couple more hours, Tony led the boys into a small, natural clearing beside the stream. The site had "lunch break" written all over it.

The horses got lunch too. The boys did not need to be fed. They figured it out on their own and had wolfed down the sandwiches, chips, apples, and Gatorade by the time Tony sat down. If nothing else, thought Tony, these kids knew how to eat.

MATT

His lunch finished, Matt wandered off into the nearby woods to relieve himself. He had not strayed far from the center of camp when he saw something glisten in the sunlight. On picking it up, he shook his head in disgust. It was an empty, recently discarded pack of Marlboro 100s. He looked closer and saw fresh cigarette butts scattered about. He had tried to ignore the horse tracks he had seen along the route, but there was no ignoring this. Had to be Fedora Man and Tonto. Pissed him off. The fire danger was bad enough, but these guys were pigs.

"Dad," he yelled, holding up the pack, "check this out."

"Looks like our territory's not so virgin after all. Throw it in with our trash."

Matt walked back to his horse, more uneasy than he cared to admit. Every time he took a leak, it seemed, he learned something he wished he hadn't. He suspected his father felt the same way. He might have misread his dad, but Matt sensed him biting back the impulse to say, "There's something wrong here." He certainly wanted to say that himself—the hunters he knew would never leave cigarette packs behind—but the last thing he wanted to do was worry Luke.

TONY

With the afternoon light illuminating the trail, Tony glassed the mountainside ahead for signs. At each water crossing, even the rivulets and dry streambeds, Tony would stop again and look closely at the trail. Nothing. Nothing, that is, except cigarette butts, the occasional candy wrapper, and steaming piles of horse manure. You didn't have to be Kit Carson to follow these guys, but Tony was getting the sense that there was more than one set of guys. The candy wrappers had been there longer than the cigarette packs.

MOOM

Sitting on top of the ridge and facing east across the valley they just hiked through, a pair of binoculars around his neck, Moom was beginning to feel just a little bit foolish. He had seen nothing in the two hours or so he had been out there. R had told him to look out for some horsemen, three in all. Pel was manning a spot some 200 yards further north. R told the brothers no more about the horsemen than that they could communicate only in Spanish and English. R's own guys spoke neither, which was why he needed the brothers to serve as lookouts.

R had given each of them a Motorola two-way radio and instructions to use it only when necessary. If Moom spotted the horsemen, he was to alert Pel, and Pel would lead the men down to the camp. Moom's job was to remain on the ridge and keep an eye out for any other people who might stray into the area. As far as Moom figured, this was pure make-work. He was wrong.

LUKE

Luke hated to admit it—and he wouldn't give anyone that satisfaction—but there was something cool about riding a horse up a mountainside in Colorado with a rifle under his leg. It all just seemed so…so…totally cowboy.

"How ya doing?" asked his father at one point.

"Not too bad. I kind of half like this."

"High praise from Mr. Buzzkill," said Matt.

Luke decided to shrug his brother off and keep on riding. This was something he wouldn't mind getting good at. Still, though, he did not want to hear anyone ask him how doing real stuff compared to video stuff. He wasn't sure how he'd answer.

Moom

Moom leaped to his feet and keyed the radio.

Pel heard Moom's faint voice and picked up his radio. "What?" said Pel. "Talk louder?"

"Sorry," said Moom, now speaking up. "Look across the valley, just below that ridge across from us."

"Got 'em. I'll make sure R's gotten the word."

There they were, three of them on horseback, cresting over the ridge opposite him and now shuffling carefully down the steep slope. They seemed too focused on negotiating the slope to look up, and clearly did not see Moom before plunging into the trees. Through the binoculars, he tracked them as best he could, which was not good at all. Still, he knew more or less where they were. He looked nowhere else.

But somehow he lost them. He was hoping they had stopped to eat or rest at the creek that ran through the valley floor, but he feared they followed the creek in the wrong direction. He had mixed feelings about the whole damned plot, but he didn't want to be the one to screw things up.

Luke

A few hours after lunch, they came to a relatively flat, sheltered stretch amidst the timber right alongside the trail. Up ahead, he could see the terrain getting steep and rough. He was more than hoping they'd take a break. He just didn't want to be the one to ask.

"This is as good a spot as any to make camp," said his father, dismounting. "We'll stay close to the trail so if Thor comes, he won't have any trouble finding us."

That was exactly what Luke wanted to hear. Climbing stiffly off his mount, he didn't fuss when his dad showed him how to set up a picket line for the horses and feed them. After removing the saddles from the horses and rubbing them down, the boys pitched their tents and stowed their gear.

"We're on foot from here on in, guys."

"No horses?" said Luke, disappointed. He was just getting the hang of it.

"It will be too dark in the morning for anyone but real horsemen, and that ain't us," said Tony. "No point taking them now. You guys ready to roll?"

"Ready as I'll ever be," said Luke.

"Grab your guns," said his father. "Can't leave them here unattended. Bring your day-packs too. Never know when you're going to need them."

TONY

After a strenuous mile or so of hiking west, Tony and his sons left the timber behind them. The uneven ridgeline lay about fifty meters ahead. This open area was close to flat, the footing relatively secure among the rocky soil and the scattered plants.

The trio walked easily to the ridgeline. On scanning the bowl-like valley below, Tony could see why hunters might avoid it. The slopes were steep and large stretches of terrain were densely wooded, maybe too dense to get a good shot at an elk. Undaunted, he followed the ridgeline north, looking for a negotiable passage into the valley and soon finding one.

"Take note of this outcropping," he said. "This is where we're crossing."

"Looks like Skeletor," said Luke of the skull-like rock formation. Tony had to admit it kind of did, stark and bulbous as it was.

"A good memory trick," Tony flattered him. "Take a look around you. Remember where we are. Mark the place and time on your maps. If we find what we're looking for, we'll need to locate this turnoff before sunrise tomorrow." They would be coming through here before light in the morning. It would be essential to have some point of reference.

"All downhill from here," he said as he left the ridgeline, his sons following close behind. Although they had gravity at their back, the going got harder, not easier. Given the slope's steep rake, Tony had to shuffle down the exposed surface sideways, his feet parallel to the ridge, leading with his left foot, his right foot anchoring the left. More than once he used his right hand to push off from the slope. Luke struggled behind him but said nothing. Matt had little trouble.

About a hundred meters down, a finger ridge jutted out of the slope, almost perpendicular to Alpha but angling northwest. For a hundred meters or so, it was level enough and just wide enough to walk across upright, and Tony did just that. He stopped at the point where the ridge sloped steeply downward so the boys could catch their breath and soak in the view. In Kansas, this humble ridge would be a tourist hot spot. In Colorado, it was just another opening overlooking another spectacular, sun-dappled valley of aspen and pine with a sparkling stream running through it. On the far side of the valley, the western side, was Bravo, the north-south ridge, slightly lower in elevation than Alpha.

"Look at this," said Tony to his sons, now joining him at the tip of the finger ridge. "Each side of this ridge has its own distinct—what's the word?—ecology." He pointed out how the north slope descended sharply from the finger ridge into a dark timber dense with spruce, fir, and pine. The south slope descended more gradually and, thanks to the sun, sported aspen, juniper, and pine, as well as open grassy patches scattered here and there. "Finger ridge begins with an 'F.' So let's call this ridge 'Foxtrot.'"

After a few minutes soaking in the wholeness of it all, Tony pulled out his 10x42 Swarovskis and started scanning for signs of elk. He'd bought these hunting binoculars used a few years back. He liked their razor-sharp images, high contrast, and true color. But even used, Angel reminded him, they cost as much as a week in Sardinia. She wasn't thrilled with that purchase, but as he told her, once you looked through them, everything else was as though through a glass darkly.

He laughed a little thinking about that comment. She had the sweetest way of scolding him. "I appreciate your Biblical references," she chided him, "but I don't think the Apostle Paul had hunting in mind when he was writing to the Corinthians." As Tony glassed the area, a good-sized business jet flew over heading southwest. It looked like a Gulfstream G5. It bugged him that it would fly so low if for no other reason that it dispelled the illusion that he and his boys were the last of the Mohicans.

"Now that's the way to travel!" said Luke, looking up at the jet with an unforced grin on his face. "Where you think they're going?"

"Aspen, I suspect," said Matt. "He's on an approach to land."

When the plane vanished behind Alpha, Tony turned his focus to the stream that ran north-south through the valley below. He checked the topo map carefully. "The stream's called Elk Creek."

"Really?" said Luke.

"No, just kidding. It's called Badger Creek."

"Too bad we're not on a badger hunt," said Luke. "I'd be more optimistic."

LUKE

The three scouted the valley floor—Tony with his Swarovskis, Matt with the more affordable Tasco binoculars, and Luke with the eyes God gave him. While his father and brother looked for signs of elk, he soaked in the vast expanse of the valley. The trees crept close to the stream on either bank, but not so close that he couldn't see the stream, at least in stretches, including one small-ish stretch directly below him. He took note of the openings in the tree cover throughout the valley, some from obvious out-croppings of rock, some from drainage, others for reasons geologists or botanists might know, but he certainly didn't.

"The woods are kind of thick," he said to his father, pointing to the dense woods between their position and the stream. "Can elk get through there?"

"They're pretty agile. I'm told they can squeeze though openings that would challenge mice, even in dark timber."

"Mice, huh?" laughed Matt.

"Okay, badgers."

"You think there's actually elk?" Luke asked.

"Unless I miss my guess," said his dad, "the water in the stream and the grass around it just might draw them out from the woods—if, that is, there's elk to be drawn."

"Can we shoot from here, Dad?" Luke asked.

"Think we should?"

"Yeah," said Luke. "How far is the stream?"

"You tell me."

He studied the stream for a bit and then replied, "Not sure. I'd just be guessing."

"To even guess you need a reference point. Try looking at the trees."

"Quarter mile?" Luke hesitated. "Don't know."

"That's why God gave us the range finder."

Luke pulled the range finder out of his pack. It looked something like a small pair of binoculars with two lenses but only one eyepiece. He had not used one before, but if it was electronic, he was sure he could figure it out.

His father let him fiddle but gave him a little advice as he did. "It shoots a laser to measure distance. At this range, it should be easy to get a reading. See that big honking rock by the stream due west? Bounce the laser off that."

Luke fiddled some more and smiled. "I got two hundred and fifty-seven meters. How long's a meter again?"

"About one ten-millionth of the distance from the equator to the North Pole," said his dad.

"That's helpful."

"You guys got to learn these things. About a yard plus ten percent."

"I know I could nail an elk from here," said Luke with a flash of pride.

"Could, son, but probably wouldn't. We got just a narrow window on the stream from here."

"And while you're terrorizing the elk," said Matt, "Dad and I are stuck on this rocky ledge."

"It is kind of cramped," his father deadpanned. "Plus, it's got a sharp falloff in front and about a ten foot drop on the right side. And if you get careless, there's lots of loose rock to slip on. Not exactly a place you want to set up on before dawn."

"Okay, okay," said Luke. "Let's keep looking."

TONY

As they hiked south down the gentler slope to the left of Foxtrot, Tony knew what he hoped to find: ideally an open area with a panoramic view of the valley. He thought he had seen one from the finger ridge, but he could not judge its sight lines from a distance. Without a good perspective on the stream, they might as well have set up shop on their deck back in Kansas. The comfort level would be much higher and the probability of shooting an elk not much lower.

"Guys, keep your eyes open down there. We need to see some signs of activity."

"Other than smoking," Matt added with a smirk.

"Yeah, other than smoking."

There was no clear path on the way south and down. They had to make their own. After about thirty meters in the open, he and the boys cut back to the left into a thicker patch of timber, all pine and Douglas fir. It was denser than Tony would have liked, but he was hoping the elk saw it differently. After a short hike, he keyed in on what appeared to be a break in the tree cover, the one he had seen from above.

"Let's head over this way, gents."

The three quickened their step and soon emerged into a clearing rich with high grass about two-thirds of the way down the slope and perhaps, thought Tony, two hundred meters above the stream. An abrupt drop-off from the front of the clearing left them with a clear view of the stream below.

"Not bad," said Luke.

The clouds had just barely parted, and the late afternoon sun threw the valley around them into spectacular relief.

"If there's water in that stream, there's bound to be some animals," said Tony, now genuinely hopeful. The boys seemed to feed on his optimism.

"Cool," said Matt.

"You think?" asked Luke, always the skeptic.

"No guarantee," said Tony, "but good bet." He took out his binoculars and surveyed the valley. He identified a few good sight lines to the stream below and looked for signs of life. He was too far away to confirm tracks, even with the Swarovskis, but he thought he could see stretches where the mud had been churned up. He chose not to say anything. He didn't want to get the boys' hopes up without being sure.

Handing the glasses off to Luke, Tony grabbed the range finder and zeroed in on a rock formation on the far side of the stream. The number on the display confirmed his own intuitive estimate: 213 meters—a little farther than he might have liked, but not bad.

"This works for me," said Tony. "Let's drag over this deadfall to use as a shooting bench."

"Sure we can do this?" asked Matt, eying the massive log.

"Piece of cake," said Tony. "Now for a little basic engineering." So saying, he pulled the block and tackle out of his daypack and went to work, tying a timber hitch around the end of the log for one block and anchoring the line for the second block to a tree across the clearing.

"You guys stand on either side of the log and guide it over straight. I'll pull." The pulleys still amazed Tony with how well they applied a mechanical advantage. For the first time since he left Dr. Heller's office a few weeks back, he was convinced he made the right decision. The boys had a lot to learn, and there was no better place to learn it than on an elk hunt in the Rockies.

MOOM

"Okay!" said Moom out loud. The lead horseman looked up as he climbed through a small clearing a few hundred yards beneath Moom and waved. Moom waved back, his heart skipping. He had done his job. The guys had stopped long enough for lunch or siesta or whatever in the woods below to worry Moom, but they knew where he was, and, for better or worse, they were on their way.

LUKE

Looking around the valley, Luke began to understand why his father was so keen on the Swarovskis. He could see everything—the sparkle in the stream, the sway of the branches in the wind, the scuttling shadows from the passing clouds.

"These are great," he said to no one in particular, "I can just about count the leaves on the trees on the far side of the valley." Fascinated, Luke panned the terrain, hoping to be the first to spot an elk. Sure enough, halfway up the opposing ridge and to the north, he spotted some movement. He played with the focus and convinced himself that yes, these weren't badgers. They were four-legged animals flitting in and out of the cover.

"I think I see something."

"Elk?" Matt asked.

"Don't know." Luke wasn't sure how to answer. What bummed him was that the animals were climbing up the far slope, moving away from the stream and their meeting with their maker, courtesy of Luke and his Remington.

"What you got there, Hawkeye?" said his father.

"Elk, I think."

"You sure?"

"No, I'm not sure." Luke intensified his focus. He looked again. "Yeah, I am sure. They are *not* elk."

"What *are* you seeing?"

It wasn't until the animals fully emerged from the tree cover that he knew what he had spotted. "Crap," he spit out.

"Ease up, son."

"They're horses, with riders."

He handed him the glasses. "Take a look."

TONY

Tony had a hard time finding them. Frustrated, Luke kept jabbing in their direction. "Can't you see them?"

"I see 'em," he said finally. He could see well enough to count the horses. There were four of them. That did not surprise him. These were the guys they had seen at Zeke's, but what worried him was that he counted three riders. Somewhere along the way they had added a third guy.

"Maybe they're heading over the other ridge and'll leave this valley to us," said Luke hopefully.

"Maybe so. Take another look, son, and tell me what you can about the riders."

"Sure."

Staring intently through the glasses, Luke followed the men as they and their horses ascended the mountainside in and out of the trees.

"Is one of them wearing a weird hat?"

"Yeah."

"Anything else?"

"The one horse has got some funny panniers or whatever you call them."

"What do you mean, funny?"

Luke continued to stare intently through the glasses.

"Well, you know how ours are big and floppy, these are like long canvas bags, like duffel bags, but longer and skinnier."

"Let me take a look."

Luke handed the glasses back to Tony. As much as he adjusted the lenses, he could not see with the clarity his son did. He handed them back to Luke.

"How long would you say those bags are?"

"How long is a horse?"

"About eight feet."

"The bags are almost that long. About six feet probably."

"You said 'bags.' Is there more than one?

"I'm guessing two. Only one of the packhorses is carrying them, and I can only see one side of him. I'm thinking there's another bag just like it on the opposite side."

"Can I see?" asked Matt.

Before Luke handed them over, Tony whispered to Matt, "There's three men."

MATT

There was no mistaking the concern in his father's voice. Matt thought he knew why but chose not to pursue it, at least not with Luke in earshot. Looking through the glasses, he confirmed that there were three men and two unusually long bags.

"Why you so interested in the panniers?" Matt asked his father.

"Just curious. Like to keep up with new hunting gear."

Matt didn't quite buy that answer. He never knew his father to lie about anything important, but like all dads, he'd fudge a little to protect his kids.

"What do you think they're carrying?" he asked.

"I don't know," his father laughed. "Fishing poles? Pool cues?"

"Cigarette cartons?" Matt joked back.

"An RPG?" asked Luke.

Matt turned to his father, hoping he would laugh his brother off, but he didn't.

"That would be a novel way to hunt," he said with a forced smile. "But I'm not sure the game wardens would approve. Let's go find some elk before these guys blow them all up."

Luke laughed, but Matt wasn't at all sure his father was joking.

TONY

As he led the boys down the mountain, sliding on their butts in one stretch, Tony cautioned them to silence. He did not want to scare the elk away, he told them, but he also chose not to talk, lest he reveal his own concerns. The Hajis—or whoever—had unsettled Thor, and Thor wasn't easy to unsettle. He sensed that Matt was a little worried too, but they had no reason to connect the guys on horseback with the Haji. Still, that third rider bugged him. *If it were Jake from State Farm*, he mused—*No, no, that's crazy.*

Try as hard as he might to stop it, that train of thought had left the station. At one moment, in fact, Tony entertained the suspicion that Luke may have been right when he said "RPG." In Shok Valley, he had seen up close what an RPG could do when launched by someone who knew how to aim one. The results were pretty horrid. On that memorable occasion, a Haji launched a round in his general direction, and he had been having the occasional PTSD moment ever since.

If it had just been him and Thor, he would have been more curious than concerned. In fact, they probably would have welcomed the adventure. But with his boys, he wondered whether the responsible thing to do was to turn around and get them the hell out of there. Dr. Heller would certainly have thought so.

No, he thought. He was here to toughen the guys up, not to hover over them like an overeager helicopter dad. Even if those riders weren't hunting elk, even if they were expecting a drug drop from one of the passing planes—he laughed at the thought—he and the boys would be in and out of this valley before they got in anyone's way. In any case, the riders seemed to be heading up and over Bravo. Out of sight, out of mind. Maybe.

MATT

As they hiked down to the stream, the pine branches whispered in the breeze overhead and the fallen pine needles cushioned their steps. Matt wished he could absorb the serenity of it all, and on an ordinary day he might have, but not today. Not now. He kept looking for a sight line up to where they had last seen those horses. The closer they got to the stream, the thicker and more consistent the cover became, and the more frustrated Matt grew. Unable to see the far ridge, he had to assume the riders were still climbing. Something was wrong. He knew it like he knew his own name. He sensed his father knew it too, but was holding back so as not to scare him and Luke.

Even in the midst of the thickest cover, Matt was sure he could find the stream. All he had to do was use his compass to head west and keep going downhill. The stream ran almost due north-south. There was no avoiding it. When they emerged from the wooded area, the stream was pretty much right in front of them.

"Here we are, guys," his father whispered. "Keep your eyes open for some tracks."

"Wow," said Luke, recoiling, "This place stinks!"

The stench washed over Matt as well. "Something must have died down here," he groaned, turning for an explanation to his father, who surprised him with a big smile.

"That, my boys, is the smell of hope."

"Hope?" asked Matt.

"Yup, and here hope is spelled P-I-S-S...as in elk piss."

Excited by the news, Luke skipped across the shallow stream on rocks poking above the water line. Matt envied him his innocence. If his brother suspected anything, he didn't show it. Matt tried to catch his father's eye without being too obvious. He imagined they shared the same concern, but he could not be sure. His dad was playing along with Luke as though nothing in the world was more important than finding elk.

MOOM

The lead horseman stopped on the upslope just before he reached Moom. He looked Hispanic, to Moom, and tough. He was smoking a cigarette. The two horsemen coming up behind him were stranger looking. One wore a funny, old-fashioned hat. The other appeared to be an Indian with a twisted braid. They trailed a fourth horse behind them, burdened with long bags on either side. Moom knew better than to ask what was in them.

"Speak English?" The lead guy asked with what sounded like a Mexican accent.

"Yeah," said Moom, a little too enthusiastically. "We've been waiting for you, I think."

"Who's we?" asked the man.

Moom was not sure how to answer. He should have figured that out before he left camp.

"R," he said, his voice lilting, as much a question as an answer.

"Show me the way," said the horseman, unsmiling.

PEL

Moom led the men across the ridge towards Pel, who met them closer to Moom's location than his own.

"I'll take it from here," said Pel to his brother. "Why don't you get back to your post."

"Got ya."

Without saying another word, Pel reached for the reins of the head guy's horse as though he ran guided horse tours for a living. He did not want the men to think otherwise.

"No," said the man, pulling the horse's head back. "You walk ahead. I'll take care of the horse."

"Whatever," said Pel. He figured the guy spoke English well enough to catch his meaning. The slope on the west side of the ridge being steeper than the one on the east side, he led the way carefully. As they descended, none of the men said a word. Neither did Pel. He knew he was playing a mind game. He doubted these guys played any games at all.

TONY

In Afghanistan, Tony learned that it was not what you knew about the enemy that killed you. It was what you didn't know. He had watched men die, and scarcely a one of them sensed where that fatal round was coming from. It almost always took them by surprise. He called Matt over.

"Keep your brother distracted," he said quietly. "I'm going to run up and see what's on the other side of Bravo here."

"You worried about those guys?"

"Are you?" he answered Matt's question with a question.

"Yeah."

"Let's just say I want to put your worries to rest. You guys keep looking for tracks. Tell Luke I'm scouting for elk."

"Roger that. Hurry back."

Leaving everything behind but his .44 and the Swarovskis, Tony plunged into the woods before Luke noticed he was gone. He hiked double-time through the scattered trees and up the rocky east slope of Bravo. He figured the horsemen had cleared the ridge. He could no longer hear them.

MATT

"Look, look, look," said Luke standing on the west side of the stream about twenty yards upstream from where they had first crossed it. Even now, Matt was pleased to see his brother's enthusiasm returning.

"Are these elk?"

Matt knelt down to get a better look and traced the outlines of the hoof prints with his fingers. Standing up, he followed the tracks about ten more yards upstream, turned around, and smiled.

"Sorry, they're badgers."

"What?" Luke all but shouted.

"Just teasing. Hawkeye, these just might be elk."

"Alright!" said Luke.

"But I'm just guessing. Dad will know."

"Let's tell him," Luke almost shouted as he swiveled around to find his father, his voice faltering as he realized he was nowhere to be seen. "Where's he at?"

"He'll be right back," said Matt as calmly as he could. "Just went to do a little scouting. Let's see if we can find some more tracks."

TONY

Tony stopped at the edge of the tree line to catch his breath. Always cautious, he concealed himself as best he could behind some deadfall and scanned the ridge of Bravo. In his north-south pass he saw nothing. To double check, he scanned the ridge again, this time from south to north. Towards the northern edge of the scan, he did a double take. *Damn!* He was sure the man he now saw had not been there on the first pass.

Tony focused the lenses. Dressed in casual outdoor clothes, the man was sitting on a rock below the ridgeline. He had binoculars hung around his neck. As intensely as he looked, Tony could not quite make out the man's face, but he had a weird feeling he had seen him some place before. For certain, he did not wear a Fedora. Nor did he have a long black braid like the Indian. And from what Tony could see, he seemed young, just in the way he held himself—younger than Jake from State Farm. It had to be some other man. Anyone other than Jake was good.

Still, Tony had no idea what the man was doing or how he got there. He did not come in the truck with Fedora Man. That meant he either came in the Bronco or had gotten there earlier. He had to be connected to the horsemen, might have even been one of them, but he did not look threatening. In fact, he looked more like a birdwatcher than a hunter, and a young one at that. Still, Tony saw no reason to test him or arouse his suspicion. Whatever happened beyond the ridge, Tony hoped, would stay beyond the ridge. This was a problem he was in no position to solve. Not now in any case—not with the boys at risk. He stashed the binocs and retreated back down the slope.

MOOM

Moom sensed the man looking at him before he saw him. Without picking up the binoculars, he slowly scanned the tree line left to right. He was correct. There was a man peering at him through the shadows. Moom kept scanning as casually as he could, lest the man know he saw him. When Moom scanned slowly back right to left, the man was gone.

Moom grabbed the two-way and then put it back down. He wasn't sure he saw anything. That's what he told himself, anyhow. In truth, he did not want to be responsible for what happened if he called this sighting in. Knowing he had to do something, he picked up the binoculars. Through the trees down below he vaguely made out the form of two men, young men—boys, maybe. They had hunting rifles and seemed to be looking for something. A man soon joined them, probably the guy Moom saw at the tree line. He made his decision. Unless these guys did something crazy, he would pretend he saw no one.

PEL

Pel led the men into the camp. These were obviously the ones R was expecting. There was no hugging, no backslapping, no introductions, not even a handshake. R's men stood off to the side, their AKs off their shoulders, ready but not pointed at anyone or anything. Without a word, R and the man who spoke English unloaded the two large bags. R unzipped the one, looked inside, and nodded. He did the same with the other. Pel did not see their contents and chose not to ask, at least not immediately. He didn't want to look stupid in front of these new guys.

Apparently satisfied that he got what he wanted, R turned towards the English speaker and said simply, "Hungry?"

"I was hoping you would ask," said the man in what sounded like a Mexican accent. Both smiled, and Pel shook his head in wonder, "What kind of bandito says, 'I was hoping you would ask'?" The bandito then turned to his two friends and said something in Spanish. They both laughed. Pel had no idea what they said. As the three men fell to eating, he had to ask himself whether the joke was on him.

MATT

"Dad," said Luke, gesturing at the tracks. "Look what we found."

His father walked over to see. He had just emerged from the trees as nonchalantly as if he had been looking for firewood. Luke seemed none the wiser.

"I'm no expert, but it looks like a gang of elk came through here and meandered around, probably just looking for a good stiff drink."

"Cool!" said Luke.

"You got the eye, son."

"Can we, like, look for some more?"

"No need," said his father quietly, shushing his son. "Let's minimize our footprint and get back to camp. We'll be ready for them tomorrow morning when the season opens. Besides, it'll be dark before we know it."

Matt looked hard at his father as he was speaking. This time he got his attention, and he nodded knowingly in Matt's direction. Matt was sure his father read the anxiety in his eyes. He must have seen that look in new recruits a thousand times. Matt wasn't ashamed of looking scared. In war, everyone is scared, his father had told him. The trick was not to yield to the fear. When Luke was distracted, Matt moved to his father's side.

"No need to get alarmed, Matt, but we probably ought to get out of here."

"What did you see?"

"A guy up near the ridgeline. Looks like a birdwatcher, but I'd bet the ZAM he's not."

Only Luke remained unaware of the threat, and that was the point. The sun was beginning to descend behind Bravo when his father led his sons up the west slope of Alpha back to the shooting spot they had identified on the way down. Upon arriving, they caught their breaths and stared down at the stream below.

"Look," cried Luke. "Elk!"

PEL

Pel hated to admit it, but R intimidated him. He knew he had to fight that weakness in himself. He had too much skin in this game not to. While the three men sat on the ground and ate,

Pel screwed up his courage and approached R. When he got his attention, he walked him away from where the men were eating.

"I need some info," said Pel.

R shrugged. "Why?"

"C'mon," said Pel, warming up to the task, "don't play games with me."

"I am not playing," said R as though he meant it. "I do not play. The less you know the better for both of us."

"I don't give a shit about the cowboys," said Pel. "I don't care if they come from Mexico or Moscow, but I do need to know what's in the bags."

"Okay," said R. "That is fair. In the one bag is a Strela, a 9K32 Strela-2. Do you know what that is?"

"Yeah," said Pel, "a Russian, man-portable, surface-to-air missile—older, but still effective. I did my homework before I ever approached you."

"Homework?"

"Research."

"Good," said R. "We will try to practice before D-Day, maybe even this evening."

As R turned to walk away, Pel grabbed his arm.

"And in the other bag?"

"A hand-held grenade launcher—you know what that is?"

"An RPG, right?" said Pel.

"That term 'RPG' makes little sense. The 'G' is a grenade," said R. "We have three of them. The RPG-7 launcher we have only one of."

"Okay," said Pel, a little weary of the word games. "What do we need with an RPG launcher?"

"The Strela is offense," said R. "The RPG launcher is defense. You never know. We may need both."

LUKE

"That's one hell of a bull," said his father, handing the glasses to his son. "Take a closer look."

Luke settled cross-legged into a sitting position with his elbows resting on his knees.

"What do you think?"

Luke was stunned. He was imagining Bambi, but what he got was a massive, magnificent animal as big as his horse with antlers spreading up and out another three or four feet.

"He's huge," said Luke, "and kind of cool-looking." Luke marveled at the animal's poise. His head held high, his uneven, reddish-brown coat shifting color in the fading sunlight, this elk seemed to absolutely own the world around him. Luke envied his confidence. "He seems so…proud."

"Don't fall in love with it," said his dad. "You're going to have to shoot it."

"And eat it," Matt added.

"No need to feel bad about that," his father added. "If hunters didn't cull the herd every now and then, the elk would starve to death."

Luke did not need the reassurance. He wasn't an eco-freak. When he dug into a hamburger, he knew exactly where the meat came from. Besides, in Call of Duty he had shot things that seemed a whole lot more human than an elk.

"Dad, can I draw a bead on him?"

"Sure," his father said after a moment's hesitation. "No ammo though. Remember, season starts tomorrow."

"Who'd know?" Luke regretted asking the question as soon as he saw the storm cloud pass over his father's face.

"I will."

MOOM

The call or whatever on the two-way came just in time. Moom was getting antsy—actually, more anxious than antsy. There was something just a little bit scary about being alone in nature as night fell.

It was Pel. Moom welcomed the call, but he tried not to sound like it. "Yo," said Moom.

"See anyone else in the valley?"

"No."

"Sure?"

Moom wondered whether Pel caught the hesitation in his voice. It was too late to reverse course now.

"Yeah," said Moom, "sure."

"Good," said Pel. "Head north on the ridge to where I was earlier. I'll meet you there. The others are on the way."

"What's up?"

"A little dress rehearsal," said Pel. "They're bringing their prayer rugs, and I'm bringing the...goods."

Not much moved Pel, and Moom was glad to hear the eagerness in his voice, even if the reason for it just might mean the end of the world as he knew it.

LUKE

Luke handed the binoculars back to his father, put his pack on the log they had dragged into the clearing, and rested his rifle on top of it. Then he fidgeted his way into a shooting position, working through the motions slowly and patiently. He brought the rifle tight into his shoulder and got comfortable.

"Remember you're 231 yards away," said Tony, "a little longer than you're sighted in for."

"Yup."

Luke placed the vertical crosshair of the scope just behind the foreleg of the elk and then brought the horizontal crosshair about a third of the way up from the belly. He thumbed off the safety and began his breathing while he laid the tip of his finger on the trigger and began to squeeze as though this were the real deal.

With the 'click' of the firing pin, Luke released the trigger and smiled knowing he would have made the kill. When he turned to his father for approval, he discovered he wasn't even looking.

Tony

With his Swarovskis, Tony was scanning Bravo. Matt was doing the same with the other binoculars. The birdwatcher had started walking north along the ridgeline, but with the sun beginning to set behind the ridge, he was fading into the shadows.

"Anything interesting?" asked Luke.

"No," said his father. "It's just that it'll be dark soon. Take just one more shot at the elk, and we'll get out of here."

Pel

"Yo, Moom," said Pel, beckoning his brother over to a relatively flat stretch of dirt and rock just below the ridgeline. As Moom approached, Pel pulled the Strela out of its canvas case and brandished the weapon before his wide-eyed brother.

"Holy shit!" said Moom. "Is that what I think it is?"

"That it be."

"What are you going to, like, do with it?"

"I know R is just jerking me off, but he is letting me practice tracking a plane."

"He's not worried about you being seen."

"Not really. He just said stay below the ridgeline and don't draw a bead until the plane passes."

Moom frowned. Pel had hoped Moom would share his enthusiasm. He could tell from the worried look on his face that he didn't.

"Where's R and the other guys?" said Moom.

"They'll be up in a minute with their rugs. Prayer time."

Pel held the weapon up one more time. "Is this cool or what?"

TONY

Tony watched as Luke lined up his second shot. While he watched, he heard the sound of a plane descending from behind that far ridge. They all did—the elk included. Unfazed, the elk looked up and went back to drinking from the stream. He must be used to planes, thought Tony.

"Check out our birdwatcher," said Matt with some urgency.

After a second Tony found the man.

"Holy shit!" said Tony under his breath.

The birdwatcher had joined another guy, and the second guy seemed to be aiming a rocket launcher at the passing plane.

MOOM

Moom watched Pel pivot with the Strela on his shoulder, his grin more natural than Moom remembered seeing since before the election.

"Got him," said Pel.

"Will R let you actually shoot it?" Moom asked. He doubted it, but wasn't sure.

"Not unless they all break their arms," Pel laughed, lowering the weapon. "I think R just wants my fingerprints on it."

Pel suddenly fell silent. He was still staring at the ridge to the east, the ridge beyond which the plane descended, his face scrunched up.

"Did you see that?" said Pel, his voice tinged with alarm.

"See what?" said Moom.

"That flash of orange."

TONY

As the plane passed, Tony pulled the hat off Luke's head, reversed it from the orange blaze side to the camo side and handed it back. He did this without asking. He could read the shock in Luke's eyes.

"I'd put that gun down too," he added. "The sun's still flush on us."

"So what's the problem?" asked Luke.

"It's a serious one. "

"How serious?"

Tony hesitated to lay this challenge on this son, but no one could see what was happening better than he could.

"Luke, there are two guys just below the opposite ridge, and I'm losing them in the shadows. I want you to look through the Swarovskis and tell me what they're doing."

LUKE

The lower tip of the sun now balanced on the Bravo ridge-line and streamed its rays into Luke's eyes. He struggled to refocus and find the men his father had been watching. The urgency in his father's voice scared him. When he found the guys, he wasn't quite sure what he was seeing.

"I see a whole bunch of guys."

"Tell me what you see."

"Two guys are standing. One guy's standing and doing nothing. The second guy standing is holding something by his side, holding…don't think me crazy, Dad."

"What's he holding?"

"A Stinger? Is that possible?"

"What about the other guys?"

"I count three other guys. They're not far from the other two. They're dropping down to their knees. Okay, now the three kneeling guys have put their heads down."

"Which way are they facing?" his father asked.

"Towards us."

"That's east."

"Does it matter?" asked Matt, his binoculars still fixed on the opposite ridge.

"It matters," his father groaned. "Mecca's east."

"Damn," gasped Matt.

"And it's sunset. Prayer time."

"The guy with the Stinger or whatever put it down and is now looking through his binoculars," Luke almost shouted. "He's looking our way."

"We're between him and Mecca, son, and until that sun drops behind the ridge, we can't hide."

PEL

Pel was not quite sure what he was seeing, but it sure as hell looked like three hunters staring back at them. Not wanting to disturb R and the other two guys prattling away on their prayer rugs, he handed the binoculars to Moom and pointed towards the hunters.

"What do you see?"

"I don't see anything."

"Keep looking."

"Which way?"

Pel could hear the nervousness in his brother's voice. Not wanting to alarm his Muslim pals until he could figure out what to do, he whispered in Moom's ear, "You don't see those three guys?"

"Oh, yeah," said Moom. "Now I see them."

Pel knew his brother well enough to know when he was bullshitting.

"How did you not see these guys earlier?"

"I don't know."

"You're lying," said Pel. "I know how you sound when you lie."

"No, I swear," said Moom.

"Stop it," said Pel. "If you saw them earlier, just don't let R know you did. They never would have let me bring this thing up here if they knew there were people in the valley."

Pel walked over to the men in prayer, knelt next to R, and tapped him on the shoulder.

"This better be important," said R.

"It is." Pel handed R the binoculars. Kneeling upright, R saw exactly what the problem was. He did not hesitate a second and did not ask Pel's opinion. He grabbed his satellite phone and barked out a command to the Mexicans so damn free of hesitation or conscience Pel doubted he could ever be that hard a man.

LUKE

"A third guy just looked at us," said Luke, "one of the kneeling guys."

"Is he armed?" asked Matt.

"If a phone's a weapon," said Luke. He watched for a minute, saying nothing, then spoke quietly, "I think he's calling someone."

TONY

On the plus side, the sun was descending behind Bravo. He and the boys were no longer easy to pick out—or pick off. On the minus side, everything else.

If he hadn't tried to spare the boys his suspicions about the guys on horseback, they might have turned around the moment they saw those long panniers—maybe even the moment he saw the extra car at the trailhead. He felt no need to apologize, but from here on in, he would treat them like men, or at least try to, and hope they could meet his expectations.

"Come here, guys," said Tony, now in a field squat, left leg forward, elbows on his thighs. "We need to talk."

His sons joined him.

"Question for you both. What do *they* think we must know by now?"

The boys looked at each other, uncertain as to how to respond.

"That they're Muslims?" Luke suggested, more as a question than as an answer.

"At least three of them," answered Tony. "Anything else?"

"I may be wrong," ventured Matt, "but it seems like they're monitoring the flight path into the Aspen airport."

"I think they were taking target practice," said Luke.

"And they know we've watched them do it," Matt added.

"I think you're both right," said Tony, "and remember it's just a week before the start of the G7 Summit."

"Are you thinking what I'm thinking?" Matt asked.

"Yes."

"That's not good, is it?" asked Luke.

"No. They're probably debating what to do about us."

"So what do we do?" asked Matt.

"We don't stick around and wait for the debate results." Tony leaped up and pulled Luke roughly to his feet. "I promised you guys an adventure. Don't say I didn't deliver."

MOOM

With the ridge behind him now cutting into the sun, Moom could see little on the far slope, and he doubted if R could see much more, even with the binoculars. By now R and his two guys were standing and carrying on in their third-world mumbo jumbo. Moom didn't understand the words. He didn't have to. R was pissed.

"How did we not see these men before?" said R in Moom's general direction, his rage barely controlled.

Moom looked around, hoping someone else would answer the question. "I don't know," said Moom, quaking, unsure of what to say.

"You do not know?" R moved closer to Moom with each angry rephrasing of the same question. "You do not know? You fucking idiot, you do not know?"

R was right in his face now, his breath foreign and foul, but before either he or R could say another word, Pel stormed over, pushed Moom back and placed himself squarely between R and his little brother. If Moom had to judge whose rage was more intense, he would have put his money on Pel.

"You never, ever speak to my brother like that again," said Pel with cold fury. "You understand?"

Moom had no idea what would happen next. The two men's faces were no more than six inches apart. He expected violence. He expected the henchmen to jump in. He expected to be dead in the next thirty seconds. But Pel proved shrewder than Moom would have thought. He didn't back down. He didn't blink. He just gave R a little room to maneuver.

"My brother may be a fucking idiot," said Pel with a grin, "but it's *my* job to tell him that."

R seemed to recognize Pel's gesture for what it was. Turning away from Pel, R said to Moom with regret, "You do understand you cost those three men their lives. We cannot let them get back to their car."

"He can live with that," said Pel.

"I'm not so sure he can," R responded with a bite. "From now on, he stays with me." As an afterthought he said to Pel, "Is that okay with you?"

Instead of answering, Pel looked over at his brother, and when Moom nodded his assent, Pel did too. At this point, Moom could care less about the mission. He just wanted him and Pel to get out of this damn valley alive.

"Back to camp," R commanded. "Our Mexican friends will take care of business."

MATT

They climbed in silence, sometimes walking upright, sometimes scrambling straight up the rocky slope on all fours. His father set a heart-thumping pace. He never ceased to amaze Matt. The old man could scurry up a hillside like a mountain goat. He would get ahead of him and Luke, stop, and if an opening presented itself, scan the opposite ridgeline and the valley below. When Luke started to falter, his father grabbed his son's pack and rifle and slung both over his shoulder. Even with the double load, there was no way Matt could keep up with him.

With Luke struggling to breathe, his father decided to rest at the tip of Foxtrot. But they did not rest for long. Scanning the ridgeline, his father said, without emotion, "They're coming. Let's move it."

Matt turned. Yes, the three men on horseback had crested Bravo and were riding fast down into the valley. On seeing them, he sensed the piss trickling down his leg but was too shocked to be disgusted. The three of them plowed on up the last and most difficult hundred yards to the Alpha ridgeline. Matt lost sight of the horsemen, but from time to time, he could hear them. They were closing the gap.

Once they reached the top, his father led them south along the ridge back towards the base camp. After about fifty yards, he dropped below and behind the ridgeline and abruptly turned back north away from the camp. Luke looked back at his brother and wheezed, "Aren't we going in the wrong direction?"

"Dad knows what he's doing," Matt whispered. "Trust him."

TONY

About one hundred meters north of where they turned, just beyond Skeletor, Tony led his sons across about fifty meters of almost-bare terrain to a dense stretch of pine.

After walking them some distance in, he whispered, "This is as good a place as any to rest." From this point on, he would speak no louder and encouraged his sons to do the same. The boys could not have gone much farther. Matt was bent over, grabbing his knees and struggling to steady his breathing. Luke had knelt down and was vomiting out of exhaustion. If there was still a trace of sunlight on the west face of Alpha, there was none on the east. It was not yet full night on this side of the ridge, but it was getting darker by the minute.

While the boys caught their breath, Tony walked back up to the ridgeline. As he walked he reminded himself never again to doubt Thor's instincts. The man had nailed this one. Once at the ridge, he discreetly glassed the valley below. The three amigos were riding hard, one with rifle visible across the saddle—an ominous sign if there ever was one. He returned to his sons.

"This is scary," said Matt, visibly shaking as he took his pack off.

"Yes it is, son, but I'm proud of you guys. Great effort. You'll be okay." Tony meant it. The boys did not panic or quit. He pulled a water bottle from Luke's pack and passed it to his son, still breathing heavily.

"Small sips."

"Okay," gasped Luke.

Matt did not need to be told.

"You good?" Tony asked. He could smell the piss. He expected to. He said nothing.

"Yeah."

"Small sips," he reminded them both. Finally, he grabbed his own bottle from his pack and took a sip himself.

"Dad, one thing," said Matt. "Why are we stopping here?"

"I headed south at first to lure them towards the camp and then turned north below the ridgeline to find a safe spot."

"Why not back to the camp?" asked Luke.

Tony put his hand gently on his son's shoulders and answered his question as indifferently as if he had asked what they were having for breakfast tomorrow. "They'd beat us to it. I expect to see them come over that ridge any minute. These guys are real horsemen. We're not. Plus, they've got horses, good horses, and we're on foot."

"What do you think we're up against?" asked Matt.

"I think you were right all along, and Thor before you. I'd bet those three guys are Mexican cartel. I suspect one of them is Jake from State Farm and that he's the middleman, the go-between with the Hajis or whatever.

"Oh, man," groaned Luke.

"My guess is the cartel guys have been supplying the bad guys with shoulder-fired missiles and everything else they need to live out here for a couple weeks and fend off an army."

"But why in elk season?" Matt asked.

"The G7 summit determined the timing. They didn't have much choice, but I think they chose this trail for the same reason we did. It's new, and almost no one knows about it. Plus, it put them where they needed to be to get a shot at an aircraft."

"How hard is that?" asked Matt.

"Not too. With a good shoulder-fired missile like a Stinger, you or Luke could knock off a plane after an afternoon's worth of practice."

"What do you think the Mexicans will do?" asked Luke, still struggling to catch his breath.

"Good question. I suspect those three guys are mercenaries. If their bill's been paid, there's half a chance they'll just take the money and run."

"You think they will?" Matt asked.

"Don't know."

"Best guess?"

"If we're lucky, we'll get back to the trailhead and find our tires slashed."

"And if we're not lucky?"

"I think they'll do whatever's necessary to stop us from getting back to the trailhead. They know we know where they got their horses. And the fact they left the one packhorse behind tells me they're more worried about us than Zeke.

Tony paused to measure the effect of his words. He needed to convince both boys that this was no kind of game, but he did not want to paralyze them with fright. Neither said anything. He continued.

"The Hajis may be suicidal, but the Mexicans probably aren't. I hate to be grim, but you need to know this is serious business. The simplest thing for Fedora Man and his buddies is to kill us off here in the mountains. No one will know what happened to us at least for a few days, enough time for them to get out of Dodge."

"So what do we do?" Matt asked.

Tony did not want to say something rash just to say it. He had seen that style of leadership too often and knew it could be fatal. He took a minute to think his answer through. "You two are going to stay here in these trees. It'll be fully dark soon enough. Keep quiet, and no one will find you. They won't even look. I'm going back to the horses to see what I can see."

LUKE

Luke could smell the piss on his brother, but since his jacket was splattered with vomit, he was not in a position to get smart about it. Besides, the very idea of his father leaving scared him silly. "When are you going?" he asked.

"As soon as our friends come over the ridge. It won't be long."

So saying, his father stopped in mid-thought and held a finger to his lips. Luke resisted the urge to ask what was up. A few seconds later he did not have to ask. There was no mistaking the sound of hooves sliding and scratching their way up the west face of Alpha. All fell silent. When his father dropped to the ground, the boys followed suit without being told. Luke could not see the horsemen, but he could hear them cresting the ridge no more than a hundred yards south of where they were hiding.

The three lay silent for what seemed an eternity as the horses headed east and their sound faded into the night. His father turned and smiled. He said nothing. He did not have to. Luke read the smile for what it meant. He was sure Matt did too. What the smile said was, "See! Trust me. I know what I'm doing."

PEL

Back at base camp, the five men sat around the fire and ate. R and his two goons talked among themselves. They made no effort to keep their voices down. Pel couldn't deceive himself. R held all the cards here. R alone could speak to everyone and understand everyone. There was control in that. Pel wished it were otherwise, but it wasn't.

After they were finished eating, Pel watched as R gathered up the three prayer rugs and walked some distance off into the woods. His brother noticed too.

"What's that about?" Moom whispered.

"I have an idea."

"Yeah?"

"Yeah. Everything we see everywhere is in Russian, right?"

"Yeah."

"If R comes back empty-handed," said Pel, "I'm guessing they plan to lay this all off on the Russians. The prayer rugs are the only give-away. I bet he's stashing them somewhere no one would find them."

"Makes sense," said Moom.

"Don't let R know we suspect this."

"Why?"

"It gives him all the more incentive to make sure we don't get out of here alive."

A moment later R returned to the camp, empty-handed.

TONY

"You sure you have to leave us?" asked Luke. The question came out less desperately than Tony might have expected. He could sense his son suppressing his urge to panic.

"Just for a while."

"We'll be okay," said Matt.

"I know you will. I may be a few hours though. I'm going to have to lay back and watch the horse camp. If I feel confident those guys have pushed on, I'll come back and get you, and we'll leave together."

"If not?" asked Matt.

"We'll try something else. One more thing, if I'm not back by tomorrow morning…"

"Tomorrow!" said Luke, almost shouting, the boy in him overcoming the man.

"Shhhh, son, c'mon," said Tony reflexively putting his hand over his son's mouth. "Yeah, tomorrow. If I'm not back, Matt, find your way down to Badger Creek and follow it—very carefully—south to the highway."

"How carefully is 'carefully'?" asked Matt.

Tony could read the fear in his eyes, but his voice did not betray it. That was good.

"Keep close to the stream for, you know, general guidance, but your priority is to stay quiet and out of sight. Use the compass when you lose sight of the stream. If you're going south, you'll get to the highway. Go as slow as you need to go. At the highway, be careful before you surface. I don't care if it takes you two days to get out. You got your packs. If the bad guys don't see you, they won't follow. As long as the horsemen don't know where you are, you're safe."

"But you'll be back, won't you?" asked Luke.

"You can bet on that," said Tony with a smile, and he meant it.

LUKE

Luke wanted to believe his father and almost did, but there was this voice within him that said this whole adventure would turn out bad—very bad. So much had turned bad in the last few years. His mom killed, his family uprooted, his life at school a daily torture.

Still, out here, in the midst of all this craziness, there was something calming about his father. He watched him draw the .44 from the cross-draw holster and swing open the cylinder with the kind of ease you'd expect from a movie cowboy. He inverted the pistol, dumped the cartridges into his hand, and pocketed them. He then fished a speed loader from his pack, inserted six new rounds, and released them. He then snapped the cylinder closed, returned the pistol to the holster, and secured it with a snap of the thumb strap as if he had done this every day of his life.

"What was that about?" asked Luke.

"Time for the hollow points," his father said grimly. "We're not worried about bear anymore. I need your rifle too."

"You don't think…" He didn't want to finish the sentence. It wasn't that he wanted to keep the rifle for himself. It was his fear that his father would have to use it.

"I don't plan on using the rifle, guys, or the pistol, but if I run into a gunfight I hate to be the guy in the old joke who shows up without a gun," said Tony. He loaded the rounds for Luke's rifle as he spoke.

That done, his father took a Gatorade bottle out of his pack and slipped it in a pocket in his cargo pants. He pulled out some food bars—Luke counted four—then filled a Ziploc with his comforting jalapeno Cheez-Its, and stuffed those in another pocket. "I'm not taking my pack. If you guys have to vamoose, leave it here and I'll come back and get it when I can."

His dad draped the binoculars over one shoulder, the rifle over the other, and said quietly, "*Hasta la vista*, guys."

MOOM

Night had fallen hard on the camp, and Moom had never felt so removed from reality. R and his two buddies played some Mideast version of dominoes in the glow of the fire as though nothing mattered more than the outcome of the game. The only interruption was a call R took on the satellite phone. He smiled at the news, whatever it was, and said only, "Stay on them." He then turned his full attention back to the game. As for Pel, he sulked in silence on the far side of the fire. He had to have a lot on his mind, like whether they'd finish the mission or just save their asses and get out of here. Moom wasn't about to bother him.

Moom tried to read by flashlight. The only book he had with him was a French book translated into English, *The Stranger*, by Albert Camus. Some girl he met at a rally told him he should read it. He bought it at a used bookstore hoping to impress her, but he never saw her again.

The hero, protagonist, whatever, killed some guy in a fight, and society turned against him because he did not feel guilty about the murder—did not feel guilty about much of anything, for that matter. The guy reminded him a little of Pel. He wasn't sure how things would turn out for the guy in the Camus book, but he wasn't optimistic. After a while, he had to put the book down. Even though he had gloves on, his hands were getting too damned cold. He had no idea it could get this cold in October. He crawled into his sleeping bag, covered his head, inched over towards the fire, and hoped when he woke up the sun would be shining.

MATT

As Matt shivered in the dark, one thought pushed out another, and no thought was so awful as to be unlikely. That was the scary part. His parade of horribles was a parade of possibles. To break the spell, he tried to engage Luke, but the talk, all whispers, meandered. As usual, it was Luke who got to the nub of things.

"What if Dad...doesn't come back?" he asked.

"He will," said Matt. He believed what he said, but his argument was too thin to share. He just had this sense that having buried their mother they were not about to bury their father. His intuition went no deeper than that.

"How do you know? Mom didn't come back."

"What's that supposed to mean?"

"I'm just saying, we've had some bad stuff happen to us."

Matt could sense the apology in his brother's explanation. "No, Luke. Bad stuff doesn't just happen. Mom didn't just die."

"What's *that* supposed to mean?"

"It means that I screwed up." Matt could taste the bile in his throat, thinking how badly he had.

"You what?"

Matt backed up. "Do you know what the word *atonement* means?"

"Yeah, pretty much."

"Well this is my chance to atone."

"Atone for what?"

Matt stalled. Words did not come easily. He needed to think this through.

"Atone for what?" Luke asked again.

"Never mind," said Matt, backtracking.

"No, tell me."

Matt thought, if not now, when? He hadn't been to confession since his mother died. He lost the habit, but this was no time to play games. Too much depended on his being straight with his brother.

"You won't like what I've got to say, but you need to hear it."

"I don't know if I need to hear it," Luke smirked, "but I'm guessing you need to tell it."

Matt wanted to go no further, but he knew the ragged state of his soul might well affect the outcome of the mess they found themselves in.

"You're right. It'll help you understand what might happen." Matt breathed deeply and bit his lip to keep from choking up. He forced himself to look at his brother.

"I'm…responsible for mom's death."

Luke raised his head from his hands and sat upright. "Be serious."

"I am. I…I…" he searched for another word but knew that only one was accurate. "I killed her," he said hurriedly, fearful that if he slowed down he might stop. "There is no other word for it. I killed her."

"Aw, c'mon," said Luke, shaking his head in disbelief.

"Yes."

"How?"

"I, like, tried to jump a light," Matt stuttered.

"Huh?"

"I didn't want to take the car out of cruise, okay? I was sure the light would turn green. I'd had a couple beers."

"Oh, Matt, damn!"

"I just kept going, and then, like, mom screamed my name. Her last word was 'Matt.' She tried to warn me. A pickup was speeding through the yellow and barreling towards the passenger door. 'Matt! Matt!' No one even, like, braked."

"No," Luke protested. "Everyone said the tweaker ran a red light."

"Sorry. The witnesses looked up after they heard the crash. They saw a green light going my way, a red light going his. He was, like, dead. No. He wasn't 'like' dead. He was dead. So was Mom. The dead don't talk, but I could, and I did, and I lied."

"Were you, like, in shock? Did you know what you were saying?"

"I had blood all over me—Mom's mostly. Yeah, I knew what I was saying. The EMTs and whatever consoled me. No one even bothered testing me for alcohol. I was the victim. They told me what I wanted to hear, and I just went with the lie. The lie was easy."

"It was, huh?"

Matt read more than a little disgust in his brother's response, but he plowed on.

"When the guy's toxicology report came back, it was, like, what everyone wanted to hear, except maybe the guy's family. They couldn't sue, and we couldn't since he didn't have insurance. Case closed."

"Did you tell Dad?"

"No."

LUKE

Luke leaned against a tree and tried to sort out what Matt had told him. He got the guilt part. That he could understand, but the atonement stuff he didn't quite get. He didn't ask for details, but he sensed that Matt had, like, a death wish.

He worried about his brother—always had, really. It made no sense, him being the younger brother and the loser in the family, but sometimes he felt sorry for Matt. He thought him too open; too innocent. Matt didn't know what it was like to be tested on almost a daily basis. He didn't know what it was like to be mocked, to be rejected, to be humiliated. His brother had no defenses. He could never say this to Matt. He would never understand, but he sensed maybe his father would.

With his brother on self-appointed guard duty, Luke leaned his head back against a tree and let himself drift. He was too tired to sort things out.

TONY

Crouched over, Tony slowly started back down the trail, always staying in the cover of the trees, ever more careful with each step as he got closer to the horse camp. When the clearing came in view, he slowed even more and crouched even lower.

For him, quiet was everything. After a few more steps, he got down on all fours and crawled. As he got closer still, he dropped to his stomach and low-crawled his way in. When he found a spot in the light brush under the concealing branches of a pine tree, he stopped. The moon, three quarters full, shone its ghostly light on the opening. He could see the camp as well as he needed to without being seen.

At first glance he saw nothing obviously askew. He did not expect to. He hoped the Mexicans might have headed down the trail to get their truck and scram, but he did not expect that. He expected them to be doing what he was doing—waiting outside the camp and observing.

The horses gave the game away. They seemed very much awake and aware of their surroundings, too much so. They should have been resting. He knew they would want to be fed, no doubt, but they did not strike him as hungry. They struck him as jumpy, anxious, unnerved, as though they knew something he did not.

Lying still in a way no one but a combat veteran could and using the Swarovskis to collect the available light, Tony continued to scan the woods surrounding the camp, looking for movement and, if not that, a straight line or a texture—any artifact not found in nature. He did not necessarily feel the presence of those guys. It just made no sense for them to be anyplace but here. Had they ridden on to the trailhead, they would have come through the site and, at the very least, scattered the horses. But nothing seemed out of order, and that troubled him.

As he waited, the moonlight crept slowly along the tree line east of the camp. After what seemed like hours but could have been minutes, a reflection caught his eye: glasses, maybe, or a button or the barrel of a weapon. On the far side of the campsite, a shoulder seemed to take shape, then another, and a head. Tony waited some more. At night in the forest, he knew how easy it was to turn a wind-shaken branch into whatever one dreaded most, but when the form repositioned itself against a tree, he was sure. If there was one man, there were likely more—in this case, two more.

His instincts were true. They were waiting for him, just as he was waiting for them. He had played this game before. He doubted if they had. It was a game he knew he could win, would win.

And win he did.

By the time the three men emerged from the shadows, his eyes had adjusted well enough that he could see their movements clearly. There was no longer anything subtle about those movements. The flash of steel in the moonlight and the plaintive wail of the trail horse as the machete creased its throat confirmed that these men were vicious beyond the call of duty.

Without speaking a word, the man with the Fedora slashed one horse after another while his amigos ransacked the tents and gutted the sleeping bags. As the last horse reared up, blood spewing from his neck, Tony backed his way quietly out of camp. The desperate whinny of the dying horses drowned whatever noise he might have made. With his last backwards glance, he saw Fedora Man severing the head of a fallen horse. They were not just slaughtering animals. They were delivering a message written in blood. There was no doubt about its meaning: no one who crosses us gets out alive.

MATT

"What's that?" said Luke, startled out of his half-sleep.

"I don't know," said Matt. He heard it too, but it was too far off, too faint to interpret. "An animal, I think."

"What kind?

"I don't know. But I don't like the sound of it." He grabbed his rifle, stood up, walked to the edge of the timber, and listened. He saw nothing unexpected, but what he heard, no matter how far away it might have been, sounded like death. The wailing lasted a minute or so before fading, and the woods yielded to the ordinary sounds of a·mountain night. They were spooky enough.

"I wish Dad would get back," said Luke.

"He will."

PEL

Pel lay on his side, scrunched into his sleeping bag, trying vainly to ward off the cold. R had kept the fire up, but it helped only a little. Lying there, he watched R and his guys play their stupid-ass game and wondered whether they felt anything at all—the cold, the anxiety, the fear. He thought not.

Around midnight, R got another call from the Mexicans. After a few grunts and nods, he heard R say, "Okay, just do not let them get by you." R then turned to Pel and said, "Are you awake?"

"Yeah."

"Here is the news. Those hunters are not going anywhere quick. Our friends killed their horses. In the morning, they will kill the hunters."

"Good," said Pel. He then turned away from R and his noisy buddies and tried to sleep, fearing he couldn't.

MATT

For no good reason, Matt recalled the distinction his English teacher once made between "anxious" and "eager." In these last few days, the meaning of each became much too clear. He *eagerly* awaited the trip to Colorado. He *anxiously* awaited the return of his father.

From the moment they'd heard the faint wailing sound, he'd stood guard standing up, rifle at the ready. Every minute was a small eternity. To distract himself, he turned periodically and comforted Luke. Of course, Dad would be here soon. Of course, he would. Yes, any minute. No, I won't shoot him by mistake. He did this as much to regain his brother's trust as he did to drive the fright out of his mind.

Still, for all Matt's mustered confidence, the moment he heard his father whisper, "Matt, it's me, son," he almost shouted out in joy.

"Didn't want to startle you," said Tony, leaning out from behind a thick tree. "I just wanted to make sure you didn't shoot me."

Luke jumped to his feet. He and Matt rushed to their father and embraced him the way Lazarus's kids must have when their old man came back from the dead.

TONY

"Get your pads out of your pack and let's sit down and talk," said Tony casually, or at least as casually as he could. The boys nestled in and listened. Tony stuck to the promise he had made earlier. He would tell his sons what he knew—at least all of what he knew that they needed to know.

"These guys are bad," he said. "They killed our horses." He thought of saying more but held back. There was no need to add detail. Killing them was bad news enough.

"In the morning, they'll be patrolling between us and the trailhead. We're going to need to find another way out of here." He pulled out his topo map, spread it so his sons could see, and illuminated it with a green squeeze light, cupping his hand around the light. "The trail is a no-go."

"How about the stream?" said Matt.

"That seems to be our best bet." Tony traced Badger Creek, mumbling calculations under his breath as he followed its course with his squeeze light. "It's about forty klicks south to the highway."

"Twenty-five miles, right?" said Matt. "That equals one hell of a long day."

"Longer than you think."

"How so?"

"We still have to deal with the bad guys on the far side of the valley," Tony explained. "They're obviously talking to our friends over here. They probably got their own horses, maybe even an ATV. My guess is that if they were going to head us off, they'd make their way to the spot where the stream intercepts the highway and start walking back in."

"So we detour through the woods before we get to the road?" said Matt.

"Exactly. We make that detour on our side of Badger Creek, the east side, at least a few klicks before the highway. Once we get there, we can flag someone down and get out of here."

"Makes sense."

"We also detour through the woods on the way down to the creek just in case they're waiting for us."

"When do we leave?"

"About an hour before first light. We want to cross the ridge in the dark for protection, but we could use at least a little light to pick our way through the woods."

"I thought we were heading out tonight," said Matt.

"We were, when we had a trail, but the bad guys are on the trail, and you don't want to blaze a new one in the dark. This is as good a spot as any. As long as we're quiet we're safe."

"We sleeping here tonight?" Luke asked.

"Going to try. Your day-pack just became your survival pack."

"I wish we had our phones," said Luke nervously.

"I wish we had a signal so we could use our phones," Matt added.

"I wish I could call in a Warthog for an airstrike, but that ain't happening either. If 'ifs' were fifths we'd all have a Merry Christmas."

"Huh?" said Luke.

"Never mind," said Tony. "Break out your survival blanket and wrap up in it. You can use the Tyvek ground cloth for whatever the blanket doesn't cover. I'd sit on your pad and find a tree to lean up against for the night. You're going to find out pretty quickly how the ground can suck the heat out of you, especially since we can't make a fire."

The boys did as asked. Tony instructed them to keep their packs close so they could grab anything they needed by feel, not by light. As he explained, the moonlight would suffice once their eyes adapted to it. If essential, they could use their squeeze lights, but only inside their packs. He then had them change their socks—he did the same—lest the damp of the sweat chill their feet.

"When you put your boots back on," Tony continued, "keep them loose for good circulation. Your feet will stay warmer that way. I know, we should have brought some heavy mittens, but who knew we'd be at war with the whole friggin' Third World. So if your hands get cold, use the socks you took off over your light gloves. They should dry pretty quickly in this air."

Luke started rummaging around in his pack and Tony grabbed him. "Quiet, quiet. What are you looking for?"

"My survival blanket."

"Okay, but open it slowly. It makes a lot of noise."

Luke obeyed. He had a long way to go, but he was doing better than Tony feared he would.

"And remember to stash the survival blanket before morning. The orange is much too easy to see."

"Okay, Dad."

Tony liked the way he said "Dad." No hint of sarcasm or spite or resentment.

"Also, put on all the clothes you have with you. You'll need them. And try keeping your arms inside your jacket. That'll help."

"Sounds like you've been in this kind of fix before," said Matt.

"Worse," Tony laughed gently, "if you can believe that." He could tell they did believe him. It was hard not to. They knew where he had been—three tours in Afghanistan, one in Iraq. He knew what it was like to spend a freezing night in hostile territory with people out looking to kill him, but he never had to share the experience with his sons. As much as he disliked the word "bonding," that's what this was—the ultimate father-son bonding experience. The boys would remember it that way, Tony mused. They would tell their own children about it and their children's children—but only, he reflected morbidly, if they all came out alive.

"Bright night," said Tony, looking skyward once the boys had found their places.

"That good?" asked Matt.

"More good than bad. With no clouds to hold the heat, these mountains will give up much of their warmth. So expect a cold night. But we can at least get oriented."

"You never stop teaching, do you, Dad?" asked Luke.

"I only have you guys for a little while. So I got to drill you down."

"Suppose so."

"Plus, I promised Dr. Heller this trip would be educational," said Tony, forcing a bit of the everyday into the conversation.

"It's certainly been that," said Matt, trying to laugh.

"Anyhow, I'll keep watch until about three, and I'll have you spell me for a couple hours."

"That works for me," said Matt.

"Love you, Dad," said Luke quietly.

Gulping hard—he had not heard those words so plainly delivered in years—Tony said simply, "Love you too. Love you both. Now get some shut eye." There was one major part of the plan he chose not to share. He was afraid they wouldn't sleep if he did.

DAY 19

MATT

"Matt," his father whispered, squeezing his son by the shoulder. "Time to take over."

"Damn, it's cold," said Matt.

"Late October, clear night, ten-thousand feet, about what'd you expect. Good to go?"

"Sure," said Matt, keeping his survival blanket wrapped tightly around him. He was not good to go at all. He had not slept—not for a moment that he could account for. Worse, the condensation caused by the survival blanket's impermeable mylar left him clammy and damp. Still, he chose not to alarm his father.

"It's about three now. If I'm not moving in a couple of hours, which is unlikely, give me a shake."

"Did you see anything?"

"No, didn't expect to. This is a tiny nook in a very big place, and the Mexicans have no idea where we are."

With that his father leaned up against a tree and, as far as Matt could tell, fell instantly asleep. Matt watched him in wonder. Over the years his dad's friends had told him, much as Thor did, that the old man was one of a kind—a work of nature. Matt was

200

beginning to see that these guys were not just blowing smoke. He wondered if some day he might be as…self-contained, as confident, as together…as the man sleeping peacefully against the tree. He would like to think he could be, but he doubted it. His father, he knew, never would have lied about something as major as the death of his mother.

TONY

"Okay, Matt, I'm awake," said Tony groggily, pushing the hand away from his shoulder. He took a moment to get his bearings, sat up shivering, and began to rub his arms. The temperature had taken a dive. He looked at the crystal clear night sky and checked his watch to confirm. It was earlier than he expected to be awakened.

He found Luke curled up right next to him and shook him awake, ready to cup his hand over his mouth if necessary. Luke's eyes opened, and Tony whispered, "Get yourself something to eat and make sure everything is ready to go."

As his eyes adjusted to the pre-dawn haze, Tony spotted Matt lying flat on his back, his survival blanket on one side, his pad on the other, and his Tyvek ground cloth at his feet. None of this computed. He could have sworn Matt had just woken him a moment ago. He crawled over and shook him gently.

"Thanks for waking me, pardner," said Tony. Matt opened his eyes and looked back at him confused. Tony continued. "No time to go back to sleep. Get yourself a bite to eat and make sure your pack is loaded. Let me get a bearing, and then we'll 'ruck up and get moving."

Tony pulled out his compass and a bag of jalapeno Cheez-Its, a weakness he passed off as a survival strategy, which it kind of was. Closing his right eye to make sure he maintained maximum night vision in a least one eye, he illuminated the compass for a quick look with his green squeeze light and then confirmed the indication with a glance at the sky. As he looked to the west to select their path, Luke startled him out of his calm.

"Dad!" he said with urgency. "Look."

Tony raised his head and saw Matt wandering through the woods in the general direction of the horse camp.

"Matt, what are you doing?" he whispered. Matt failed to answer. He just kept walking. Tony did not dare yell. He jumped up, ran after his son, and grabbed him by the shoulders. Matt struggled to move forward. Tony stepped in front of him, held him by his arms, stared into his eyes, and saw nothing.

"Matt, what are you doing?"

"Doing?" said Matt, his voice slurred, his breathing slow and shallow. Tony grabbed his wrist and felt his pulse. It was weak, as he feared it would be. The fact that Matt was not shivering he took for the ill omen it was. He was beyond shivering.

"What's happening?" said Luke anxiously, trailing close behind his father.

"Hypothermia. Bad."

LUKE

"Oh, man!"

"He must have fallen asleep without his survival blanket or pad. We'll take care of it, Luke. I've seen it before."

His father picked Matt up and threw him over his shoulder. Matt was compliant and completely silent. "Luke, get your pad out and put it next to Matt's." Tony then sat Matt down on his

pad and turned to Luke. "Now sit down behind Matt and strad-
dle him with your legs."

Luke looked up, confused. This was too weird, too early.

"Now take your coat off and your fleece off too."

"What?"

"Not so loud."

"Sorry," Luke whispered and did what he was told. His father
took the coat and fleece off Matt and pulled his son's wool shirt
over his head to expose his back.

"Luke, now raise your shirt to expose your chest. Then put
your bare chest against your brother's back and wrap your arms
around his body."

Luke flinched when flesh met flesh. Matt's back was that
cold. Shivering, he watched his father pull a small gear bag out
of his pack, dump the contents on the ground, and grab the duct
tape. His dad then put Matt's fleece on Matt's front, Luke's fleece
on Luke's back, and taped them together.

"What?" Luke had not quite figured out what his dad was up
to, but he was beginning to see where this was all heading.

"Trust me and keep your voice down."

Luke watched in awe as his father taped the coats front and
back, grabbed the boys' survival blankets and ground cloths,
wrapped them around both him and Matt, and secured them
with more duct tape.

"We've got to get him warmed up," he told Luke. "We've
got to add heat because his body isn't making any." Luke was
amazed at how his father seemed to know exactly what he was
doing, as if he had practiced this routine every other day just for
the heck of it.

"Okay, now it gets a little interesting," he said to Luke as he
picked up a one-quart freezer bag, turned his back on him, and

pissed into the bag. When he finished he took the bag over to Luke. "I bet you won't see this in a Ziploc ad."

"Hope not," said Luke, grimacing as his father passed the bag to him underneath the coats.

"Now take it and hold it against Matt's bare chest."

Luke complied wordlessly.

"Okay. Give me the fire starters out of your pocket and get Matt's out of his pockets."

Luke grabbed all he could find and placed them on the ground. His father took out his stainless steel water bottle, nearly full, set two rocks together, and leaned the water bottle against them. Placing his own two fire starters and the four Luke had gathered under the bottle, he ignited them with his lighter. He then scrounged around for some loose kindling and added it to the gathering flames. As the fire heated up, he poured a little Gatorade powder into the water.

"Should we be making a fire?" asked Luke, not sure he had the right to ask a question.

"No, we shouldn't, but we have to."

Luke held on to his brother and watched in stunned silence. Worried as he was about Matt, the strangeness of what he was doing trumped every other sensation. The word "surreal" kept popping into his head. He wasn't quite sure what it meant, but it seemed like exactly the right word for the occasion. After a few short minutes, his father stuck his finger in the water and nodded approval. With his gloved hand, he picked up the bottle, put it to his lips, and licked it around the edges.

"Doesn't that burn?" Luke asked.

"Like a son of a bi…, but I got to cool it off for Matt."

His father then held the bottle to Matt's lips.

"You got to swallow this."

After Matt drank some, Tony paused and gave him more. He then put the bottle back on the waning fire and added a few small sticks lying close. Then he gave the bottle back to Matt again.

"What's going on?" Matt asked in a dull voice.

"You guys were a little cold this morning. I wanted to get you warmed up. Here. Drink some more of this."

Matt tried to lift his arm, but the coats and the tarp restrained him. Luke watched helplessly as his brother struggled.

"Ease up, bro," said Luke. "We're good."

His father slowly poured more of the warm liquid in Matt's mouth. "Just let me do the work for the moment, and you stay wrapped up."

"What's going on?" Matt asked his dad, this time more alert.

"Best I can tell you dozed and rolled off your pad. The cold ground sucked the heat right out of your body. We're just lucky it's not raining or snowing."

"Wow, sorry."

"No need to apologize. How do you feel?"

"A little dopey, but okay, I guess."

Matt tried to turn, but Luke blocked his way. "Hey, what are you doing? Let go."

"Not my idea," said Luke.

"Relax guys, you're keeping each other warm."

"Do you want me to tell him what else is keeping him warm?" His father answered with a look that Luke had no trouble interpreting. *What a weird friggin' night,* Luke thought. *Totally, totally weird.*

TONY

"Matt, you need to start moving around. Wiggle your fingers and toes, and I'll unwrap you in a minute. We can't stay here much longer."

Confident that Matt was okay, Tony unwrapped the boys and instructed them to pack up. On his own, Luke tossed the Ziploc bag off into the woods without Matt seeing it. Tony nodded his approval. There would be no lecture about littering this time.

"Did I fall asleep on watch?" Matt asked almost desperately as he packed his gear.

"It happens. No big deal." Falling asleep on watch was about as cherry as it gets, but Tony decided then and there not to tell Matt how badly he'd screwed up. He did not want to sap Matt's confidence, not with the day they all had in front of them.

"There is one slight change in plans," Tony told his sons as they prepared to leave camp. They looked at him nervously.

"I'm going to go with you to the stream bed," he said calmly, "and then I'm going to come back up to the ridge."

Both boys look stunned.

"Really?" asked Luke.

"Yes, really."

"Why?" asked Matt.

"Three reasons. One, I can make sure no one follows you—not the guys behind us or the bad guys from across the valley. I'll be more help to you up here than I would be down below."

"And two?" asked Luke.

"Thor. I can't let him wander into this. He wouldn't let me walk into a situation this FUBAR, and I won't let him. Once I'm sure you're well on your way and no one's following, I'll head back down parallel to the trail and keep a watch on it."

"Sure?" asked Matt.

"Sure," said Tony. "I don't expect to see anything, but if I run into Thor, I'll join up with him, and we'll wing it from there."

"But…like…" Matt stuttered, "won't the horse guys see him first?"

"They might, but if they do, they've got no reason to pick a fight. I expect they'll let him pass."

"But if not?" asked Luke.

"I need to be there."

"Can't we come with you?" Luke pleaded.

"No, and that brings us to the third reason. If the three of us try the trail, we're loud and slow. Alone, I move quietly, and no one on this planet can keep up with me."

"Not even the guys on horseback?" asked Luke.

"Not unless they're racing to the trailhead. And I don't think they will be. I think they'll be wandering around looking for us."

"I suppose," said Matt.

"Plus, if I get to the trailhead before you get to the highway, I can make sure the highway's secure."

The sun had yet to break through, but the sky was beginning to brighten, and dawn was all too close. It was going to be brighter than Tony wanted when they crossed the ridge. They needed to get moving.

"Time to go."

Tony led his boys past Skeletor, over the ridge, and down the route they explored the day before. They moved slowly in the half-light and much more quietly than yesterday. They found the finger ridge, Foxtrot, without any trouble. As the boys caught their breath, Tony assessed the valley with fresh eyes. The flow of it troubled him. Although the Alpha and Bravo ridges ran in more or less parallel lines, each culminated in a larger mountain to the north from which emerged the stream below. What worried him was that the bad guys could come across the valley or around the rim or both.

"Are we dreaming this, Dad?" asked Luke quietly, as they were about to head down.

Tony had been in ops before that went bad, and this one had the same feel. Still, he was not about to let his sons pick up the slightest sense of unease.

"It's got to seem that way, doesn't it," he said, "but you guys are doing okay, and when it's over, think of the stories you'll have to tell when those little snobs at school start talking about their Colorado *ski trips.*"

PEL

Some sorry ass cop was jabbing him in the back with a baton. "Fuck off," said Pel.

The cop continued.

"I said, fuck off, pig," Pel repeated, this time more angry than annoyed.

With the third jab, Pel sprung up ready to fight. There was no cop. Just R, staring down at him, his face unreadable in the early morning light.

"It is time to get to work," said R.

"Work?"

"Yes, and wake up your brother."

"What kind of work?" asked Pel, struggling out of his sleeping bag and feeling around for his boots.

"Hunting."

"Hunting what?"

"Hunting people."

"The Mexicans didn't find them?" said Pel, now standing and stretching.

"Not yet."

"Damn, it's cold," said Pel as he struggled to find something better to ask.

"Did you expect something different?" asked R.

From the tone of R's voice, Pel knew this was going to be one cold-assed bitch of a day, and whichever way it ended was going to be ugly.

MATT

Matt had been thinking along the same lines as his brother. This whole enchilada was too freakish to be real. Stranger still was the whole sleep deal. He was still not quite certain what happened, and he had the sense that no one was going to tell him, at least not straight up. *Maybe*, he thought, *that was the way it ought to be.* Maybe he was better off not knowing.

As they followed their dad's indirect route through the trees down towards the streambed, another odd thought snuck into Matt's still-cobwebbed brain. Was it only about twelve or so hours ago that they had climbed down here with no greater concern than finding elk tracks? It seemed like a year ago, when he was still an innocent, eager to go elk hunting with his dad and his annoying little brother. Now they were squaring off against a small army of jihadis or whatever intent on blowing some head of state, maybe even their own president, out of the sky. This was unreal—too freaking unreal.

The closer they got to the stream, the more anxious Matt grew about getting there. He could tell Luke felt the same way, and probably more so. Around his father they felt safe, they always had, and especially so in the last twelve hours, but their father would leave them soon. Was that possible? Was it? Yes, it was. With their father gone, Luke would look to him now. He would man up, he told himself. If they were to survive, he had to.

"Here we are, guys."

Although the sun still had a ways to go before cresting the ridge behind them, night had gradually given way to day. It was beginning to warm up, and so was he. The climb down had gotten the blood flowing.

"We're good from here, Dad," said Matt, looking down the stream.

"I know you are. Keep a good pace, and you should reach the highway before dark. You got a long day ahead of you, but you'll do well."

"If we need you?"

"Forget what I said about the three shots. Fire once. I'll assume you're shooting at something other than an elk."

"Got you."

They stood silently for a moment, staring at the stream. *It looks just as it did yesterday*, thought Matt. There was something oddly reassuring about it. The water just kept flowing. The stream did not know it was their lifeline to the world, and it didn't much care.

"I'll need the Swarovskis and maybe the range finder, but you take the other binoculars," said his father, handing them off to Luke.

"Thanks, Dad," said Luke. "I think."

"I'll also keep the .44 and Luke's rifle. Matt, you keep yours. You shouldn't have to use any of your rounds, but you've got five of them just in case."

Matt had a thought. He just wasn't sure it was a good one. "Dad," he said. "Take *my* rifle. If we need to make a long range shot, Hawkeye here is the one who should make it."

"Good idea," he said finally. "That's real leadership. I'm proud of you."

"Thanks," said Matt, relieved his father understood his motives.

"My mission is to get you two out of here in good health. You understand that."

"Yes," said Matt.

"Your primary mission, if I don't do it before you, is to tell the authorities what's going on here. Understood?"

"Right."

"If they give you any grief, ask for Thor by name. They'll know you're not screwing with them."

"What's Thor's last name?" asked Luke.

"Olafson. But just ask for Thor. Tell them how we took the trail to Crow Creek and from there headed northwest on a sec-ondary trail all the way to this valley. And make sure they know what they're up against."

"Gotcha," said Matt.

"Okay then, if we are both to accomplish our missions, you must keep moving and get to the highway. Understood?"

"Yes, Dad."

"No matter what you hear."

Matt looked away. He did not want to make a promise he was not prepared to keep.

"Matt? Understood?"

"I hear you, Dad," said Matt, carefully dodging the question.

Matt hugged his father. Luke did the same. The three stood in the half-light for a long moment without moving or speaking, the cheerful pitch of the morning birds and the relentless rush of the stream filling the void. Matt did not want to leave his father, and he was sure his father did not want to leave his sons, but they all knew this one last moment of near-peace could not last.

"I'm proud of you boys and I love you. Now get to the highway and get us some help. And remember, as long as you're quiet and stay hidden, you'll be as safe as a baby in her mother's arms. Now get out of here!"

TONY

Tony watched uneasily as the boys made their way down the stream. They were not ready for this yet. No one's sons ever were or should be. Satisfied they were in no immediate danger, he scurried back up the hillside towards Foxtrot, pausing wherever an opening allowed him to scan the valley below and the ridgeline above. If he saw anyone moving anywhere, a shot from him would draw all attention his way and away from his sons.

The sun had crested Alpha and was flooding the east slope of Bravo, but a rush of cold air alerted him that the sunshine would not last long. Angry nimbus clouds were erasing the blue from the sky west to east. He sensed it was becoming cold enough to snow. He would rather have snow than rain or sleet. Good visibility was not his friend, but then again neither was a soaking, freezing rain. No one had predicted this, but then again no one had predicted a showdown on a Colorado mountainside with some deranged Third Worlders.

After a hard scramble he reached the flat tip of Foxtrot. From there he could see the valley below with more detail than he could from the ridge above. After glassing it, he climbed back up to the top of Alpha, rifle in hand, and crossed it quickly to avoid easy detection. Once below the ridge, he headed back in the direction of camp to look for any sign of Thor or the three horsemen of the Apocalypse. Seeing none, he headed up to the Alpha ridgeline and down again to Foxtrot to make one final check on his sons.

From across the valley, he could see the snow falling even before it reached him. With the visibility still sharp, he scanned the valley again for sign of the bad guys. The only movement he saw now was a small gang of elk making their way through the trees to the stream below.

Moom

"Snow," said R, "great."

Moom did not know R well enough to know whether he was being sarcastic. He guessed so. Trailing behind, struggling to keep up, Moom was unable to see R's face.

R had not been kidding about making Moom stick to him. To make it worth everyone's while, R gave Moom a job—bagman. Moom got to carry the bag holding the RPG launcher and wear the chest carrier holding the grenades. Climbing the slope back up to the ridge was hard enough without the bag or the snow. Now, it was damn tough. Moom wished he was somewhere else, anywhere else.

Given the possibilities, he would much rather be with Pel. Pel had asked for Moom, but R said no. As compensation, he let Pel use one of his AK-47s and sent him to patrol the valley from the south end of the ridge. The two foreign goons R sent around the rim of the valley to the north. R had actually used the term "pincer movement" to describe what they were doing. The Mexicans would herd the hunters back into the valley if they didn't kill them first, and R's people would finish them off if the Mexicans didn't.

Moom was already grabbing his sides to catch his breath. In a way, he welcomed the exhaustion. It helped him forget about the cold. It also gave him something to think about other than the image of three guys, a father and his sons, maybe, getting snuffed in such an oddly peaceful setting.

LUKE

Luke shuddered and pulled the zipper of his coat up to his chin. As he and Matt wound their way south through the trees that lined the stream, he was paying so much attention to the rock-littered ground that he failed to notice the change in the sky. But there was no ignoring the snow. It came down heavy right from the start, in big fat flakes. Matt turned back to look at him.

"This is good," said Matt.

"Think so?" At this point Luke knew his brother would say whatever he had to in order to encourage him. He got that. His motives were all well and good, but they forced him to question everything Matt said or did.

"Actually, yeah. It'll make it that much harder for anyone to see us. To hear us too."

"What about footprints?" said Luke.

"As long the snow keeps falling, it'll keep covering our tracks."

Luke nodded. That was a good answer. It made sense. His brother wasn't his father—no one was—but he was beginning to trust him.

"You okay?" Matt asked.

"Yeah."

"Keeping up?"

"Yeah."

"Cool."

Matt smiled, turned around, and resumed a pace just a half a heartbeat slower than the old man's. Luke struggled to stay with his brother, but he wasn't going to bitch. His bitching days were over.

TONY

Satisfied for the moment that no one was following his sons, Tony headed back up the slope to the ridgeline. He had not gotten far when a muffled clatter of hooves sent him scurrying back down the slope to Foxtrot, the finger ridge.

PEL

By the time Pel reached the ridgeline, now facing east, the snow had killed the visibility, but he could still hear. There was an urgency to the sound of the horses cresting the far ridge. As jacked up as this scenario was, Pel still wanted a piece of it. He hurried down the slope towards the action—AK at the ready. He would show R just how hard-ass he could be.

TONY

It shocked him those guys were this close. They could have crossed the ridge anywhere. Crap luck, that's all. He knew what he had to do. Without turning to look behind him, he ran to the tip of the finger ridge, jumped off to the right, and slid down the steeply angled slope in front of him as if he were sliding into second base, left foot extended, accelerating as he slid.

If it weren't for that damn rock hidden in the scree, his escape would have worked fine, but there it was—protruding just enough. About ten meters down the slope, his left foot crushed hard into it. The momentum pushed the upper half of his body forward, and he cleared the ground, now flying face and arms forward into the juniper bushes below, his rifle lost in flight. He landed softer than he had any right to hope in a welcoming bush, but the damage had been done. So intense was the pain shooting up his leg, Tony feared he might pass out. Before that happened, he had to do his best to hide. He dragged himself deeper down towards the tree line, reaching a small shelf. If they didn't see his fall he had a chance.

MOOM

"Can you see anything?" R asked. They both peered from just below the ridgeline in the direction of the sound.

"No," said Moom.

R pulled a water bottle from his backpack and handed it to Moom. "Why am I asking you?" he laughed. "You did not see anything when things could be seen."

Standing by R's side at the ridgeline, Moom took heart at R's jest. It meant more to him than it should have.

"Your brother did you wrong bringing you out here," said R, with what sounded like a touch of sympathy. "He is tough guy. You are not, but you are good brother."

"So is he," said Moom. He meant it.

"Time will tell," said R. "Follow me."

TONY

At the shelf's edge, the slope descended in a narrow chute steeply through the trees for another twenty or so meters. The snow was falling steadily now in big, wet flakes. That was good. He wasn't sure if the guys had seen him, but if they hadn't seen him, they probably heard him. He lay still, assessing his situation. Although the wounds to his face and arms were superficial, he knew his left ankle was totally whacked. It was throbbing madly, probably broken. Had he two good ankles, he would have slid further down the slope and sought refuge in the trees below. They could never have kept up with him. But there was to be no more running, no going back for his rifle.

His inner badass yearned for a shootout, but facing three homicidal desperados with God knows what kind of weaponry, he could envision no scenario in which his six-shot revolver would give him a fighting chance. Odds favored lying low rather than shooting it out. He didn't survive Afghanistan by playing Sgt. Rock. Even if they found him—and there was at least a chance they wouldn't—he had to bet they would grill him before they would kill him.

He still had his day-pack. As quietly as possible, he pulled it off his back and groped through its contents. The only thing he found of possible use was the bear spray. He slipped the narrow canister into his right jacket pocket.

He then stretched out face-down and pulled his jacket hood over his head. Pushing the pack, he finessed his way through the branches of a deadfall tree shielded by junipers. As he maneuvered, his thoughts drifted to the times he and Angel's father had gone pheasant hunting, the first hunting he had ever done. The two of them would walk the fields and blast the pheasants that took flight. The birds that survived were the ones that stayed put. If you didn't step on them, you didn't see them. If you didn't see them, you didn't shoot them. The lesson was there to be learned.

As best he could, he buried the pack. He then pulled out the bear spray, ripped off the plastic safety guard with his teeth, and put the canister back in his pocket. That done, he burrowed in among the deadfall and the junipers, insulating himself from above and below in the hope that those guys had neither seen nor heard him.

MATT

Scared as he was—and he could not deny that—Matt never felt so alive. He could almost hear the soundtrack from *The Last of the Mohicans* playing in his head. Like Natty Bumppo in the film's opening, he was running through the woods, his brother by his side. The difference was those guys were hunting. He and his brother were being hunted. If anything, that difference made the experience all the more intense.

As he and Luke negotiated their way through the woods along the stream, he began to see a way out of the jam they were in and maybe even out of the quiet mess he had made of his own life.

TONY

For some endless time, Tony lay still—zen-like—keying in on the sounds of men scrambling down the slope, cursing in Spanish. He heard no horses. He did not expect to. In their position, with the snow and all, he would have left his horse at the ridgeline. They probably did just that. Listening closely, he heard one of the men saying he saw Tony, or thought he had. The others were skeptical, but they joined in the search. They sounded like the kind of men who would litter a trail with cigarette butts. They were cocky and careless and loud, and they were getting closer.

He saw no more viable course right now than to will himself into the sweet borderland between dream and reality, the warm breeze from the Tyrrhenian Sea separating the curtains and washing over him, and she, ever so lovely, leaning in and whispering now, "The evil ones are in the wire." She left as soundlessly as she came, the breeze cooling in her wake. It was sharp now, and bitter. *The evil ones are in the wire?* he thought. *I'm in Colorado, Angel.* He was in Colorado, but the sudden press of steel on the back of his neck reminded him that the evil ones were real and very much in the wire.

"*Oye carnal. ¿Lo encontraste?*" asked one of the guys from a distance. Yes, thought Tony, the *cabrón* with the gun in my neck found me.

"*Si, aquí tengo al buey,*" said the man with the gun proudly. Consoling himself with the knowledge that the boys had gotten away, Tony waited. He did not rule out a bullet to the head, but he expected an interrogation, likely an "enhanced" one—maybe very enhanced. He braced himself for either possibility. He had still not looked up but he could hear the other men approach.

"*Ven a hablar con él,*" said the man with the rifle in his neck. Good, thought Tony, they wanted their English speaker to come talk to him.

"Roll over, hands above your head," said a second man. He spoke English with a Mexican accent so stilted it seemed practiced, theatrical even.

"No problem," Tony said in English. He did not want to let them know he broke his ankle or spoke Spanish. He rolled over and looked up. It was Jake from State Farm, except this time he wasn't wearing his khakis. Standing next to him was the Indian. Damn, if he'd ever doubt Thor again. The three of them were hovering above him now—Jake, Fedora Man, and the Indian.

"Crawl out of there," said Jake. "Keep your hands where I can see them." Tony complied, emerging at the shelf's edge.

"Okay, on your knees. Keep your hands up."

This was difficult. The pain shot through Tony's left ankle like an electric shock when he knelt upright, facing uphill, but he preferred this position to the one he had been in. No longer helpless, he surveyed the Mexicans, all armed and with an interesting array of weapons.

Fedora Man had an '03 Springfield much like the one his father-in-law had left him. That, Tony suspected, was to keep up the pretense of elk hunting. Jake had a Beretta M9, but the Indian held the firepower, a MAC-9. Easy to conceal and fully automatic, it could spew 9 millimeters like water out of a hose.

Jake, the Beretta in his right hand, crouched in front of Tony, patted his sides, pulled his jacket half-open, peered down into the jacket, paused, and straightened back up. Tony stared back at him.

"No satellite phone?" Jake asked.

"No. No phones at all," said Tony.

Tony could not believe what just happened. Jake had left Tony's .44 in its holster. He had to have seen it. The revolver was too big to overlook.

The Indian, standing with Fedora Man a few feet back, was growing impatient. "Just keel 'em," he said in English, presumably so Tony would have no doubt about his intentions.

"No," said Jake, adding in perfectly fluent Mexican Spanish. *"Necesitamos información de éste pendejo."* He put the muzzle of his Beretta under Tony's chin.

"Where are the other two?"

"They're just boys. Leave them be."

"Where are they?"

"They're my boys. What kind of man gives up his sons?" He hoped to appeal to a Latin sense of family and honor, but a boot to his shoulder from the Indian convinced him that the appeal did not work. Laughing, the Indian walked back to Fedora Man, and the two conferred feverishly in Spanish. Tony understood every word. He had about sixty seconds left to live. The two were going to give their partner no more time than that to prove his worth. If need be, they would pull the trigger themselves.

"Keel 'em!" repeated the Indian.

"No," Jake yelled back.

"¡No seas pendejo y mátalo!

"You hear my friends," said Jake, now crouching right in Tony's face. "They want me to kill you. I want you to give me some information. I want to know where your boys are."

Tony looked hard at his interrogator. Something about his eyes told him he didn't want to kill, but Tony was not sure why—prudence probably, cowardice maybe. His amigos sensed his hesitance as well. They had just called him a *pendejo,* a pussy.

"Keel 'em. *¡Ya, mátalo!"*

"Necesitamos sacarle información," Jake shouted angrily. As Jake turned around to challenge his bloodthirsty partners, Tony grabbed for the man's pistol with his left hand and yanked the muzzle down and away from his body to neutralize it. In that same moment, with his right hand, he pulled out the bear spray.

When Jake instinctively reached over with his left hand to free the weapon in his right, Tony pushed the canister past his left side, and delivered a fog into the bewildered faces of the two Mexicans behind him. In the back end of that same motion, he stuck his right foot between Jake's legs for leverage, wrapped his right arm around his shoulder, and yanked them both ass over elbows down the side of the mountain.

PEL

Pel could hear something happening. He wasn't sure what, but he oriented himself to the sound of it and plunged ahead. Damn, this was cool.

MATT

Something stopped Matt in his tracks just as he was hopping from one rock to another. He halted astride the stream and turned his head back north. It felt like a hand on his shoulder. The sensation chilled him.

"What's wrong?" said Luke, just a few feet behind his brother but still on the left bank.

"Shhh!" said Matt. "Listen."

They both fell silent.

"I'm not sure I hear anything," said Luke.

"I'm not sure I did either," said Matt.

"Now what?

"Let's just stop here for a second."

"And do what?"

"Listen."

TONY

As they fell backwards, Tony managed to knock the Beretta from Jake's hand. Tumbling down the hill, the man shouted something at Tony over and over, but the only word Tony was sure he could make out was "asshole." It was not until they came to rest at the base of a large aspen, Jake on top of Tony, now struggling to get up on all fours, that Tony understood what the man was saying.

"I'm ATF, you asshole. Undercover."

Yes, of course, thought Tony. He should have figured it out himself, not that it would have made any difference. They were where they needed to be.

"Army, Special Forces," Tony whispered. With his left hand he pulled the ATF agent back towards him. With his right, he reached into his jacket, unsnapped the holster flap, and grabbed the pistol. "Do what I tell you."

"It better make sense."

What Tony knew about himself is that when he gave an order, people listened. No one in the 3rd Special Forces Group could match his command presence, and this was no time for a debate.

"Trust me."

"You got the gun," said the agent. "I'm not sure I have a choice."

LUKE

"I don't hear anything," said Luke.

He stood and listened some more. They both did. All Luke heard was the wind and the snow. Until this moment, he never realized that falling snow could be noisy. That only made sense.

Rain was noisy. People wrote about the noise rain makes all the time. They wrote songs about it even. But in the wind, among the trees, snow had its own soft, whooshing, shushing sound, and no one ever talked about it.

"I don't hear anything either," said Matt, "at least not anymore."

TONY

"When I give the order, roll hard to your left."

The ATF agent nodded. They could both hear the two Mexicans sliding down the hill after them, coughing and cursing all the way. Tony pulled out the .44, and cocked it, a move not recommended in any safety class he ever attended, and held the gun on his chest.

The agent was blocking his view of Fedora Man, and the Indian was directly behind Fedora Man, but neither could see the .44. Tony hoped to take out the Indian first to neutralize his MAC-9, but Fedora Man was in the way. *Damn!*

When the Mexicans were no more than about five meters away, Tony whispered, "Roll." The agent did as commanded and rolled hard. Tony swung his .44 up and out and focused on one point: front sight—front sight—front sight. Distracted by the agent, Fedora Man didn't have a chance. As the sight passed above his right hip Tony squeezed the trigger. The bullet blew through the man's chest to the right of his solar plexus, through the ribcage and out through his back, knocking the Fedora clear off his head.

The powerful muzzle blast flipped the barrel of this double-action revolver upwards. Now it was a race to the next trigger pull. Tony pulled the front sight down and when it crossed the Indian's right shoulder, he squeezed long and hard but in one smooth motion. Staring wide-eyed into this big silver cannon, the man panicked and pulled the trigger of his MAC-9. In a one-second burst, he watered the stunned ATF agent with as many as ten rounds, ripping his right side vertically from thigh to face.

The man had no time to savor his kill. The second round from Tony's .44 blasted through the man's stomach, exploding his guts every which way. Tony looked to his right, "Damn! Damn!" shouted Tony as the ATF agent went limp. "Damn! Damn! Damn!"

PEL

"Holy shit," said Pel out loud. Hearing nothing more, he called R on the two-way.

"What happened?"

"Don't know," said R. "No one is answering satellite phone. Where are you?"

"Down by the creek."

"Stay there until I call you."

MATT

The sound from the gunshots raced down the valley. Matt, still frozen in place astride the stream, turned upstream and listened intently.

"Hunters?" asked Luke.

His brother knew the answer, thought Matt, but he was just hoping for some other, more innocent explanation.

"Shhh!"

A sullen echo of the shots passed them, faded quickly, and left the boys standing stunned in the noisy silence of a mountain squall. The screaming—or whatever—had stopped as well. Matt wished he were clever enough to distinguish one gunshot from another, but he wasn't.

"I have no idea, but some of those shots sounded like full auto. That wasn't Dad, and those weren't hunters."

"What should we do?"

Matt gathered his thoughts. He did not want to alarm his brother any more than he had to, but he did not want to deceive him either. They had some hard decisions to make very quickly. They had walked about a mile down the streambed. It was another twelve hours at least to the highway, but, if they hurried, a half-hour or so back to where they last saw their father.

"Let's listen some more."

LUKE

Luke stared up the streambed in the direction of the shots. No more than fifty yards upstream, a solitary elk stood proudly indifferent to the world around him. Luke had never seen anything more majestic. For this elk, he thought, nothing had changed. Although the elk had no way of way of knowing this, his prospects were brighter than they were a day ago.

"We better hurry and get help," he said urgently.

"Not so quick," said Matt.

His brother looked more determined than Luke had ever seen him. If this had ever seemed like a game, it no longer did. He knew what he had heard better than Matt did. He just couldn't bring himself to say it out loud. That was an automatic weapon.

If Dad was in a shootout with the bad guys, the bad guys got off some shots, maybe even the last ones.

TONY

Now up on his knees, the report from the .44 still echoing in his ears, Tony grabbed the hand of the agent. He was alive, but barely. He could scarcely talk. He had taken at least one shot in the jaw. That could wait. Blood was spurting out a severed artery in his right thigh. That could not wait. Tony stuck two fingers in the wound and applied direct pressure. In his experience, that usually worked, at least in the short term. The agent would survive the leg wound, thought Tony, but barring the miraculous, the multiple shots above his waist would kill him. The bullets had blown out a kidney and ripped open his intestines. They were spilling all over the place. There was little Tony could do but console the man.

"Can you hear me?" he asked, squeezing the agent's hand. "Blink once for yes. Two for no." The man blinked, fear pulsing from his eyes.

"Terrorists?"

One blink.

"Five of them?"

One blink.

Tony had hoped the bad guys would choose discretion and hightail it down the far side of Bravo, but he doubted it. His four tours had made him a pessimist. There was no underestimating the crazy, suicidal impulses of these people. Too many actually prayed to die fighting. He prayed to stay alive, and his God, he was pleased to remember, gave his people the courage and the will to do just that.

"Thanks for the intel. We got help on the way. We'll medevac your sorry ass out of here and have you out caroling by Christmas."

Two blinks.

"That wasn't a question," said Tony, smiling warmly. "That was a promise." If there was one kind of lie God permitted, Tony figured, it was the lie told to a dying man.

"Got a wife?"

One blink.

"Kids?"

One blink. His color was fading quickly.

"I'll tell them myself how nobly you lived and how bravely you fought. You saved my life, brother. I'll never forget it."

The agent's eyes teared. He must have sensed he was a dead man, but he struggled through his anguish to speak. Tony squeezed the agent's hand, leaned over, and listened, his ears still buzzing.

"Loaded for bear..." said the agent faintly, imperfectly, the words drowning in blood.

"They coming after us?" asked Tony.

This time when the agent closed his eyes he did not open them. Tony watched the life drain out of his face. He had seen it before. He made the sign of the cross with his thumb on the agent's forehead and said out loud, "Angel, this is a very good man. Help him over." The snow fell on Tony's lips as he looked skyward and reminded him, if he needed reminding, that he still had to fight not just the Haji, but the elements.

MOOM

It was cold and getting colder. Standing in place alongside R, Moom could barely move his jaw to speak. He knew it was not his place to speak in any case. He watched as R tried to dial up the Mexicans, his frustration growing with each failed call.

"What do you think has happened?" R turned to him and asked. The question threw Moom.

"Me?"

"Yes, you. You are the only one here. I want second opinion."

R seemed to be looking for a serious response. Moom decided to give him one.

"I think, like, the Mexicans are all dead." He watched R recoil in surprise.

"Interesting. Why do you think that?"

"If one of them was alive, even if his phone had been destroyed, he would have called out. Sound travels in this valley."

R stared at Moom for a long second, then nodded, "I believe you are right."

"I have one more thought."

"Tell me."

Moom took his time to respond. He wanted to share his intuition, but he did not want to let R know it was reinforced by what he had denied seeing earlier when on lookout. He chose his words carefully.

"I think it's a father and two sons," said Moom. "I think my brother and me ran into these guys at a gas station in Missouri on the way here. If I'm right, the man, the father, is one seriously tough dude."

MATT

Matt saw nothing, heard nothing more. Being isolated in this streambed, with no visibility beyond the trees on either side, was maddening. He wanted to reassure his brother, but who knew what the right thing to say was? They had no precedent for the jam they were all in.

"Hand me your rifle." Matt held out his hand.

Luke hesitated, then complied.

"I've got to get back to Dad."

"We promised not to," Luke protested.

"I know, but I got some…atoning to do."

"C'mon, you remember what Dad said."

"I remember, but the mission's changed."

"Who changed it?"

"I did." Matt had heard his father talk more than once about what makes the American Army different from others. It was rule number forty-seven or ninety-five or whatever: when the strategy isn't working, devise a new one. The Army trusted its guys to change tactics at the squad level if need be, and that, Matt figured, was the level he and his brother were at. But this was no time for history lessons.

"I got to believe Dad's alive and needs me." Just saying this out loud made Matt shudder. "You go on," he said, holding Luke's shoulders from behind and giving him a little push. "You can make it to the highway. I know you can."

"I know I can, numb nuts," said Luke, turning back to face his brother, "but I'm not leaving you."

"C'mon, Dad would want you to," Matt said harshly. "Now get your ass in gear."

"No. Sorry. If you can change your marching orders, I can change mine."

Matt had to respect the kid's stubbornness, but he knew better than Luke did what lay ahead.

"C'mon, man, get out of here!" he said, now pushing Luke hard enough to make him stumble.

"No!" Luke insisted. "Remember what Dad said?"

"About going back? Yeah, I get it, but that's settled."

"No, about being a team?"

"Yeah, so?"

"I can see breaking one promise," said Luke, "but I don't see, like, why we have to break two."

Matt shook his head in dismay. He wanted to say, "You fool, this isn't a video game. You don't kill digital bad guys, keep score electronically, and rag your friends after you beat them. This is real, and you've never even been in a fistfight, let alone a firefight."

"We're just a couple of doofuses," he wanted to scream at his brother, at the heavens. "Do you know how crazy this whole scene is? Do you know what little chance there is that all three of us will get out of this fix alive?"

But he said none of this.

"Okay, you stubborn little douche," said Matt. "Let's go see if we can maybe, like, help."

TONY

Sitting amidst the carnage, scanning the area for threats, the snow falling unevenly, Tony wondered whether it was a good or bad thing that he felt almost nothing about what had just taken place: no anger towards the Mexicans, no regret about his own role in their deaths, and, as much as he respected the agent, no heartbreak. All of his emotion he reserved for his sons. That he had heard no gunshots before his own incident, and none after, told him the boys had gotten away safely. This thought brought him at least a wisp of peace.

He understood his current position to be untenable—he could see almost nothing—and thus indefensible. He decided to return to the level tip of Foxtrot above. From the finger ridge, he could survey the valley one last time, cross Alpha, God willing, and make his way through the woods along the trail. With luck, he would run into Thor—if, that is, he could make it up the slope. He was not optimistic. He knew from experience that injuries like his often got worse before they got better.

He would sort out his emotions later. He ran through a quick checklist of things he had to do. First step was a combat reload. He replaced the two .44 rounds he had fired with fresh ones pulled from his pocket. The second step was to take care of his ankle. He was no expert in these things, but it felt broken. So he took out his SAM splint—really, just a lightweight sheath of molded aluminum alloy with a foam backing—and fixed it in place with duct tape. The splint did not return anything close to mobility to the ankle, but it stabilized it and allowed him to put a little pressure on it, at least for the moment.

That done, he surveyed the damage. The one satellite phone had been shot through, and he could not get a signal on any of the cell phones the men carried. He checked their pockets and found nothing but cigarettes. As to the weapons, there was a MAC-9 with an extra magazine, the '03 Springfield, and a Beretta M9 somewhere up the slope. He drank the dead men's water and pulled Jake's parka off his body.

The parka had a few holes in it after the shootout and was more than a little bloody, but it was a good one. Seeing no easy way out of the valley, that extra coat could help keep him alive overnight. Tony tied its sleeves around his neck. He then put the MAC-9 and Springfield straps across one shoulder and pocketed the magazine. Never knew when the extra rounds would do him some good.

He found the Beretta just a few meters above his position. So loaded, he began his hike. It was more of a crawl really—painful, exhausting, and hell on his ankle—but he told himself he could do it. He had to.

When he reached the juniper bushes where the Mexicans found him, he paused to catch his breath and ease the pain. The snow was still falling and didn't show any signs of abating. He could not chance another stop after this one. The climb up to Foxtrot was longer, steeper, and almost fully exposed. He would be no more capable of defending himself during this stretch than an elk, maybe less.

While resting, he took a moment to sort out his strategy. One thought that nagged at him was that the boys likely heard the shots. He knew what he told them to do, but he feared they would do the opposite. Then there were the Hajis or whatever. They would have heard the shots too, and if they were anywhere in the neighborhood, they would have a strong sense of where the shots came from. His extra weapons notwithstanding, if they came after him, he had no reason to believe he could defeat them, not five of them anyhow, not with them "loaded for bear"—whatever the hell that meant—and he suspected the worst.

His ankle negated his mobility, but remaining where he was left him with little visibility and max vulnerability. Having sorted out his options, none of them promising, he began the slow, slippery, painful climb back up to Foxtrot. The falling snow provided just about the only cover he would have until he got there. He could only pray the enemy did not see him, and, if they did, that they were still too far away to shoot him.

As he climbed, Tony looked for his rifle and found it peeking out of the snow, halfway up to Foxtrot. A quick inspection showed no obvious damage to the scope, and the barrel was clear. Carrying two weapons on one shoulder, a third on the other, the pack and parka on his back, and the glasses around his neck, he had to pause every ten or so meters to cope with the pain. It grew more intense by the moment and slowed him more than he anticipated.

If the ankle weren't problem enough, the snow and the slippery rocks demanded that much more energy and focus. He was crawling now more than he was hopping, grabbing on every rock and root to pull himself up, his left leg worse than useless. Had he known it would take this long, he might have plotted another exit strategy, but he had gone too far to turn back. The finger ridge was within reach. Just a few more meters, Angel, just a few more.

Moom

Scanning the valley with the binoculars, Moom saw the guy first. He thought for a moment of not telling R what he saw, but the cold had limited his options. If he could not get back to camp soon to warm up, he was afraid he might get frostbite, or worse. His thin cotton gloves were a joke, and his feet were as numb as his hands. He handed the binoculars to R and pointed.

"Look over here."

It did not take R long to zero in on the guy climbing up towards the ridge. Even through the blur of the snow, the guy stood out against the white of the slope. R did not hesitate to act. He barked orders into his two-way radio in whatever language it was he spoke. Moom figured he was telling his two third-world homies what to do. He had no doubt they would do it, or at least die trying.

That done, R made another transmission, this one in English.

PEL

"Okay," said Pel. "I can see him now." R was calmly speaking to him, sharing his thoughts. He believed there were two others, likely boys. He wanted Pel to head downstream a short distance to see if he could see any signs of them and, if not, to angle up from the south towards the ridge the man was trying to reach.

"Sounds good," said Pel. He was eager to get going again. He was enjoying the chase, and it was too damn cold to stand in place. With the AK at the ready, he headed downstream.

MATT

Matt sensed his father was alive. He sensed the horsemen were dead. He had no firm reason to believe this, but he chose to believe it nonetheless. He was in too much of a hurry now to seek cover in the trees. Carrying Luke's rifle, his gloved right hand resting at the balance point just forward of the trigger guard, he walked purposefully alongside the stream, thinking feverishly about how he might help his father fight off whoever. Luke kept pace right behind him.

As he walked, Matt looked anxiously for some break in the tree line so he could scan the west slope of Alpha. Seeing none, he decided to climb a swell on the west bank and hope that he could see something from up there. It was not an easy climb—maybe twenty-five feet, but at a sixty or so degree angle. He had to crawl through the snow and mud on hands and knees, grabbing at every root and bush to reach its crest.

The snow had eased. The visibility improved. Matt could see the slope above the tree line. It did not take him long to spot what looked like a figure sprawled out at the tip of Foxtrot. His heart pumped double time.

"I see someone, I think," he said to Luke more calmly than he felt. He reached down and helped Luke up the last few feet. His brother had the binoculars.

"See where I'm looking?"

"Yeah."

"Tell me what we're looking at." Matt held his breath.

"It's Dad!" Luke shouted.

"Shhhh! Shhhh!" whispered Matt. "Thank God!"

"He seems to be kind of moving around on his butt, scanning the valley."

"Good, good, good," said Matt. Without ever trying to, he was learning to compress his emotions, to keep them in check, to sublimate them until the job was done. When he wrestled, he didn't celebrate until the ref held his arm in the air. He never gloated mid-match. No time to start now.

"Is he hurt?"

"Might be. When he moves, he moves funny."

"Bad?"

"Don't think so. Don't know."

Matt had an idea. Although he had no doubt how his father would react, he would still want to know where his sons were. All plans would hinge on that knowledge.

"Can you give me the glasses?"

"Yeah, sure." Luke did as asked.

"I got a job for you."

"Yeah, what?"

"I want you to grab your orange bandana and flash it. The orange will stand out against the white."

"Couldn't the bad guys see it too?"

"They might," said Matt. "So hold it inside your jacket and open your jacket at an angle only Dad can see. We've got to get his attention."

PEL

Walking along the streambed, Pel thought he could see vague imprints in the snow, maybe footprints, but the snow was falling so quick and heavy, it was impossible to tell. Besides, he didn't want to chase a couple kids down the stream. He could always do that later.

He thought for a moment about dialing up R, but hated the idea of asking permission. In the way of a compromise, he figured he would go another hundred or so yards downstream and, if he didn't see anything, he'd head up towards the man on the ridge. This so beat marching down Boylston Street.

TONY

With the snow easing, Tony sat out on the farthest, horizontal edge of Foxtrot before it angled downward. From there, he glassed the bowl from the northwest to the southwest. Although much more exposed than he would like, he could see better from here than anywhere else in the valley.

He still saw no sign of the enemy—thank God—but he suspected they had to be on the way. He turned his attention now to the stream and followed its course to the south, and there he saw something he really wished he had not.

Even through the snow, he had no doubt he was looking at Luke, standing on a rise and flashing a bright orange object under his jacket. Standing next to him, staring through the binoculars, was Matt. Proud as he was of their courage, worry smothered pride like paper on rock. Oh God, he wished that they had not come back. He raised his arm and pushed his palm repeatedly in their direction. He hoped they read his message right. Deep down, he knew it would do no good. He had raised his sons too well.

LUKE

"He's waving at us," said Matt, his eyes still glued to the binoculars.

"Can I see?"

"Yeah," said Matt, handing the glasses off to his brother. Luke quickly located their dad. The message was clear.

"He wants us to turn away, go back down the stream."

"That's what I thought too," said Matt. "While we got his attention, I want you to do something."

"Okay." Luke was not at all sure where this was heading, but he was starting to think his brother could make good decisions. Maybe there *was* a reason they made him captain of everything.

"Very slowly and deliberately," said Matt, "I want you to do what I am doing."

Luke looked over at his brother. He was shaking his head "No."

TONY

There was no mistaking the message. His sons were refusing his order. He saw no point in waving them away. They understood what he meant and rejected it. He wasn't sure how to feel about that, wasn't sure at all. They had never done this before.

He wished he could have preserved their innocence a little longer or at least trained them a little harder to be ready, but it was too late for all that. The boys were growing up by the hour.

MATT

Matt handed the binoculars to his brother. "It's time for me to go."

"Go? What? You're leaving me?"

"Kind of got to," said Matt. He expected his brother to resist, and he did just that.

"I thought we were, you know, like a team?"

"No, not 'like' a team. We are a team, Hawkeye. You stay here, and you got a sight line on Dad and anyone who gets near him." What Matt thought, but did not say, was that here his brother would be far enough away to stay out of trouble.

"Matt, c'mon!"

"I'm serious. You keep watch with the rifle."

"You sure?"

"Yeah, totally."

"We're pretty far away."

"It's the best spot we've seen so far. I don't expect we'll find any place better."

"What about you?"

"I'll slice through the woods and see if I can find my way to Dad before someone else gets there. No time to debate. Gotta go."

Matt put his pack on his back, patted the six-inch Buck knife to make sure it was still on his belt, and turned to leave.

"Take the gun," said Luke.

"No, you've got to keep it. You're the sniper."

"Don't leave yet," said Luke, grabbing his brother's arm.

"C'mon, man. I gotta go."

"I got an idea."

"What? C'mon." Matt thought Luke was just trying to hold him back. He underestimated his little brother.

Luke quickly pulled the Tyvek ground cloth from his bag.

"Cut a hole in this and wear it as a poncho. It's as white as the snow. It'll camouflage you."

Matt looked at his brother in wonder. "Makes sense." *This kid's smart*, he thought. In less than sixty seconds, they had made a poncho that covered Matt to his knees and cut out a wrap from the same sheet to cover Matt's head. Matt pulled the Tyvek from his own pack, gave it to Luke, and urged him to do the same.

"Find a comfortable place to shoot from," Matt said. "And make sure your rifle's resting on your pack just like in practice. It'll recoil differently if you rest it on a log."

"Okay."

"Wish I could spot for you, but you'll figure it out."

LUKE

Luke had another thought. "Dad needs to know you're coming."

"Good point. Give me that bandanna, and I'll see if I can get his attention."

Luke did as asked, then focused the binoculars on the ledge while Matt flashed the bandanna in that direction, shielding it as best he could within the Tyvek.

"He's looking at us," said Luke.

"Good. I'm out of here." Matt pointed with both hands in the direction he intended to go, sort of like the famous image of that guy pointing down the third base line in some World Series or another. He then slid down the rise.

"Be careful, bro," Luke whisper-shouted.

Matt crossed the stream heading for the trees. Luke watched his brother as he veered off north and east through the trees, and he worried. He worried about Matt's need to make things right, worried that Matt was so hell-bent on saving his soul he would sacrifice his life to do it. He wanted to talk to him about it before he left, forgive him even, but he couldn't bring himself to say anything. It didn't much matter, he supposed. Matt would have shut him out in any case.

Luke figured if he got busy he wouldn't feel quite so alone. But busy wasn't enough. He needed to do what his father and brother instructed him to do, and do it right.

Working quickly, he found a spot where he could set up shop. The position was close to perfect. A large tree had fallen nearby, and although the branches hung over the stream, the trunk remained on the rise. It was broad enough so that he could put his pack on the front edge, rest his rifle on the pack, and rest his arms on the remainder of the trunk—a position much like the one he assumed on the shooting bench at the range. Better still, sitting on his pad and leaning into the tree, he was perfectly aligned with his father's position on Foxtrot, a line of sight blurred only by the falling snow.

His position set, Luke draped the Tyvek ground cloth over his body, keeping himself dry and blocking the wind. Now, with the snow falling even harder, his position was close to invisible. The problem was that the longer he sat, the less heat he would generate. He had to keep his hands warm—his trigger finger especially. And it was then that he had this inspiration.

For any hope of an accurate shot he had to have an idea of the range. Rummaging through his pack, he pulled out a pad and pencil. Unable to see much of anything in the snow, he figured it would be a good time to do some math. From yesterday, he knew the tip of Foxtrot was 257 meters due east of the large rock near the stream they bounced the laser off of. The stream flowed more or less straight here—straight enough for his calculations, but not so straight he could see that rock through the snow. So he decided to pace off the distance.

If nothing else, the walk would keep him warm. Once he got the length of this leg of the triangle, it would be no big deal to calculate distance from his shooting spot to his father's ledge. That would be the hypotenuse of the triangle. He slid down the incline on his butt, rifle over his shoulder, and began to walk, counting his paces.

MOOM

Through the snow, Moom and R had watched the man climb the slope opposite them. Once he reached the ridge sticking out into the valley, R turned and said, "Let us go, me and you."

Moom knew this would not be easy. R had him wear a chest carrier with three RPG rounds and carry the RPG bag. All R had to carry was his AK-47. Sliding and stumbling down the slope, Moom struggled to keep up.

Watching the man from behind, Moom marveled at his self-assurance and his toughness. He was a lot like Pel in that way, but in R there was no bluff, no game-playing. He was one hard dude. There were times Moom wished he could be like that. Right now, though, the thing he envied most about R were his boots and gloves.

TONY

The way Tony figured, he had little choice but to stay put, at least for the time being. His ankle had only gotten worse. Much worse. He packed snow on the swelling—it would help some, but it was no cure. His pants had worn through and his knees were bleeding. To move now, he had to shuffle on his butt. He joked to himself they might have to use the block and tackle to get him off this finger ridge and over Alpha, but he wasn't sure he was joking.

Luke had a bead on his position, however distant, and Matt had disappeared. He was confident Matt was heading his way, but he couldn't be sure. In the meantime, he layered up to ward off the cold. The snow was falling hard once again, so there was little for him to see. On the plus side, the near-whiteout condition gave him cover to scuttle about like a crab.

Once the snow eased a little, he scanned the valley again with the Swarovskis. The enemy was nowhere to be seen. That did not surprise him. He imagined the Hajis had lingered on, or even beyond Bravo and let the Mexicans do their dirty work for them. How hard could it be, they all must have figured, to take out an elk hunter and his two kids? Not much harder, say, than herding wayward goats or setting a roadside IED. That said, shots had rung out throughout the valley, and the Mexicans were no longer taking their phone calls. The enemy had to suspect something unfortunate happened to their *amigos*.

And they had a mission. Likely, that mission was to pop a plane out of the sky—a week or so away. Now, though, some random hunters had compromised their plans, and they would not let those hunters get back to civilization. The more Tony thought about it, the more clearly he understood he had to get his boys out of this valley, with him or without him.

Tony glassed the valley once again. He didn't see Luke near the stream where he had seen him before, and he did not see Matt. The lack of a visual on Matt didn't worry him overly— he was likely on the way—but not seeing Luke scared him. Uncertain of their whereabouts, he would remain in place.

In surveying the Alpha ridgeline to the northeast, he soon spotted something—or someone—about two hundred yards away, above the tree line and just below the ridge. He did not like what he was seeing, not at all. A man with a transmitter of some sort held to his mouth had his binoculars trained squarely on Tony.

MOOM

R stopped to take a call on his two-way. He seemed to like what he was hearing. When finished he turned to Moom and said, "We are closing in."

Moom did not know what to say. He was too cold to speak in any case. He followed R towards the stream down below and wished he were somewhere else.

TONY

Tony swapped out the glasses for the Remington and spun around on his butt until he was facing north. He hoped to get a shot off but did not expect to. Even before he could put the scope on the man, the man retreated over the ridge. This was not good. Despite the snow, Tony transitioned to prone with the rifle fixed in the direction of the ridgeline behind which the enemy had sought cover.

The man was just one of five, and they had him made. They knew where he was and, maybe, knew he was immobile. He was confident they would come for him as soon as the snow cleared, maybe even before. He did not like his options. Not at all. Even if he could climb to the Alpha ridgeline, he would be much too exposed. If he slid down to the trees in search of Matt and Luke, he would be leading these thugs right to his sons and would slow them all down. Then, too, Thor would be entirely vulnerable if he did show up.

Right now, there was nowhere to go worth going, at least not until Matt arrived—if Matt arrived. Until then, he could at least improve his position. The rocky surface of Foxtrot's horizontal stretch was about two feet higher than the ground immediately to its south. That two-foot drop would give him at least some protection from the likely snipers to the north. So he slid off awkwardly, jarring his ankle and sending a jolt of angry energy through the left side of his body. He fought the urge to throw up and, as best as he could, ignored the cold and pain and waited in position. This he could do better than anyone.

MATT

Matt angled through the woods with caution. By now, an inch or two of snow covered the tree roots and rocks, and these were difficult to negotiate even when visible. As he maneuvered up the slope, he struggled to keep his footing and asked himself whether he had set out on a fool's errand.

And yet there was something epic about the snow and the woods and the nature of the task at hand. Initially, at least, the adrenalin rush drowned his fear; suppressed his anxieties. Succeed or fail, he had the chance at least to atone, but failure at this stage seemed more likely than success. Armed with a knife, he had to somehow elude—or overcome—as many as eight armed men.

One advantage he had was stealth. Luke was a clever kid. His idea was great. As long as it snowed, Matt was well camouflaged in his Tyvek. He assumed he had another advantage as well: strength, both muscular and cardiovascular. In close quarters he would prevail, not because he could wrestle and do a little mixed martial arts, but because, like his father, he had the power to endure. "Persistence" the old man called it. He had a point there.

LUKE

Luke took long strides to measure out a yard with each step, looking warily around as he walked. Of the eight bad guys they had spotted, he had no idea how many were left alive, possibly all eight, and he had even less idea of where they might be. He hoped the snow and the Tyvek would give him cover enough. He counted under his breath, "thirty-five, thirty-six, thirty-seven, thirty..." then stopped mid-number. He saw movement out of the corner of his eye.

PEL

Losing the feeling in his fingers, Pel decided to sling the AK over his shoulder. His hands free, he took his gloves off with his mouth. He then slipped both his hands down his pants and rubbed them furiously against his legs. They stung at first, but gradually they regained sensation. Once they did, he withdrew them and put the gloves back on. For the moment, he could think about something other than his hands and feet.

What he thought about was just how cool the damn experience was—walking through the woods in the snow, an AK on his shoulder, an opportunity for real action up ahead. He had a hard time believing that just a few weeks ago his big thrill was throwing a newspaper box through a picture window. Come whatever, those days were over.

LUKE

Stopping and staring, Luke watched something cutting through the woods about a hundred yards or so in front of him and to his right. No, it wasn't something. It was someone. The man was heading in the same general direction as Matt. Without thinking much about the consequences, Luke ran through the snow-covered grass and into the trees to catch up.

MATT

As he ducked and weaved through the trees and up the slope towards his father's position, Matt thanked God for the snow and the wind and the Tyvek. They muffled the sound of his footsteps and obscured his movement through the woods. If anyone were prowling around, Matt was confident he would see that person before the person saw him.

LUKE

From the moment he entered the woods, Luke felt as dumb and vulnerable as a clay target at a skeet range. Still, he reasoned, if the guy he saw was a Haji or whatever, he could not allow him to sneak up on his brother or his father. The Tyvek and the snow gave him cover just enough not to feel totally foolish. He gripped his rifle and prayed he would not have to use it.

He walked as quickly as he could, slipping occasionally in the snow on the steeper stretches. Within minutes, he caught sight of the guy, and from the looks of his weapon, it was no kind of deer rifle. From Call of Duty, he knew it was an AK. Scared and uncertain, he kept about fifty yards between him and the man, ducking behind the occasional tree when the guy paused.

His mind raced. Shoot a bad guy in Call of Duty and you score points. Shoot at a bad guy in the woods and he shoots back and kills you. Running out of time and space, Luke walked even quicker. He still had no idea what he should do right up to the moment he stepped noisily on a branch and then tripped trying to regain his balance.

PEL

Pel turned at the sound. "Holy shit!" he muttered. It was some kid lying out in the snow with a rifle just out of his grasp. From the looks of it, he must have fallen. Pel just stared for a moment, trying to process what he saw.

LUKE

Luke looked up. The man had turned at the sound and was staring at him. He crawled desperately through the snow to retrieve his rifle, too afraid to maintain eye contact and sure he was about to get shot.

"Matt," he heard himself cry out. "Matt!"

PEL

When the kid went for his weapon, Pel knew what he had to do. It was the same answer to all of his problems of late—Medvedev, Chelsea, the pizza kid. He had to kill the little dude. He pulled the AK off his shoulder, but *damn!* His movements were slow, clumsy. The cold was part of it. Part of it was the anxiety, the fear, the whatever. But most of it, Pel knew, was that he had never gotten around to learning the weapon.

MATT

Matt heard what sounded like his name being called. His name? He took off on a dead run through the trees, looking alternately up and down—down to avoid the roots, up to see what the hell was happening. Holy Jesus! There was Luke lying helpless in the snow and a man with a rifle leveled right at him. Matt dashed forward, his breath strained, his legs burning.

PEL

"Shit!" said Pel. When he pulled the trigger, the damn rifle didn't fire. He fumbled around the AK until he found what might be the safety and he pushed the lever down with his right thumb. Just in time—the boy had grabbed his rifle. Pel re-shouldered the weapon and jerked the trigger hard and fast. The first four rounds fell short, but the little plumes of snow kept marching towards the target.

MOOM

Moom and R both turned in the direction of the noise and fell silent when it ended.

"That sounds like ours," said R. He patted Moom on the back to assure him. "The sound is coming from where your brother went. It is a good sound."

Moom wasn't quite so sure.

MATT

Matt could see the spent cartridge casings spinning up and away through the air. Faster, he had to get there faster. The makeshift Tyvek poncho slowing him down, he ripped it off as he ran. At the last step Matt lowered his shoulder and hit the man square in his side at the bottom of his rib cage. He heard a fifth shot, but God only knows where the bullet impacted. With the man lying there stunned, Matt yielded to his instinct and looked up to check on Luke. That was a mistake.

PEL

Regaining his senses—he felt as if he had just been hit by a truck—Pel saw what hit him. It was a kid no older than Moom. He lunged at the kid, now turning, and caught him with a blow to the mouth. The kid rocked back, and Pel, now on his knees, came around with his left to the kid's nose. He had him reeling. This was going to be quick work. This kid would last no longer than Moom would.

LUKE

Luke cleared the snow from his eyes and looked down range. He could not believe what he was seeing. The guy and Matt were on their knees, and the guy was slugging him. Still lying in the snow, Luke tried to aim his rifle, but cold and fear paralyzed him. If he managed to shoot, he was as likely to hit Matt as he was the other guy.

MATT

This guy was ferocious. Matt tried to roll away, but the guy grabbed his jacket with his left hand, spun him around, and delivered a looping right towards his face. Matt brought both forearms up vertically, but the force of the blow drove his forearms into his face. Another punch split Matt's arms but pushed him far enough back that he was able to escape the guy's grasp and stumble to his feet. With his vision blurred, and the blood flowing freely from his nose and mouth, he knew he had to do something or he would soon be dead.

PEL

Pel sprung right up after the kid. Now free to throw his whole body into a punch, he was sure the next one would be the last one. A few kicks to the head and game over. He grabbed the kid's jacket with his left hand and loaded up his right for the finisher.

MATT

Matt watched as the guy leaned back and lunged forward. He had telegraphed it. Matt jerked hard right, and the blow glanced off his forearm, scraped his left ear, and went on out into space. He had an opening. Pulling the guy to him, he reached out with his left arm and wrapped it over and around the guy's extended right arm above the elbow. He then pulled the arm in tight, locking it to his side.

The guy let go of Matt's shoulder and pulled back his left hand in a fist. As he did, Matt grabbed the man's coat around his back and brought him in close, cheek to cheek. With no separation, the guy could do no more then launch powerless jabs at Matt's side.

Matt had never experienced such strength or fury up close. The guy reached up to gouge Matt's left eye but missed, leaving himself slightly off balance. Matt didn't wait. He slid down, lowering his center of gravity. Stepping one foot behind the man's leg and pushing on his other with everything he had, he forced the guy backwards.

The game had just changed from boxing to wrestling, and now all advantages, save weight, were Matt's. As the guy fell, Matt reached for his right leg. Lifting it, he slammed him into the ground as hard as possible.

PEL

"Mother fucker!" Pel shouted, or tried to. No air came out of his lungs. The slam left him breathless. Now, the kid had his legs wrapped around his own and was leveraging him over on to his stomach. As hard as he resisted, the harder the kid pushed. *Damn, damn, damn!* The little shit had him.

MATT

Now on top of the guy's back, Matt encircled his neck with his left arm, grabbed his own right bicep with his left hand, pushed the palm of his right hand into the back of the guy's head, and forced his neck into a vise. With one leg looped around the guy's body and the other anchored at an angle to it, the dude was toast.

LUKE

Matt had him! He did! He had him. Spared the need to shoot—and the guilt of not shooting—Luke scrambled to his feet, slipping with every step. "Thank you!" he cried out as he rushed towards his brother.

PEL

Pel had one last move to make. Channeling his dwindling energy, he grabbed the kid's left wrist first with his right hand and then his left hand. In one superhuman act of will Pel started prying the arm off. The kid was strong, but he was stronger, and at this moment he was the one fighting for his goddamn life.

MATT

Holy mother of God! Matt had never wrestled anyone nearly this tough. The guy had an iron grip around his left wrist now and was a moment away from yanking Matt's arm from his throat. If he succeeded, he had no doubt the guy would overwhelm him and kill him. It was only then that Matt remembered he had one more move to make, and he knew he had to make it.

PEL

He had him. The kid could not hold on any longer, and once he let go, Pel would kill this ballsy son-of-a-bitch one way or another. Then, without warning, the kid let go entirely, his left arm and his right arm both. Freed, Pel rolled to his right until he felt a punch in the side of his neck that didn't stop at the surface. It just went deeper and deeper and *sorry I fucked your life up, Moom, sorry, sorry, sorry....*

LUKE

Not a thousand kills in Call of Duty equaled the rush of emotion Luke felt as he watched his brother take down the guy who tried to shoot him. When he reached his brother, Matt was on the man's back, the handle of his knife sticking out of the man's neck. The man's blood was flowing freely, staining the snow red. Nothing in Call of Duty prepared him for the sight.

"You okay, bro?" said Luke.

His rib cage heaving, his head down, Matt hesitated before looking up. There were tears in his eyes. He tried to talk but couldn't. Luke knelt beside his brother and hugged him.

"You were freakin'…awesome."

Matt sighed, shook his head, and said, after a long moment, "That was close." As he brought his face up, Luke was aghast to see it. Blood was still flowing freely from Matt's now crooked nose. Matt tried to stem the flow on his sleeve.

"Are you all right?" asked Luke.

"Not really," said Matt. "Not really."

MATT

Matt wondered if the emotion would come later—if a week from now or a month, he would bolt upright from his sleep in the horrible recognition that he had just killed a man—but he doubted that would happen. He killed two people with his car and suffered for it every day during the last two years. This time, he killed a man to save a life, maybe two, maybe twenty. If he felt anything, it was relief.

"How about you, bro?" Matt asked, leaning back after he regained his composure. "You okay?"

"I think so," said Luke. Luke stood and helped Matt to his feet.

"Thanks man," said Matt. Still struggling to breathe, he had a hard time coping with the reality that the fight was far from over.

TONY

Tony knew the rounds came from a semi-automatic weapon, but that was all he knew. He could envision positive scenarios to explain them, but the negative ones came easier. Whatever happened, the shallow protection of Foxtrot shielded him from the Haji threat to the north but left him fully exposed to the threat from the south. He rotated back around. Sitting down now and using the inside of his knees for support, he began scanning the area. He hoped to see Matt emerge from the trees southwest of him, but he wanted to be ready for whoever did.

LUKE

"Now what?" asked Luke.

"You need to get back to that rise we were on. You're going to keep me and Dad covered."

"I started to do the math, man. It's, like, too far away."

"You did the math?"

"I started to. I was walking off the distance. That's how I saw this guy." Luke pointed to the man lying on the ground. "Wow," he added. "Still can't believe this."

"You can't come with me."

"I can't?"

"No, you can't," Matt protested. "I don't want you here. Forget that rise. Just get your ass downstream and don't stop until you get to the highway."

Luke had never seen his brother this intense. After what Matt had just done, he earned the right.

"You sure?"

"Yeah, and I'm not going to argue."

"I hear you." Luke had to agree. This was no time to argue.

MATT

Matt wasn't at all sure sending Luke away was the right thing, but he did not want him in the mix. He had more than enough to deal with.

As soon as Luke left, he frisked the man he had just killed. The man's driver's license identified him as Peltier Adams from Cambridge, Massachusetts. He was no Haji. He had no cell phone, but he did have a two-way radio and a weapon. Matt picked up the AK and figured out how to engage the safety. He grabbed a spare magazine as well, and the radio. This guy wouldn't need any of this, not today, not ever.

LUKE

As he promised, Luke headed back down the slope towards the stream. That was the only part of the promise he planned to keep. With Matt out of sight, he turned north. He hoped to find his way to the shooting site they had picked out the day before.

He did not have to go far. After one false start, he found the spot and settled in behind the log they had positioned in place. With the snow easing once more, and the visibility improved, he took out the binoculars and zeroed in on the area between the tree line and Foxtrot—the area where his brother was most likely to emerge. He had a good sight line to his father from here and was close enough to cover him.

He watched his father scan the valley with his binoculars, swiveling back and forth between the ridgeline to his northeast and the tree line to his south. His dad must have known Matt was on the way, but the rounds from the AK had to have rattled him. He desperately wished he could reassure him.

MATT

The odds had just gotten better. For the first time in hours, he began to think he and his family just might get through this mess. Much depended, though, on the condition of his father. If he couldn't move freely, all bets were off.

After a miscalculation or two, Matt found himself in the edge of the woods southwest of the tip of Foxtrot, thirty or so yards away. It was hard to see anything through the snow, but his father appeared to be kneeling awkwardly against the edge of the finger ridge, the binoculars pressed against his eyes, looking alternately northeast and in his general direction. From the way he moved, Matt could tell his father had almost no mobility.

Fighting the urge to rush in, he lay among some tightly clustered trees and scanned the whole area. He had to be careful. His father had heard the rounds from the AK and could only suspect the worst. If he burst out of the woods, he would leave his father too little time to distinguish between friend and foe.

Matt thought of yelling out to get his father's attention, but if there were bad guys lying in wait, that would surely alert them to his presence. So when his father turned in his general direction, he discreetly waved his orange bandana and hoped to catch his eye.

TONY

Tony almost shouted out of relief when he saw the orange. It told him much of what he needed to know. He raised his rifle vertically to signal he got Matt's message.

MATT

Climbing to his feet, Matt hustled towards his father's position as quickly as the snow allowed. But as he looked up at his father, a sight beyond him froze the smile on his face. Two armed men were crossing over the Alpha ridge behind his father, no more than a hundred or so yards away.

"Get down," Matt yelled as he dropped lower to the ground and raced to reach his father.

LUKE

Luke watched the two men cross the ridge and stop at a small shelf just below it, their weapons at the ready.

Tearing off his gloves, he grabbed his rifle and swung the magnification on the scope to 9X. With a shot this long, he needed all the visual help he could get. The problem, he discovered, was that the setting so narrowed his field of view he couldn't find the guys through the scope, at least not at first. His stomach churning, he collected his wits, targeted the ridge, and scanned across, each passing second a hammer-blow to his self-confidence.

Yes! He found them. They were settling into position in the snow and lining up a shot. He placed the reticle's crosshairs in the center of one of the men's chest as they sat, rifles raised, preparing to shoot.

C'mon, Hawkeye, he told himself. *You can do it.* He began increasing the pressure on the trigger until the rifle thumped in his shoulder. When the scope settled back down, all Luke could see were the men's reactions. They ducked and looked around as if unsure where the shot came from. Luke didn't know where the shot hit, but he knew it was close enough to scare them.

He racked the bolt and hurriedly took aim again. In his haste to fire, he jerked the trigger. When the scope settled back down, he was staring at an empty mountainside. He didn't even want to know where that last bullet went.

TONY

At the sound of the shots, Tony swung round on his knees and watched two guys, their concentration blown, claw their way back over the ridge before he could fire.

MOOM

Moom was stumbling down the slope, trying to keep up with R, when he heard the shots. He and R both turned in the direction of the noise.

"The shots came from down there," R said, pointing downstream. "Call your brother."

Moom did as told. He got no response. He tried again.

"Maybe he is trying to lay low."

"What?" said R.

"Maybe he does not want anyone to hear him."

"I cannot afford sentiment here, son. Very maybe your brother is dead."

"No!"

"Sorry," said R, now rubbing Moom's shoulder, "but you must prepare for that."

Moom had been preparing himself since he heard the shots. He just didn't believe, didn't want to believe, anyone could kill his brother. He tried to force the thought out of his mind, but he could not begin to. He was in agony, physically sick. It just did no good for him to show it.

R picked up his two-way and said something in his native tongue. He seemed relieved when his man answered.

MATT

Still kneeling, Tony grabbed Matt by his jacket and pulled him to the ground in the shallow cover offered by the shelf of the finger ridge.

"I got a lot to tell you, Dad."

"No time to talk," said Tony after a very quick embrace. "Who fired back in the woods?"

"A bad guy, an American I think, shooting at Luke. He missed."

"Thank God for that!"

"I killed him."

His father just looked at him but said nothing about his nose or the blood on his clothes. He seemed sad, regretful, resigned. He patted Matt on the side of his face. "I'm sorry, so sorry for dragging you into all of this. We'll talk about that later."

"Okay."

"And those two shots," said Tony, pointing to the ridge behind him, "Luke?"

"Got to be, but he's not where I sent him."

"Where is he?"

"I got a hunch." Matt took the binoculars from his father and glassed the shooting spot south of their position.

"Bingo," said Matt. "He's holed up behind the log at that site we identified yesterday."

"I don't want him anywhere near here."

"That's what I told him, but he didn't listen."

TONY

The information was coming so fast Tony had to work hard to process it. For now, he limited himself to essential information.

"The horsemen are dead."

"All of them?"

"Yeah, long story. I'll tell you later, but now, I want you to go back in the woods, get your brother, and get him the hell out of here."

"Back down the stream?"

"Change of plans. Once you get out of this hot spot, maybe a klick or so south, I want you to cross over the ridge, this one," said Tony, gesturing to the ridge above them, Alpha, "and head down the trail. Look for Thor."

"And who takes care of these guys?" said Matt, pointing in the direction of the ridge above them and to the north.

"I do."

"I watched you, Dad. You can't move."

"I'll be okay."

"Dad, c'mon," said Matt, almost pleading. "There's got to be a bunch of them still out there."

"Did you hear me? I'll be okay," Tony said emphatically. "You got an AK, I see."

"Yeah." He held up the weapon.

"Take this too," said Tony, handing Matt the Beretta. "I already checked. It's loaded and ready to go. Just click the safety off and pull the trigger. It'll do its job."

Matt smiled, slid it into his jacket, and zipped up the pocket.

"Now, go get your brother and get the hell out of this valley."

"Dad?"

"You heard me."

"Okay, I hear you. I hear you."

"Get out of here. I'll cover you." With that, Tony pounded Matt's chest.

"Sorry, Pops," said Matt. Before he could restrain his son, Matt was beyond his grasp, running the length of Foxtrot, then charging up the Alpha slope beyond.

MOOM

Moom watched as a guy scrambled up the slope in front of him. Moom wondered if he was the guy who killed Pel. He looked young. Moom could not find it in himself to hate him.

R had the binoculars but was not looking in that direction. Moom waited until the man was near the ridgeline before shouting out as if he had just discovered him, "Look."

R turned, nodded, and took out his two-way.

MATT

Despite the snow cover, Matt climbed up the mountainside even quicker than he did the last time—whenever that was. He was losing track. When he crossed the ridge and dropped below the ridgeline, he took cover behind Skeletor, the same outcropping they had passed in their hairy flight from the valley.

When was that? Could it possibly have been just last night? Twelve hours ago? Sixteen? It seemed like years ago, back when he was just a stupid kid who fell asleep on watch and hightailed it down the stream with his little brother. Now, he was disobeying his father and heading into harm's way to protect him. He had let one parent die. That was enough.

The whole thing was mind-blowing, but he had no time now to let his mind be blown. He needed to think and plan. The outcropping would protect him from the north, at least for the moment. The bad guys could not come around the back side of the ridge without confronting him, and if they tried again on the front, Luke would take them on.

Matt was not at all sure what they would do, but he was confident they and their buddies—and who knew where in the hell they were—would do something.

LUKE

Luke twisted the power on the scope back to 3X and began watching again. He wished Matt was still there to tell him what to do. But then again, Matt did not tell him what to do during his cyber battles, and he won a whole lot more of those than he lost. This was different. He didn't need anyone to tell him that. The cold and snow alone changed everything. Throw in some seriously nasty dudes, and this was a whole new world. Everything was harder, not just the physical things like walking and shooting, but the mental things like planning.

A thousand thoughts crowded his brain, and he struggled to sort them out. The conclusion he came to was this: he would stay where he was. From his position, he could see the tip of Foxtrot where his father was. He could see up the ridgeline to the north where the bad guys hid. He could see the spot where Matt crossed Alpha. He could see just about everything he needed to see, including the western slope of the valley and the stream below. The problem was that he still wasn't sure he could shoot what he could see.

He remembered what his father had said about combat. It could turn a crack range shooter into a spineless deadweight. Luke's first two shots hit nothing except maybe dirt and snow. He half-wanted another chance to prove himself, and he was scared shitless he would get one.

TONY

Other than remaining vigilant, Tony realized there was little he could do, at least not at the moment. Luke had defied Matt, and Matt had defied him. Troubled as he was by their defiance, he admired their initiative and admonished himself for making it necessary.

With the snow ending, he could climb neither up nor down without exposing himself. Hell, a one-armed, one-eyed Haji could pick him off in the time it would take him to clear Alpha— if he could clear that ridge at all. He knew he had to move soon, but he needed more information before deciding where.

If nothing else, by staying in place, he would draw the enemy's attention to himself, not to his sons. In the meantime, it made no sense to worry about his position, no sense to regret past mistakes, no sense to plot tactics—at least until the other guys showed themselves.

What he could do was trust in the judgment of his sons, trust that he had raised them right, trust that they would not expose themselves to any more danger than they had to, and ask Angel to intercede on his behalf—with whoever up there had a mind to listen.

MATT

The snow had stopped falling, but the skies remained grey and the ground fully white. Matt edged out in a kneeling position from behind the outcropping, facing north, the AK at the ready. Still partially sheltered by the rock, he could see up and down the ridge and its largely treeless east slope. He hoped to spot the bad guys before they saw him, and he was prepared to wait as long as he had to. He wished he hadn't left the Tyvek behind as it offered some protection against the wind. Now, it was the cold he feared, and sooner or later the cold would get to him. It had last night, and that was sooner rather than later. He wished he had his rifle too, but the AK would have to do, and there was always the Beretta if push came to shove.

It did not take long before he saw movement, fleeting and distant. He suspected the bad guys were waiting for their comrades. They had the advantage of being able to communicate over distances. He had the advantage of having a father who could kick all their asses, even if with only one leg. He suspected, too, that they'd had a better night's sleep than he had, but there was no way in hell he was falling asleep on this job.

Matt was plotting his next step when he heard a whinny over his shoulder. Thor! *Thank God*, he thought. He listened intently as a horse moseyed its way through the trees back and below him. He wanted to shout out, "Here I am!" but he checked himself. He didn't want to give himself away. While he waited, he turned forward every few seconds to make sure the bad guys stayed in place.

Glancing back, he spied the horse the moment it emerged from the trees and laughed bitterly at the sight of it—"Hi ho, Silver." Of course, it wasn't Thor. It was just a stupid, rider-less horse the Mexicans had left behind. He should have suspected that. However hastily they had tied old Silver up, if they tied him up at all, he worked his way free, probably out of hunger or just plain boredom.

Disgusted, Matt turned back around to keep his eye on the bad guys. He ignored Silver, but Silver did not ignore him. The horse started trotting right towards him, looking for a friend, or at least a feedbag. Matt turned and tried to stare him down, but Silver did not read the visual cues and kept on coming.

Unaware of anything but his own needs, Silver stuck his nose in Matt's face. Matt retreated behind the outcropping and tried to shoo him away, but the horse had already blown his cover. An unmistakable snap above Silver's nose, the sound of a small object traveling faster than the speed of sound, confirmed that fact to the satisfaction of both Matt and horse. While Matt pressed himself against the rock wall, Silver reared up in shock and pivoted away back towards the woods. Another shot nicked Skeletor's forehead. Fifteen seconds later, a third shot smacked Skeletor's nose. When Matt chanced a quick look, he could see the two guys shooting while they worked their way around for an open shot.

The plan he conceived in those harried seconds was crazy, but he saw no other option. If nothing else, he would be doing something other than sitting in place, waiting to get shot. He was sure his father would understand. No, he wasn't sure at all, but there was no time to ask permission. Forgiveness would have to do.

Matt held the AK in his left hand and felt to make sure the Beretta was still in his right jacket pocket. A supersonic crack right past his head startled him into action. He sprang up from behind the rock and made a mad dash for the woods. At least two shots snapped right by him, but the trees provided just enough cover for him to strap the AK over his back and mount the horse, which had nervously found its way to shelter.

Matt looked up and saw the bad guys running towards him in the open area below the ridgeline. With their weapons on full auto, they were spraying every which way. Scared beyond reason, Matt wheeled Silver around, dug in his heels, and shouted to high heaven. Startled, Silver shot out of the woods. With his left hand glued to the saddle horn, Matt pulled the Beretta out of his pocket with his right, fired, and started galloping towards the guys like some mad Cossack. Even from a distance, he could see the fear in their eyes. He did not expect to hit anything, but he and Silver set off the instinctive panic reaction mounted horsemen have been inspiring for millennia.

The men turned and ran back up and over the ridgeline. As the second man crested the ridge, he gathered himself, pivoted, and began to fire. Matt ducked behind the horse's head Indianstyle. He felt, or thought he did, a momentary thump of resistance, but the horse had no quit in him. Silver seemed hell bent on pursuing the men whether Matt wanted him to or not.

TONY

Tony could hardly believe what he was seeing. A Haji had come leaping over the ridge about one hundred meters north of Skeletor and was tumbling head over heels down the mountainside. Tony was more than ready. Moments earlier, after hearing the first shots fired, he had knelt into a shooting position facing northeast—the direction the shots had come from.

Despite the urgency, Tony was pure calm as he slowly applied pressure to the trigger. He did not know for sure where he hit the tumbling man, but by the way he jerked, he knew he hit him somewhere. Tony ran the bolt and quickly turned his attention to the second Haji, who had stopped on the ridgeline to fire. The man sprayed a few random rounds back over Alpha, but before he could take good aim, a round from Tony caught him dead square in the chest. The man cratered in on himself and slid haphazardly down the mountainside.

LUKE

Luke was looking more or less in the right direction when he saw the men come flying over the ridge, but before he could even aim his rifle, someone beat him to it and blew them both away. It had to be his dad. He sure as hell was a badass.

MATT

Silver was enraged. Matt could feel it. And probably dying. Matt could sense that too. Still, he had little choice but to keep a death grip on the saddle horn as the horse clambered up the slope and over the ridge.

For just a moment Matt felt as though he were suspended in space. He could see the whole world. He could see the ridge beyond, the pines and aspens below, and the hint of a blue sky above as the sun peeked through, illuminating the valley with a mystical light made all the more magical by the blowing snow. He tried to soak it all in the seconds before Silver plunged madly down the slope.

TONY

"Oh, my God!" Tony sang out in surprise and relief on seeing Matt safe and well and astride the bloody, defiant horse. No sooner did the horse clear the ridge, however, than his forelegs collapsed beneath him. Matt's momentum thrust him, arms flailing as if to fly, over the horse's head. The boy and horse careened alongside each other, heads first, then sideways down a slope whose many sharp edges were only barely cushioned by the snow. As Tony watched helplessly, the two finally bounced to an abrupt stop at the tree line.

MOOM

Drawn by the sound of shots fired, Moom watched the two men tumble down the slope, followed unbelievably by another man on a horse. A horse? From a distance he could not tell who was who, but he had a strong sense that the odds had just shifted.

"This is not good," said R, who had watched as well. "Let us get closer. We will take out shooter."

"Yeah," said Moom. He had little choice but to follow. Their original mission was dead. Moom knew that. He was not sure what R's plan now was, but Moom's plan was to get out of the cold and make his way out of this mess alive. He could think of nothing else, not even his brother.

TONY

Looking now through the binoculars, Tony could see Matt lying prone, face fully in the snow, head facing downhill parallel to the horse. The horse was clearly dead. Tony could not be sure Matt wasn't. Without a moment's reflection, Tony decided to go to his son's aid or die trying. Given his exposure and his ankle, the latter seemed a more likely outcome than the former.

LUKE

Luke had heard the phrase "emotional roller coaster" before. It was one of those clichés that well-meaning people said about him after his mother's death. It made no sense as far as he could see. Roller coasters go up. His roller coaster only went down. That was no roller coaster at all.

At this moment, though, the phrase made perfect sense. On seeing his father level those guys he could not have been higher. Then, as he watched Matt's horse collapse underneath him, dread pulled him right back down to earth as sure as gravity.

Where Matt and the horse stopped tumbling he could not see from his angle. Foxtrot blocked his view. When he turned his binoculars back towards his father, he saw him crawling across the finger ridge in the general direction of his brother. Even from a quarter mile away, there was no mistaking his desperation.

MATT

Matt felt the gentle tug on his shoulder and cursed himself even before he opened his eyes. *Damn it*, he thought, *how could I have let myself fall asleep again?*

Upon opening his eyes and lifting his head, he quickly absolved himself. No, sleep was not the issue. He fought through the fog in his brain to make sense of what the issue was. The larger picture came into view first. Yes, he was in Colorado. Yes, they were on an elk hunt. Yes, the hunt had turned deadly. But how to account for lying nearly helpless in the snow with a dead horse alongside him? At that moment at least, the answer escaped him.

But he was not imagining this. The pain shooting up his side from his hip to his head affirmed it was real. If he remembered right, his father was lying low on the south side of Foxtrot, and his brother was at the shooting spot south of Foxtrot. Propping himself up, he waved his free arm in hope that his father would see him.

TONY

Scrambling exposed across the tip of Foxtrot, Tony knew he shouldn't shout out when he saw Matt wave, but his paternal instincts overwhelmed his well-schooled sense of caution.

"Matt, you okay?" he yelled, his voice echoing throughout the valley.

"Think so," Matt shouted, now struggling to stand up. "Stay where you are. I'll come to you."

Immensely relieved, Tony turned in Luke's direction and held out both his arms with his thumbs facing up. Not wanting to leave himself any more vulnerable than necessary, he shuffled back over Foxtrot to the position he had just abandoned on its south side. He then picked up the binoculars and turned back towards Matt.

MOOM

"Give me the bag," said R, "and hang on to this," he added, handing Moom his satellite phone.

He and R had reached a point almost directly underneath the jutting ridge where the shooter hid out. Moom had hoped it would not come to this, but it obviously had. R, now on knee behind a log, handled the grenade launcher as deftly as other guys his age might handle a fly rod or a 9-iron. He had obviously done this before. Moom's job was to hand him extra grenades if he needed them. Moom would do his job, but he no longer felt conflicted about the mission. He hoped R would miss.

TONY

As he refocused the eyepiece, he sensed a rush of noise and energy. Almost instantaneously, the ground heaved in front of him, and he was thrown up in the air. Now on his back, he rolled over and stared at exactly what he feared most. His body shredded in a hundred different ways, his ears ringing madly, he pulled himself back up on the surface of the ridge in the hope of finding protection on the far side.

MOOM

"Give me another," R barked. Moom thought for a half-second about saying no, about turning and leaving, but he did as told. He wanted to get his ass out of the valley alive.

LUKE

Luke barely had a chance to absorb the good news about his brother when he heard a sound he half recognized from Call of Duty. Before he could compute what he heard, he saw a projectile explode short of his father's position. The sound of the explosion reached him a second or so later. He suspected it to be an RPG, likely an RPG-7, the most commonly used rocket propelled grenade in the world. Having experienced plenty of these in his video universe, he jerked his head towards the initial sound and searched the lower valley for the distinctive cloud of grey-blue smoke that followed a launch.

The cloud wasn't hard to find. Off to his left, across the stream, a north breeze was pushing the smoke away, right to left. At its source, he saw the shooter and another guy in a small clearing. Behind them was an ugly scar left in the snow by the blast of the RPG. That scar would have given the game away if the smoke hadn't. The shooter was on one knee behind a dead-fall log. The other guy knelt next to him, handing him a round for the next shot.

Without much in the way of thought, Luke dropped the binoculars, jumped to the far side of his shooting log, and laid his rifle across his pack. The RPG guy had reloaded for a second round. Luke knew he had to account for the range, but the distance was pure guess. He suspected these men were farther away than the men on the ridge, but he wasn't even sure of that.

To account for the fall of the bullet over distance, Luke put the crosshairs on top of the shooter's shoulders. To account for the wind, he aimed slightly right of center. With no time to squander, he squeezed the trigger.

MOOM

Moom heard an odd sound like a snap. He wasn't sure what a bullet sounded like, but he sensed that was exactly what he heard. R didn't even flinch. He turned his head slowly in the direction a bullet might have come from, and Moom turned with him. He saw nothing. R turned back and prepared to fire.

LUKE

When the scope settled, Luke saw a chunk of the deadfall fly away just to the left of the shooter's leg. *Damn!* He had aimed too low and not far enough right. Three shots he had taken now, and he still had not hit shit. The pair glanced in Luke's direction, but the shooter quickly refocused on the task at hand. Through the scope he watched in horror as the backblast from a second shot widened the scar in the snow.

MOOM

"Another," R raged. "And take the AK and fire in direction bullet came from."

Moom pulled a third grenade from his vest and handed it to R. He then picked up the AK that R had stood against the log. He turned in the direction that R designated and started pulling the trigger.

TONY

Tony did not see the second round coming, but he sensed it. He could do little but flatten himself on the ridge's rocky surface, cover his head with his pack, and wish he had his Kevlar. Then all went black.

LUKE

Luke yanked the bolt back, and then rammed it forward, chambering another round. As he did, he recalled the "one-way" comment his father made at the range. He had laughed the comment off. He shouldn't have. Elk may not shoot back, but these guys did—Elk Qaeda. There was such a thing as "two-way," and this was it.

He heard the rat-tat-tat from a weapon on full auto. The rounds were landing wildly, but not so wild they could not hit him. Luke was in a race for his father's life, his own as well. He had to adjust his aim. As best as he could judge, his last round fell about three feet lower than he aimed and a foot and a half left. To hit the RPG shooter in the chest, he figured he would have to aim about two feet above his right shoulder and a foot farther right.

That point had no clear reference. Luke would have to estimate it, but his grip was so tense his heartbeats registered in the scope. He stopped himself, took a breath, and prayed. The RPG shooter was within seconds of pulling the trigger, and Luke knew it. He could not afford another miss.

As his mind raced, he felt a gentle hand on his shoulder. He exhaled that last half-breath and settled in. He heard no sound, felt no cold. His heartbeat seemed to soften. Time ceased to pass. His very universe narrowed to two pieces of wire crossing on a point in space. The shooter was making his last hurried adjustment for another launch when Luke sent a signal to the tip of his finger and squeezed gently. The rifle struck into Luke's shoulder. The scope's eyepiece settled in front of Luke's right eye half a second after the shot. A tenth of a second later Luke saw the man's abdomen rip open in a ghastly spray of red mist. As the man went down, the rocket took flight. Luke came up on his left elbow, quickly racked the bolt, and pulled the rifle back to his shoulder to line up his next shot. He had to be extremely careful. He had one target left but only one round to stop him. He felt nothing. He had no time to.

MOOM

Moom felt the blood splatter on his face before he even heard the bullet, if he heard the bullet at all. He had thought R invincible. He had thought his brother was. He was wrong on both counts. The bloody mess that was R cleared his mind. The only game now was survival, and if he did nothing, he knew he could not expect to live another twenty seconds. He had no one to ask what he should do. He was on his own.

MATT

As best as Matt could figure from a hundred or so yards away, an RPG round struck near his father's position. When it did, he instinctively buried himself in the snow. A second round from an RPG struck near the first, and a third round soared in a lazy, aimless arc over the Alpha ridgeline and exploded out of sight. In between, he heard a mess of automatic weapon fire and maybe a shot or two from a rifle. The wayward third RPG shot left him anxious but hopeful. He could not be sure.

Once his head cleared, he forced himself to his feet. Nothing seemed broken, but he had bruised the hell out of his whole right side. Walking would not be easy. Climbing would be even harder. Although now unarmed—he had no idea where the Beretta was or the AK—he was determined to reach his father. From the distance, he could see him lying on the rocky tip of Foxtrot. He wasn't moving.

LUKE

Luke peered through his scope and watched the second guy drop to his knees and face in Luke's direction. The guy had to know Luke had him dead to rights, but what he did next forced Luke to rethink everything.

The guy slowly made the sign of the cross and remained in place with his hands in prayers. If he counted on Christians to be too merciful to shoot a defenseless man, even one who used his left hand to bless himself, he was right—at least in the case of this one young Christian.

MOOM

I guess the left hand was correct, thought Moom. He hadn't been to church since his grandmother took him a few times a dozen years ago to offset the influence of her heathen daughter. Moom figured he would remain in place for a minute. If he was still alive a minute later, he would nod his thanks, leave the gun and the carrier vest, and walk back to the camp unarmed. Once there, he would warm up and head out. He wanted to put this life far behind him and, if arrested, he could never escape it. At eighteen, he would be tried as an adult. He would cop no mercy from anyone.

As the seconds passed, the adrenalin subsided, and the cold and fright took over. If the shooter didn't kill him, he feared the weather still might.

LUKE

Stunned by the gesture, Luke waited and watched, his finger on the trigger guard. After a minute, the man stood and turned towards Luke. Only then did Luke see that he wasn't a man at all, at least not a full grown one. As best as he could tell, the guy was not much older than he was. He wondered if he had shot the kid's father or brother.

Luke wondered too whether the kid expected to be taken prisoner, but Luke had little time to think that option through. The guy nodded as if to say thank you, turned, and walked slowly west, up and away from Luke. Luke watched him go. If he felt any guilt at all about shooting the older man, he had just atoned, perhaps at the risk of his and his family's life.

Luke had no time to dwell on this stuff. He picked up the binoculars and stared up towards Foxtrot. The angle was such that he could not find his father. Scanning the slope to the north he saw Matt limping up and over the finger ridge.

MATT

"Matt!"

Matt stopped. Was he nuts or did he just hear his name echoing across the hillside? He stopped to listen. He heard nothing more. He pounded the side of his head with his palm. It still hadn't cleared from the spill.

LUKE

"Matt!" Luke yelled again, but all he heard in response was the wind rushing through the snow-burdened trees. At several hundred yards or more, he could not expect his brother to hear. Still, he took great heart seeing Matt reach Foxtrot. He figured Matt would tend to their father, and that left him free to check on the guy with the RPG.

To gauge the distance, Luke looked at the chart affixed to his rifle stock. For a bullet to drop thirty-eight inches the target would have to be five hundred yards away. His bullet had dropped at least that much. Wary of the young Haji, Luke began his trek through the woods, holding his rifle in front of him the way soldiers did in Call of Duty's World War II version.

He had no trouble finding the site. The smell led him the final few feet. Upon arriving, he almost retched. Even the stabbed throat he saw earlier did not prepare him for this. When he forced himself to look at the man, sprawled lifelessly face up, his entrails steaming in the snow, he understood at a glance why his father took no interest in video games that simulated war.

Bracing himself, Luke searched the man for a satellite phone, but found only a two-way radio. Damn, he thought, the kid probably took the satellite. Eager to get moving, he scooped up the abandoned AK and the RPG launcher. He shouldered both, along with his own rifle and his day-pack. Even before he took a step, he groaned under the weight, but he couldn't leave these weapons behind. The kid could come back any minute and make short work of them all. Luke worried that this might have been his plan from the beginning.

Luke looked up at Foxtrot, saw Matt tending to his dad, and figured that he simply had to make this climb, burden or no burden, snow or no snow.

MATT

Worried less about the threat from the bad guys than the well-being of his father, Matt cleaned the rocks and debris off his legs and backpack. Lifting the pack, he found his dad unconscious but breathing. On the surface, at least, he did not seem badly hurt, or so Matt tried to reassure himself. The pack likely saved his life.

Matt tended to his father the best he could. He laid out his pad and rolled him onto it. He found a bloody parka nearby and covered his father with it. He raided both of their first aid kits for whatever salves he could apply to the man's many wounds. While he worked, the sun broke through fully overhead, altogether indifferent to the drama below. Matt checked his watch. It seemed impossible, but it was not yet noon.

LUKE

Luke had to stop every ten yards or so to rearrange the weapons and ease the burden. His lungs burned, and his eyes watered. Twice already he had fallen. Twice he had struggled to stand up. He thought of shucking the RPG launcher, but quickly thought better of it. He had no choice but to continue his hike through the woods and up and over to Foxtrot. He willed himself to carry on.

MATT

From the sounds he had heard and could interpret, Matt was hopeful his brother was alive and well. Still, for all his manufactured confidence, only the sight of Luke emerging from the trees and struggling up the slope put his heart at rest.

"Hawkeye!" shouted Matt. Luke stopped where he was, his hands on his knees, his chest heaving. Seeing his brother in distress, Matt slid off the ridge and limped and slid down through the snow to help him.

"Wow," gasped Luke when Matt reached him.

Matt took the weapons from his brother and put them on his own shoulders. He then turned and headed back up to their father. Luke followed, too exhausted to talk.

LUKE

"Take a look," said Matt.

Luke knelt down beside his father. Matt did as well. He looked pretty bad—shredded clothes, cuts, bruises starting to form.

"His pulse seems okay, I think," Matt continued. "His breathing's okay."

"That's good," said Luke, still struggling to catch his breath.

"He doesn't seem to have any deep wounds, no spurting blood or anything like that. I got knocked silly myself with the horse," said Matt, pointing in the horse's direction. "Did you see that?"

"Yeah. Totally whacked."

"Dad got it worse, but he seems to be coming around."

"Hope so," said Luke nervously.

Luke was never sure what came over him at that moment—worry about his father, love for his brother, longing for his mother—but he could not speak. All he could do was sigh—a deep, wrenching sigh that moved Matt to embrace him like a son.

"I killed a guy," said Luke when he could gather his words, "a real guy, someone's father or brother, I don't know. I shot him and killed him." He was shaking now and couldn't bring himself to stop.

"I killed a guy too," said Matt. "You saw him. Dad must have killed five guys, all the horsemen, those other two guys. We had no choice."

"I know, but…" Before Luke could finish his sentence, his father groaned and muttered, "Angel." With that one word, Luke could feel the heaviness drain from his chest.

"He's coming around," said Matt.

"Maybe it's over."

"I wish," said Matt, "but we got to get him out of here. We can't spend another night out in the open."

"Right."

"So tell me what happened."

Relaxing just a little, Luke shared his story. Matt shared his and his father's as well, at least what he knew of it. They looked at each other wide-eyed.

"Are we the same two wusses that spent last night cowering in the woods?" asked Matt with an unbelieving shake of the head.

"I don't know," said Luke. "I let the one guy go."

"I almost did," said Matt. "If you hadn't stumbled into the mix, I probably would have."

"Did we do okay, Matt?"

"I think so."

"Will Dad think so?"

"I suspect he will."

MATT

Matt wheeled his brother around to face the slope north of their position and pointed to the two bodies lying openly in the snow.

"Grab the binoculars, Hawkeye, and see if you can verify that they're dead."

Luke did as asked.

"Well," he said, "the one guy's chest is blown open."

"Yeah," said Matt wryly, "that's usually kind of fatal. How about the other guy?"

"His back's to us, but I don't see any obvious wounds."

"Okay," said Matt. "I got one more job for you. We need a satellite phone. One of those guys may have one. If I could walk halfway good, I'd go, but I can't."

"I understand."

"Here, take this." Matt picked up Tony's massive .44, flipped open the cylinder and checked to confirm each primer was smooth, thus unfired. He then closed the cylinder and handed the gun to Luke. "Use both hands if you need to shoot. You got six rounds. It's ready to fire. I'll cover you just in case the second guy is still with us."

Luke held the .44 like a small rifle. "I'll start with the seriously dead guy."

"Makes sense, but be cautious with the second guy."

"I will."

"This may sound stupid, but when you get about fifty feet away, make a snowball and throw it at him. If he doesn't respond at all, he's probably safe to search."

"Sure," said Luke with a shrug, "pistols, snowballs, whatever!"

LUKE

As he clawed his way up the slope, Luke was thinking this whole scenario was too farfetched even for a video game. Here he was in a snowy Colorado valley, armed with a .44, about to search two dead or dying terrorists for a phone, with the directive to throw snowballs at the less dead of the two them. In Call of Duty, he shot just about every weapon there was, but he never threw a snowball at anyone, let alone a guy who had already been shot.

The guy who died of the chest shot had barely crossed the ridge when he fell. Trying not to look at his wound but unable to avoid the stench, Luke searched in and around him. He found a knife, a pistol, and an AK and gathered them up, but there was no phone—not even a cell phone. He turned back to his brother. Matt was kneeling on his pad with his rifle resting on his pack.

When he caught Matt's attention, Luke shrugged with his hands open and empty. Matt nodded. He understood.

The second guy had fallen about twenty yards downhill from the first guy and about that same distance to the north. Luke half-walked and half-slid down the snowy slope until he was parallel with his body. He found a spot where the footing was secure, bent over and picked up some snow. Just enough sun had hit the slope to melt a little moisture into it. With the pistol tucked under his arm, Luke gathered some snow and found himself reflecting on how ideal this snow was for snowballs, a thought, he laughed to himself, that had to be in the running for the most trivial observation ever made during a firefight.

Luke missed short on his first throw. On the second, he hit the man in the back and got no response. He walked closer for the third throw, packed a snowball as tight as he could, and smacked the guy right in the head with it. Nothing. More confident now, he walked up to the man, noticed the large pool of blood, and shivered. He then knelt down next to the body and rolled it over. His father's bullet had caught him in the thigh. He appeared to have bled out. A two-way radio was on his belt. This would do him no more good than the one he picked off the RPG guy. There was no satellite phone.

Luke then searched the man for a pulse. He did not find one, but then again he really didn't know if he was doing it right. He grabbed this guy's gun and ammo, too, and hiked back towards Matt and his father, scanning the valley below and the ridge beyond as he hiked. He still wasn't sure letting the young Haji or whatever walk away was the right thing to do. Time would tell, he thought, and sooner rather than later.

MATT

Matt shifted slowly and painfully to a standing position. The pain reminded him of how he felt right after the accident with his mom. Then, it was a kind of throbbing stiffness that intensified for about twelve hours and then only slowly faded away. The emotional pain from the accident had never gone away, but in the mad rush of experience in the last few hours, Matt felt it easing, even if just a little.

As Luke walked back, Matt watched him with something very much like pride. He wasn't sure he ever felt that way before about Luke, but the kid was really pretty cool. Together with their father they had done the unthinkable. They had taken out a whole gang of seriously bad people. He still wasn't sure he believed it.

The only threat now was environmental, but that, he had to admit, was a mighty big "only." He would worry about that when he had to.

"No phone?" Matt asked when Luke returned.

"No."

"I think we're officially screwed."

"Now what?" asked Luke. "Smoke signals?"

Matt suspected his brother was joking, but even if he were, he nailed it.

"Actually, yeah," said Matt. "If Thor's out there we've got to let him know where we are. And if he doesn't come by, maybe some other hunter will see it."

"And if no one comes?"

"If no one comes by, say, mid-afternoon, we'll have to make some plans about staying overnight."

LUKE

Luke had little confidence in his ability to build a fire, and Matt had even less, but he was the only one mobile enough to climb back over Alpha and do it.

Luke had just begun his hike up the slope when he heard the neighing of a distant horse, or at least he thought he did. He stopped in his tracks.

"Matt, listen." Luke heard it again. So did Matt. Luke jumped back down and grabbed the weapon he was most comfortable with, his Remington. Matt grabbed his as well.

"Did Dad get all the horse guys?" Luke asked.

"I think he said he did."

Luke began to position his rifle. With one round left he wasn't going to miss. All kinds of thoughts flooded his brain, all of them negative. Were there more of the horse guys? Had the boy he let walk free called in reinforcements? He stared hard up at the ridgeline. The outline of a man on horseback, rifle drawn, forced its way into his view.

MATT

There was no mistaking that silhouette. It almost blotted out the sun. Matt shouted out a joyous, "Thor!" He had no idea how tense he had been until he watched his father's epic friend walk his horse down the slope. They would be saved.

"Howdy, pardner," said Thor when he reached Matt's position and promptly wrapped Matt in a bear hug worthy of a real bear. Having taken care of Matt, he turned to Luke. "Come here, boy. You're a sight for sore eyes," he said, smothering the boy in a monumental embrace.

"Dad's hurt," said Matt, gesturing towards his unconscious father.

"I could see that from above," said Thor without a hint of anxiety. "I know you guys have stories to tell, but let's take a look at the old man."

Thor wasted no time with pleasantries. He knelt down next to his buddy, checked his wounds, and felt his pulse. Matt searched Thor's face for any signs of worry.

"Well?"

"I think he'll be okay. He doesn't break easy."

"How did you find us?"

"Those RPGs kind of caught my attention. That's not a sound you soon forget."

Matt tried to tell Thor what they had been through, but as he told it, the whole story sounded more and more improbable. Luke filled in the details, all equally outlandish. For his part, Thor just listened wide-eyed until he noticed Tony stirring. He cupped his head in his massive paw, and whispered, "Tony, can you hear me?"

TONY

She soothed his head gently with her hands, kissed him on the forehead and said, "All's well." So saying, she turned and walked through the curtains billowing gently in the wind.

"Angel," he said as she parted. "Angel."

"If I'm an angel, hell's looking more inviting all the time," said Thor.

Tony blinked his eyes, struggling to make sense of the huge head hovering over his own.

"Thor?"

"At your service."

Tony forced a smile, but then the images of the last two days came rushing forward, crowding out thoughts of his Angel and pushing him hard into the present.

"The boys?" he burst out, now trying to sit up and look around.

"We're good," said Matt as he leaned in to embrace his father.

"Totally," added Luke, and he did the same.

"And the enemy?"

"Dead or gone," said Matt, "all of them."

Tony patted the back of Matt's head and then Luke's. He struggled through a flood of emotions, the intensity of which he had not felt since Angel's death, but he didn't break. When he regained full control, he said softly, "Your mother watched over you."

"I'm sure she did," said Matt.

Sitting up now, Tony got back to business, or tried to. He had plenty of wear in his voice. "Thor, remind me never to question your judgment."

"I'll make a note of that."

"You nailed the Hajis, but we both misjudged Jake from State Farm."

"How so?" said Thor.

"He was one of us. ATF."

"Was?"

"Was. I'll fill you in when I get a chance. How the hell do we get out of here?"

"Help's on the way."

"It is?"

"Yup. I called it in a little while ago," said Thor, pulling an object off his belt. "I got this cool new satellite messenger."

"How did you know we needed help?"

"In all my experience," said Thor, "I've never known a horse to cut his own head off."

"Cut off?" gasped Luke.

"Sorry, guys, pure evil, didn't want to scare you," said Tony.

"When I saw that," said Thor, "I had a feeling you guys were in a pretty serious jam."

"You don't know the half of it," said Matt.

"No, *you* don't know the half of it," Thor smirked. "And you won't know until Zeke finds out what happened to his horses."

MOOM

It was after dark by the time Moom reached a two-lane highway. He had seen the helicopters and heard the emergency vehicles, but traffic seemed to be flowing normally. Despite the miles he had walked, he had nearly lost the feeling in his hands and feet. He had to take a chance. He held out his thumb and hoped for the best. He waited only ten minutes before some grizzled old guy in a ratty flatbed picked him up.

"Where to?"

"Denver airport?"

"Will downtown Denver do?"

"Do great."

They hit a roadblock a mile or so down the road. There were several cars in front of them. Moom tried to see how closely the cops were checking ID without seeming too obvious. His driver's license could be a problem. The name Mumia Abu Adams just might raise some eyebrows, but at this point he had no choice. He kept quiet as the truck edged forward.

When the truck reached the checkpoint, a cop motioned for the driver to lower the window. This one still had a hand crank.

"What you looking for?" asked the driver. The cop peered into the cab and then scanned the empty flatbed before waving the truck through.

"They're saying Muslim terrorists. Keep your eyes open."

"Wow," said the driver, "will do." He pulled away without incident, but about a hundred yards past the roadblock, he turned to Moom and held out his hand.

"Mark McCoy," said the guy.

Moom grabbed his hand and shook it.

"Adams," he said, "Sam Adams."

"Like the beer?"

"Like the beer."

DAY 22

MOOM

After about eight hours on I-70, and a couple hours of sleep at a rest stop, Moom saw a sign ahead that read, "Welcome to Lawrence, Home of the University of Kansas."

This must be it, thought Moom. *This is destiny.*

The autumn day was crisp, sunny, maybe seventy degrees, still warm enough in Kansas for the co-eds to wear what co-eds everywhere wear on warm days. Driving down Lawrence's main drag, Massachusetts Avenue, his windows open, Moom couldn't help smiling.

DAY
23

TONY

Tony labored his way to the pulpit of a small chapel near the Arizona State campus in Tempe. He had not yet mastered the aluminum crutches that supported him, but he was getting better. Reaching the pulpit, he set the crutches against it and hopped up the two steps to the microphone.

Before speaking, he surveyed the audience. There were no more than a hundred people in attendance. Most, he surmised, were from the Phoenix ATF office. Judging from the long hair and beards, he suspected a few were undercovers like the man he had come to honor, Peter Zapotec. When Peter's wife Jennifer had asked him to speak at the memorial service, he did not hesitate. Even the restrictions put upon the content of his eulogy could not dissuade him.

"I was with Peter when he died," said Tony. "He died saving my life and the life of my sons, and he helped stop a much greater evil. I am prevented from telling you anything more specific than that he died in the line of duty. I can say, though, that in all my days on the front lines of Afghanistan and Iraq, I have not seen anyone acquit himself more nobly or selflessly. The man died a hero's death."

Tony had written his remarks in advance, in small part to ferret out emotional landmines, in large part because the ATF brass wanted to review what he intended to say. They cited the preservation of "ongoing operations" as the reason for their scrutiny. He wondered, however, if they needed to edit out anything un-PC to keep their jobs. Not willing to risk the lives of other agents in the field, Tony stuck to the script.

"I will keep this short. My contact with Peter did not last more than five minutes. In those minutes, I got to see the heart of a soldier. In speaking to Jennifer, I learned that what I saw was who Peter was. I am honored to have known him, however briefly. As long as America can produce men like Peter Zapotec, this nation will endure. May God bless your soul, Peter. Thank you for your service."

DAY 26

"Quoting the great Jeff Foxworthy, if you name your son Dale Jr., and your name's not Dale, you just might be a redneck."

The boys laughed. "What's that got to do with anything?" asked Matt.

"Well," said Tony. "I didn't name you Dale Jr., which means I don't expect you to drive like him, but you kind of are."

"Oh, sorry," said Matt. "It's just that I've never gotten to drive the ZAM to school before."

Tony may have been the only father in North America happy to see his son drive like a teenager. The change came not after Matt's heroics in the valley but days later, when his son opened up about his mother's death and his own role in it. He wished Matt had come to him earlier, but he was proud Matt came to him at all. When he told Matt this, and he watched his son sob shamelessly in relief, he realized mercy was as much a two-way exchange as war.

"Excited?" asked Tony.

"Sort of," said Matt. "First day back and all."

295

"How about you, Luke?" asked Tony, turning to face his son in the back seat.

"A little, I guess. I supposed I'd be more excited if people knew what we'd done since we've been gone."

"Or if we could talk about it," said Matt.

"Well," said Tony. "I got some news for you guys."

"What?" said Luke.

"Don't tease us," said Matt.

Tony picked up his smart phone. "New item on Drudge. Red light with a siren. Brace yourselves."

"Okay," said Matt, "we're braced."

"Good. Here's the headline: 'Kansas Family Thwarts Colorado Terror Plot.'"

"Let me see that," said Matt, nearly swerving into a parked car.

"No," said Tony. "Pay attention to the road."

"What else does it say?" asked Luke excitedly.

"Subhead: 'ATF Agent Dies, Six Terrorists Killed, Mexican Cartels Working with American and Chechen Radicals.'"

"Holy Mother of God," said Matt. "How did the news get out?"

For his sons' sake, Tony regretted the publication of the story. He knew what could happen down the road with the family identified, but it was too late to worry about that. He might as well let them enjoy the glory.

"Well," said Tony. "You got two kinds of people working in the government, the kind who suppress the truth, and the kind who reveal it. Someone in the truth camp apparently leaked the story to Drudge."

"What's that mean for us?" asked Matt.

"If nothing else," said Tony, "the news should improve Hawkeye's chances with the ladies."

"Can't get any worse," said Luke.

"As promised," Tony added, "let's not say a word to the media, at least for now. That may change. In fact, our whole lives may change."

"Change majorly?" asked Luke.

"I don't know," joked Tony. "Maybe once the movie comes out."

"Yeah, who plays you?" Matt asked.

"Brad Pitt's too old. Maybe Bradley Cooper?"

The boys laughed, but just a little nervously. As Matt parked the ZAM, Tony could see they were more on edge than they had been since he dispatched them down Badger Creek.

"First things first. We have to check in with Dr. Heller."

"Does anyone at school know yet?" Matt asked.

"We'll find out soon enough."

At Heller's request, the meeting was set for a half hour after school started on Monday morning. She knew that he and Matt had been injured and that they had to spend an extra week out west, but that may have been all she knew. He could imagine her greeting him with a litany of "I told-you-sos."

To reach Heller's office, the three had to pass down an empty corridor with classrooms on either side, all of them with classes in session. Still on crutches, Tony made more noise than he would have liked. The boys flanked him. When they passed the first classroom door, he made brief eye contact with Matt's math teacher. Tony heard what happened next before he saw it.

"They're here!" the teacher shouted.

"Guess they *do* know," said Tony to his sons. "Brace yourselves."

In seconds, the hall flooded with students and teachers, all of them, it seemed, wanting a piece of Tony and his sons. This was the kind of greeting reserved for returning astronauts and small-market Super Bowl champs—an unceasing flurry of back pats, handshakes, and high fives. As Tony and the boys struggled to get through, a chant sprang spontaneously from every throat.

"A–Cer–O, A–Cer–O, A–Cer–O."

Heller was waiting for them at her office door.

"What was that all about?"

Tony smiled, a bit breathless after the hero's gauntlet they had just run. "Did you see this morning's Drudge Report?"

"What's the Drudge Report?"

The students pushed their way down the corridor to Heller's office. "A–Cer–O, A–Cer–O, A–Cer–O."

"Let's go inside," said Tony, "and I'll explain."

Once seated, Tony instructed the guidance counselor to pull up the Drudge Report on her computer. She managed after a few false starts. The headline was linked to a Reuter's article. She read the opening sentence out loud: "In an effort that one federal official described as 'absolutely heroic,' a father and his two teen-age sons prevented an Islamic terror cell working with American radicals from shooting down the plane carrying the president to the G7 Summit in Aspen."

"Wow," she said, too astonished to say much more. "Wow!"

"Keep reading," said Tony.

That she did. When finished, she just shook her head in wonder. "I really don't know what to say."

"Just promise me you won't try to medicate Luke. I have a feeling he is ready to *engage*. Luke, what do you say?" said Tony.

"Yes, sir," he said, smiling. "Engage!"

"And Matt, I know, is ready to get back to practice."

"Can't wait."

"Wrestling might just seem a little anti–climactic, don't you think?" Heller ventured.

"No," said Matt. "A team's a team, winning's winning."

By this time the commotion in the hall had subsided, and the students had returned to their classes. Matt and Luke knew where they had to go and stood to leave.

"You okay to drive, Dad?" asked Matt.

"Yeah, of course."

"Good."

"Okay, then," said Tony firmly, as though giving an order. "Be cool today. Don't let your heads swell, and see you guys after school."

"Will the boys need any...added security?" Heller asked as they turned to leave.

"No, they'll be okay," said Tony. "They can take care of themselves."

"Sure you can drive?" Matt asked as they headed out.

"Sure. Adios."

The door closed behind them.

"I know you have to get back to work, Dr. Heller," said Tony, hopping up to his feet, "but I was wondering if I could buy you a cup of coffee some day after school this week?"

"It's Tanya," she said. "Sure, why not."

* * *

Tony hopped down the now-empty corridor a happy man, his heart skipping a beat in a way it had not since Angel's death. His boys were strong again—whole again. And he was confident he and they could withstand whatever media tsunami came their way. Stepping out into the parking lot, he was relieved to see the first media wave had not yet reached this particular shore.

There was no one in the lot—almost no one. Tony halted in place at the sight of two thin, young, heavily tattooed white men walking furtively among the cars. When they reached the

ZAM, one took out his cell phone, knelt down behind the vehicle, and took a picture of the license plate. Tony in turn hobbled up closer to the men, held out his cell phone and took a photo of them.

"If six dead ain't enough," said Tony, "we can easily make it eight." Startled by his approach, the men hustled off without saying a word. As he watched them leave, another Yogiism forced its way into his mind.

"It's not over," he thought, "until it's over."

ACKNOWLEDGMENTS

For their editorial and/or technical advice, we would like to thank Dave Chan, Mark Chan, Perry Clark, Greg Finch, Tim Godfrey, Janie Godfrey, Larry Laporte, Doug Malcom, Deidre Malcom, Emmett Perry, Ted Roembach, Jay Manifold, and, of course, Bill Freeman.

ABOUT THE AUTHORS

An independent writer and producer, Jack Cashill has written eleven books in the past thirteen years, most recently *TWA 800: The Crash, the Cover-Up, and the Conspiracy*. Jack serves as executive editor of *Ingram's Magazine*. He writes regularly for *American Thinker* and WorldNetDaily and has a Ph.D. from Purdue University in American studies.

A program manager by profession, Mike McMullen is a skilled hunter, backpacker, and outdoorsman, a veteran Boy Scout leader, and the proud father of two young U.S. Marines and a future U.S. Air Force officer. This is his first book.